TRAPPED

TRAPPED

Dewey Hensley

COPYRIGHT

This novel is a work of fiction. Although set in Louisville, Kentucky, the places and incidents are products of the author's imagination or are used fictitiously and are not to be construed as factual. Any names or real people are historical references to well-publicized places, cases, or events. Any resemblance to actual events, locales, organizations, or persons, living or dead, is coincidental.

DEDICATION

This work of fiction is dedicated to all those who spend their lives creating strong children and repairing broken men.

("I Must Have Been...")

"I must have been incredibly simple or drunk or insane
To sneak into my own house and steal money
To climb my fence and take my own vegetables.
But no more. I've gotten free of that ignorant fist
That was pinching and twisting my secret self.
The universe and the light of the stars come through me.
I am the crescent moon put up
Over the gate to the festival."

Rumi

Translated by Coleman Barks

CHAPTER 1

Although he dreaded their fingers, Carter Sykes would do anything to protect children. As he hurried toward the playground's back fence, kids and teachers approached from the opposite direction, fleeing the urgent pops from the street and the gray smoke rising on the gentle May wind.

Carter swerved to avoid the children as their little hands stretched toward him. He initiated contact, patting those who wandered too close on the shoulder. Carter didn't fear the snot and germs clinging to their fingers, nor was he concerned about staining his blue dress shirt, red tie, or khaki pants—Goodwill sold plenty of those. Instead, he evaded the Traps.

One first-grader, a faded Wonder Woman sweatshirt hanging from her thin shoulders, bounced off her classmates like a pinball. Carter saw her stumble and fall. He rushed to her side, kneeled, and shielded her from the stampede.

"Mr. Principal," she said, her eyes wide, "What they doing? They scaring me." Another explosion caused her to cover her ears.

"Don't worry, Shandi," Carter said. "You're safe."

Teachers herded the students around the principal like shepherds retreating from wolves on the horizon.

"Come with me," Carter said as he stood and waved to Ms. Robertson. She propped open a door to the school fifteen yards away.

Without warning, Shandi appeared at his side and grasped his left hand.

Carter stopped. The world shifted when she gripped his fingers. His core tightened. His brain tumbled into a canyon, and slow-motion images commandeered his vision. As the Trap took its usual form, Carter widened his stance to retain his balance beside the little girl. A scene battered his mind—showing a woman's face and bright lights obscuring the winter sky. He felt the frozen pavement numbing the little girl's legs as she stared up into the face; the bright lights hurt her eyes, and cold blades of wind sliced through her thin jacket. To him, these visual and virtual events persisted forever. However, like even the worst nightmares, the fear and pain only lasted a few moments outside the Trap.

When the Trap ended, Carter searched Shandi's face. *This world doesn't care what it steals,* he thought. She gazed back at him; her intense brown eyes, like rich soil, confirmed she was unaware of what he had witnessed. His presence. It's how it always was.

The principal tightened his grip on her hand and forced a smile. "It'll be all right," he said, "I'll get someone to help you."

Shandi wiped her nose with her sleeve, streaking the WW emblem with a wet swoosh as she squeezed Carter's hand. "You good, Mr. Principal."

Carter towed the first grader to Ms. Robertson at the entrance.

"Please escort Wonder Woman inside when you can. She's in Ms. Jude's class," Carter said above the children's chirps and the commotion on 39th Street. He guided the first grader's hand toward Ms. Robertson.

"I am so proud of you, Shandi. You can get through anything," he said.

As he turned, he unclipped the walkie-talkie from his belt. "Vickie?"

"Yes, I'm here," she said, calm but urgent. "Nothing from the police yet, although the dispatcher said, and I quote, 'They'll be there when they get there.' I called Minnis Elementary, and they are experiencing the same situation. Several downtown schools are on lockdown."

Carter dodged more sheep as he crossed the playground. "Tell Lamar to stay inside. Keep kids away from the windows. Bring aides to the office to help answer phone calls. Tell parents their kids are safe, and they can pick them up, but warn them getting through the crowd will be tough."

"Got it," Vickie said.

Carter returned the radio to his belt as he approached the fence dividing the schoolyard and the street. Kids were still crisscrossing the playground to find their teachers. With only three school days remaining before summer vacation, the teachers had selected today as the official Field Day. The kids spent half the day outside competing in various games and filling their bellies with popcorn and snow cones, and now they scrambled across the grass as if playing a frantic game of tag.

The teachers had planned the event based on weather forecasts. The sun peeked through the gray clouds, and the breeze was no more than a gentle breath. However, the local weatherman didn't foresee a police officer shooting an unarmed teenager several blocks away from West Louisville Elementary in the early hours of Wednesday morning, nor did the city government and school district anticipate the massive protests the killing sparked.

Louisville and its people fluctuated even more than the Kentucky sun and rain.

So many protesters filled 39th Street that Carter couldn't see where the line ended. At the front, a young African-American woman spoke into a red megaphone. Her dark brown skin and short onyx hair drew Carter's gaze. She raised her high cheekbones toward the sky as righteous indignation inflated her crimson University of Louisville tee shirt.

"No justice," she shouted.

Without pause, the crowd chanted, "No justice."

"No peace," she called out.

Without pause, "No peace."

Carter rested his elbows on the chain-link fence, his red tie draped across the railing like a tiny banner. Across the street, spectators sat on porches and stood in their yards watching the spectacle on the pavement. One white-haired man pointed his brown finger, warning marchers to stay off his manicured yard. Others cheered and joined the marchers' chants. Several abandoned white houses, their windows covered with plywood and spray-painted graffiti, resembled fractured skeletons jutting from Louisville's gray dirt.

Although Carter hadn't spoken, the protesters grumbled when they saw him. They formed a wildly diverse crowd. Many, including their leader, appeared college-aged or a little older. However, each generation, young to old, was represented. Carter imagined a kaleidoscope—their clothing was a mixture of reds, blues, blacks, and greens. Their hair colors added purple, green, and maroon specks to the stained glass.

When the principal waved to get the leader's attention, the young woman lowered her megaphone and veered toward the fence. Carter read the amusement and caution on her face. She halted three yards short as though she feared he'd hurdle the boundary and grab her.

"Thank you for stopping." Carter waited for acknowledgment, but she pushed aside a strand of her ebony hair and stared as if he were a fence post. Others joined her, and many pressed against the fence. Their combined weight forced the metal posts to tilt. Carter hadn't witnessed so many people marching since the Second Gulf War twenty years ago.

"I appreciate and respect your opinion." Carter directed his words to the leader, ignoring the others. "I'm concerned for my students and families. How long do you plan to block the street? We have buses and parents arriving soon. Also, could you save the M-80s and firecrackers until you get farther from the school? It scares the kids."

The woman's caustic smile became a smirk. Her strong shoulders and statuesque form reminded him of a gymnast or a swimmer. She raised the megaphone again. "The boss wants to know how long we plan to be in the streets." Carter saw the barbed wire and chain tattoos encircling her slender wrists.

A roar rippled across the crowd.

One person shouted, "As long as we wannabe."

Someone else yelled, "Tell the man we'll leave when he stops killing our kids. That's how long." Laugher followed, accompanied by several whistles and chants of "Shut him down. Shut him down."

"Let me explain," Carter said.

The woman ignored him, basking in the shouts like sunshine. She retained her wicked Mona Lisa smile, glanced at him, and then turned away, returning the megaphone to her lips.

"The boss wants to mansplain because we're too stupid to understand," she said into the mouthpiece. The crowd grumbled; it sounded like strange thunder erupting from the sun-kissed blue-gray sky.

More protestors approached. One volatile young man, dressed in a black hoodie and sand-colored camo pants, caught the principal's attention. The protestor's intense stomp—his Army surplus black boots torturing the pavement—suggested he planned to hurdle the fence. A neon-red cloth mask hid all but his eyes and pale white forehead. Without apology, he pushed others aside to press against the barrier near Carter.

The crowd's chatter and boos hung in the air like the firework smoke. Many pointed their phones, recording the exchange between their leader and the school principal. Several young men and women, their faces masked, joined Neon Red. They ground their shoulders against the metal mesh. Others cheered.

Carter said, "Hey, you don't have the right to do this." His words prompted more marchers to charge and push against the fence. Carter's focus bounced between Neon Red and the leader.

The metal bars shifted, creaking like a distant, wounded crane.

"You're going to get hurt," Carter warned. "The posts won't break. They'll uproot, and you'll fall."

Neon Red grunted. He and the crowd pushed even harder until the fence surrendered. The young man rode the collapse as if surfing toward Carter. The fence's concrete base unearthed and bucked into the legs of several protesters, causing them to yelp in surprise and pain as they fell. Only Neon Red leaped onto the school grounds. He stumbled toward Carter as if winning a marathon.

Carter backpedaled to avoid the fence's sharp prongs and bars. As he stepped, pain radiated through his right knee. He gritted his teeth when Neon Red approached him. "I'm warning you to stay off these grounds," Carter said, his voice a growl.

Neon Red lunged toward Carter. However, he stopped before making contact. He was gauging the principal's response. When Carter didn't flinch, Neon Red stepped so close that Carter heard the laughter beneath the red mask.

"You. Stop doing that," the leader yelled at Neon Red. But the young man disregarded her words and jerked toward the principal again.

This time, Carter grasped Neon Red's collar, pulled the younger man closer, and stared into his eyes. He tugged down the neon red mask to reveal the protester's face. Carter considered head-butting and hip-tossing him to the ground, but he sensed his kids and teachers watching from a distance. Besides, Neon Red's laughter had evaporated—replaced by surprise and fear.

Although the kid was at least six feet tall, the principal stood taller by two inches. Carter's muscular arms lifted the protestor onto his toes. He stared at the protester's pale skin and perfect teeth. "I'll remember you, kid," Carter said, shoving him backward.

The young man tried to retreat as though it was his idea, but his feet tangled in the fencing, and he fell onto the metal and concrete. Two marchers helped him stand. Unintentional laughter rose from some protestors, then stopped when Neon Red glared into the crowd.

"Screw you, man," Neon Red shouted over his shoulder at Carter. He kicked the slanted post as his friends helped him scuttle away.

Carter faced the young woman with the megaphone. *It seems volume is more impactful than reason in 2023*, he thought. Despite her initial words commanding Neon Red to stop, the leader smiled as if the confrontation pleased her now—as if it confirmed her cause. With their cell phones lifted, others stood beside her like digital bodyguards.

"We have buses arriving to pick up my kids in an hour," Carter said. "If you are in the street, the drivers can't..."

"Break the chains! Break the chains! Break the chains!" the protesters shouted in unison.

The leader, assured and confident as if she had achieved all she needed, nodded and strolled down 39th Street like a pied piper. Her deliberate pace signaled she was in no hurry to clear the street. Carter's words were inconsequential.

As the marchers filed by, Carter rolled up his shirt sleeves and attempted to raise the overturned fencing. When it refused to budge, he turned and gazed at his school as he rubbed his knee. The students and teachers were inside now. He hoped they'd missed his exchange with the young man.

It would be impossible for the bus drivers to reach the loading area, so he considered alternatives. Everyone praised him for his ability to adapt to leadership challenges, calling it one of his best qualities. He often wondered if it might also be a negative trait. His world fluctuated as much as the May weather.

The damaged fence rattled behind him, and he heard the words, "I know you," as a warm hand clutched his forearm.

Carter spun.

The world shifted again.

This time, the current was more profound than earlier. Carter took a shallow breath. Darkness narrowed his vision. He stared into a crater as deep and dark as his forty-one years of life. Over time, he had learned to keep his balance and composure. He clenched his jaws and closed his eyes like earlier.

He remained standing; however, Carter Sykes fell into a Trap.

***

It's a woman this time. She examines her hands, so Carter also sees the red and green glitter dotting her fingers and scarred knuckles. She calls out the man's name.

"Honey," she says. She searches the immaculate kitchen and living room, but no one is there.

Honey? That can't be his name.

The woman examines her carnival reflection in the stainless steel refrigerator. He senses her shame. It is brief. She straightens the shoulder strap of her mini-dress. Carter sees her brown hair, streaked with burgundy highlights, falling to her cleavage. She bends her slender leg to slip away her vinyl stiletto-heeled shoe. Her chest, arms, and thighs have tattoos, but Carter struggles to identify them in the distorted metal mirror.

A man, his brown hair collected into a tight ponytail, enters the kitchen from the hallway. His trimmed goatee divides like a crevice when he smiles. Behind the man, at the end of the hall, Carter sees an open bedroom door. The early morning sun fills the kitchen. She asks what he is doing, but the intense pounding inside her chest suggests she knows all too well.

Honeyboy grins, reaches for her sparkling hand, and draws her close. He hugs her, overpowering. His hand pats her back to assure her things will be fine.

"You're tired, Babydoll, and you just left work, so you have to rest," he says, dancing her away from the door and nudging her along like Carter might redirect a student toward the cafeteria at school—gentle yet controlled.

But Babydoll turns away from his pressure to peer past his broad shoulders through the open bedroom door.

She sees her, so Carter sees her—the teenage girl, her hair darker than a starless sky and her skin a flawless caramel. The teenager curls into a ball like a cat on a windowsill, except her pupils aren't steady jewels mounted in a feline's face. Her eyes dart in each direction as though she would run away if not for the cords tethering her to the headboard. Babydoll gazes at the girl's young face, her bare shoulders, and the tears rolling across her cheeks. The abducted girl's fear becomes Babydoll's, which Carter Sykes feels in his brain and heart like acid melting his skin from within.

***

When the Trap released him, Carter felt dirty—his soul stained and tainted. Whenever he stepped into someone's trauma, he sought to pass it to someone else—to regurgitate it from his system so someone better could solve it. He was the finder, not the doer. This one was complicated.

When Carter turned, the woman released his wrist.

"You have been on my couch before, you naughty boy," the woman said. She stood on the schoolyard side of the uprooted fence, her hands on her hips as if imitating Carter's stance a moment earlier. Instead of a short, form-fitting dress and exaggerated heels, the woman wore jeans and a black tee shirt with a red University of Louisville emblem on the front. Her pale skin and burgundy-streaked hair lacked the clown makeup and hairspray seen in the refrigerator reflection, and she didn't glitter in the May afternoon sunlight. Her thin frame displayed sharp angles and shallow holes as if carved from the lightest maple wood.

Other than inside the Trap, he couldn't place her.

Babydoll shouted to her friend—a shorter, red-haired woman in her twenties. She was heavier and more compact than her friend and wore and identical UofL shirt. "He doesn't recognize me, Kelsey," Babydoll said. "Let's give him a clue."

Both women laughed, stepped closer to Carter, and turned their backsides toward him. They performed a synchronized dance, gyrating their hips and bouncing their butts.

Protesters cheered as the young women performed for the principal. Several young men who had stopped to enjoy the show whistled and catcalled. Many others laughed and pointed at Carter as though his stoic reaction entertained them more than the dancing.

However, Carter Sykes stared at the ground instead of the spectacle. The Trap burned inside his head; he longed to release it to anyone else who agreed to save the girl. That would extinguish it.

Finally, he focused on the dancers.

And he realized how he knew the young woman.

CHAPTER 2

As Carter drove his Toyota Camry toward home, downtown Louisville revealed itself—the tall buildings carved into the skyline, the silver moonlight spilled onto the Ohio River, and the illuminated bridges spanned the river like scud missiles frozen on the horizon. Although it was now spring, the Kentucky wind carried the cold air from the water through Carter's open car window. He appreciated the breeze and the view of the city.

However, the daily trek to his small Shotgun home on Swan Avenue presented Louisville's cracks and the weeds rising from those crevices. The city's fragrance rode the same wind—the Butchertown pork processing plant, the rotten eggs of the sewers, and, he imagined, the bourbon and beer rising above the local bars. The ten blocks to Broadway showed him the people and their shadows hunkered between the neon lights and brick walls. Dark angels wore halos of smoke and artificial smiles painted on by regrets, their bodies bought and sold repeatedly. Lost men lingered at the bus stops or hid beneath tattered tarps or makeshift cardboard shelters, their scarecrow legs exposed to the world.

People had lined the streets three weeks earlier in May to celebrate the Kentucky Derby.

Today, people filled the downtown again as the peaceful protests and the violent riots merged throughout the late afternoon and evening hours.

Carter had stayed at school working until 9:00 p.m., leaving only when he was confident all the students, teachers, and staff had made it home. The closed streets, burning cars, and people blocking his route turned this short drive home into a long journey.

At Broadway and Liberty Street, four young men staggered into the street. Carter braked, but it didn't matter. The shortest man gave Carter the middle finger while the other three shook their fists or glared. Anger shaped their faces—anger at a person they did not know. The incident that sparked the protests mirrored other events around the country, highlighting the conflict between the ideals of the law, the reality in which people live, and the reluctance to find peace somewhere in the middle.

When Carter turned on Barter Street toward his house, several people stood on the sidewalk around a burning barrel. The flames illuminated their faces like a strobe light. Before the riots in the streets, he had seen these men—the outcasts, the strays, the ones imprisoned inside their minds. *There are many kinds of Traps, after all.*

Their homelessness wasn't a product of the protests or riots—it was the consequence of ideological mud-wrestling. *Our world doesn't solve problems; we hammer every red-hot crisis until it becomes an opportunity.*

His phone rattled in the cup holder.

"Hey, Vick," Carter said. "Everything okay?"

"I don't know," she said. "You looked pale today, like the vampire in my daughter's favorite movie."

Carter leaned back and massaged his right knee as he steered clear of a boy and girl, holding hands as they walked in the street.

The Trap hacked at his thoughts. He blinked to allow the images to dissipate before replying: the open door, the ponytail, and the man's face, the woman's sparkling hands, the girl's terrified, cobalt eyes. Traps were the demons he couldn't exorcise until he passed this problem to someone else.

"It's May, and the kiddos get released back into the wild next week," he said once the images faded. "I'll visit the sun this summer. Who knows? I may become a Parrot Head, looking for my lost shaker song."

Carter pictured Vickie's signature headshake. She often checked on him like a fearful mother. Everyone, including the teachers and parents, trusted her and sought her advice. She had chaired the school's Principal Selection Committee six years earlier, and according to the rumor mill, she'd fought for Carter and convinced the committee he was the best choice. He often said her presence at the school mattered more than his.

"Walking outside would require you to leave your cave," Vickie said. "I don't see it happening."

"Did you just call me a caveman?"

"If the loincloth fits," she said.

Carter chuckled. "Just a long day."

"All your days are long, Carter. It's my job to keep you alerted on the latest gossip. There's a video all over social media showing what happened on the playground today, but I haven't seen it. Some teachers have commented on YouTube, defending you for putting that kid on his butt."

"The teachers don't need to do that," Carter said, gritting his teeth. "Nothing escapes scrutiny nowadays."

"You fared well in the staff lounge chatter. Everyone appreciated your stance. However, the teachers revived their old complaint—they don't know you."

"I'd prefer they talk about anything, or anyone, else," Carter said. It wasn't modesty; he often struggled when others shared kind words.

"So, you refuse to talk about yourself, and you don't want others to speak of you either," Vickie said. Her voice sounded small on his cell phone. His Camry was too old for a Bluetooth system. "Perhaps they wouldn't be so talkative if you shared a little more. You can't be a mystery and act all surprised when people try to solve you."

"Are you and Denzel bingeing those British crime shows again?"

Vickie ignored his attempt to change the subject. "Don't get me wrong. It was positive talk laced with bewilderment. Ms. Robertson said that when you helped Shandi Gibson today, it warmed her heart. However, Ms. Jermane said you are too secretive and don't speak her "love language." Then Ms. Callen reminded us how her husband's adopted sister told her you grew up in foster homes. Even Mr. Dunn weighed in, claiming—"

"My story's not important, Vickie," he interrupted. "Besides, I can't help it if I'm a boring dude."

Vickie's tone shifted. "That's where you fall off the train, Carter. Everybody's story matters to other people. It's how we build trust. You should come to church with us sometime. Denzel would love it if you did."

Carter eased the Toyota around an Amazon box and a shopping cart blocking the street. The cart's front wheels mounted the cardboard like a hound in heat.

"Last Sunday, our pastor's sermon was called, Be Your Authentic Self. Don't take this the wrong way, but I thought of you." Vickie said. "Others trust you when they know you're genuine. They see you are strong and vulnerable. Even I can tell you've dug in deep, but we've never talked much about you growing up or your time in the Middle East. That cave's pretty deep, Mr. Caveman."

"And sometimes people no longer trust you when they see the real you, Vickie."

He recognized her frown, even on the phone. "Everyone trusts you enough, and they suspect you're not perfect, Carter."

The phone glowed like a ghost in the dark car. Carter parked near the curb and killed the engine.

"I'm home, Vick," he said. "Could you do me a favor?"

"You're the boss."

"Tell Lamar I'll be late tomorrow morning, so he'll cover the cafeteria when the kids arrive for breakfast."

"Sure," Vickie said. Carter noted she didn't question why he'd be late. He appreciated it. "I'm sorry for the intense talk after a tough day. It's my job to nag you toward happiness and heaven."

"You're good at your job," he said with a chuckle. "I'm considering paying you overtime for evening naggings."

"See," she said. "That's not my love language at all."

***

"You look pale today." Carter heard the words when he plodded through the front door of his two-story home. His sister didn't greet him in the living room. Instead, he watched her shuffle toward the kitchen.

"So I've been told," Carter said, his words trailing behind her. He placed his keys in a small basket by the door and switched on the overhead light.

An antique chair and table sat on a tattered red and blue rug. Both needed repairs, but that was the case for Carter's entire house and furniture. Every item was a thrift store special he had vowed to fix and finish, yet somehow, he never found the energy and time.

An old coat rack, one leg shorter than the others, leaned against the left corner, and a mirror with a damaged frame hung to his right. A scratched cherry coffee table separated a pale burgundy sofa and an entertainment center more suited for a 1970s Brady Bunch set. The center's faded and chipped oak clashed with the wall's Columbian blue paint and the cream-colored love seat.

He stretched his rubbery arms, and his head ached with an urgent thud. The young girl's tortured face hung in his thoughts like a horrific painting on a gallery wall.

When Carter entered the kitchen, his sister leaned against the granite counter near the sink. He opened the refrigerator door and allowed the cold to roll over him. The light inside shined on his face like the flames from the burning barrel down the street.

"I bet it's been hopping around here with the protests, riots, and fires," he said.

"Let's not mention that," Becca said, her tone as sharp as a Ginsu knife. "Tell me what's making you resemble a ghost."

Becca always expected him to explain the world since they were kids. She had always counted on him to be an expert on the people, the planet, and the stars. When he didn't know the answer, her disappointed expression hurt him, even all these years later. Back when she was five, and he was ten, he could make her laugh and feel safe at the same time. The way they grew up, safety and happiness were scarce, so finding either equated to discovering lost treasure.

"The protesters blocked my bus routes, requiring me to use my brain." Carter grabbed a Corona Extra from the dented white refrigerator and closed the door. He sipped the beer with his left hand and tapped his temple with the index finger.

"Wow, that's a workout for you. I hope you stretched first." After over thirty years, she was the one who made him laugh. "But big bro, I know you as well as you know yourself. A crappy day at school didn't plant that constipated expression on your face."

Carter breathed and eased into a rickety chair, placing the beer and the bottle cap on the scarred brown kitchen tabletop. "You see right through me, Becca," he said. "I fell into two Traps for the price of one today. The first was with a kid. I can deal with it tomorrow. The second is a different story."

"As much as these things drain you, Carter, you should be more careful about getting touched." She stepped closer. He felt her soft hand on his shoulder but did not turn around. "No one understands what it is like to live another's trauma—to feel the panic and pain you feel, all because they touch your skin. That's a damn hard road, my brother."

"At least it isn't everyone and all the time," Carter said. "I'm thankful it doesn't register on my radar unless it's extreme."

"The problem, Cart, is that you shouldn't pack other's suffering when you're not strong enough to carry your own."

Carter rotated his shoulders and rolled his eyes. "I'm not worried about the person who touched me. It's a girl I saw in the room behind the man. The fear and pain on her face..."

Becca wrapped her arms around his neck and hugged him like they were kids. Back then, she wanted a piggyback ride. The painted sunflowers of her white cotton dress pressed against his back.

"Do what you always do, Cartie. Tell the right person so they can fix it. Isn't that your penance? You fall into a "Trap," watch like a creepy voyeur, then pass the responsibility on so someone else can solve the problem. I still picture you hiding behind that old living room couch. That didn't work out well, did it?"

Carter bristled. A heavy brick tumbled inside his stomach. He hammered it until it crumbled into red dust.

But his sister was right. Ever since he first recognized his curse or gift, he had passed along each problem like a UPS driver delivering a package and walking away untethered. He planned to do the same with both playground Traps. Untethered. Walk away. The admission stung him. The urge to silence Becca and shed responsibility filled the void left by the crumbled brick.

"I think I'll go..."

Becca whispered in his ear. "Where? To your special club to drown in bodies? Maybe Banger's to watch those naked angels dance around a silver pin? Oh, I know. Since you're so distraught, you'll call one of those ladies who help you forget. Do you have enough cash? Isn't that your chosen medicine—a stranger who doesn't even know your name?"

Carter trembled, placed his hand on the wooden table, and stood. The unstable table rocked, and his beer bottle cap bounced and then clanged against the hardwood floor.

Becca no longer whispered. "Calm down, Carter. It's tough for a little boy to keep his balance with so much shame and guilt in his backpack." She stepped away and turned.

Carter inhaled as he viewed her profile. Blood splatter stained the sunflowers on her dress. The exit wound on her side was a massive crater so wide and bottomless that Carter peered at the antique cabinet behind her. A second hole on her shoulder resembled a train tunnel exiting a mountainside. His skin tingled, and the dried clay in his belly formed a brick again.

But Carter's expression didn't change. He sipped his beer, stood in the kitchen, and stared silently at the unstable table he'd never repaired.

Rebecca Sykes was gone.

He dug his cell phone from his pocket. He scrolled through his contacts, dropping his thumb onto the "right person so they can fix it." He tapped a short text message, his fingers so eager that he forced himself to slow down until the words made sense.

When he completed the message, he lowered himself into his chair and stared at the wobbling table, picturing a teetering scale, shame on one side and the need to save that girl on the other, endlessly rocking.

CHAPTER 3

"There's my favorite customer," the woman behind the counter announced as she wiped her hands on her coffee-colored apron. "I wondered when you'd bless us this week."

"Sure, but you didn't care enough to form a search party," Carter replied, raising his eyebrow. "What if rogue second-graders held me hostage?"

The barista knuckled her cheeks as if wiping away tears. "Crybaby. That'll teach you to monopolize the monkey bars at recess." Then, her broad smile returned. "The usual?" she said, grasping a large paper coffee cup from a stack near the register.

"Unless you now have an extra large coffee of the day, it will have to do." He glanced at his watch. It was only 5:45 a.m., so he had a few minutes to spare. The barista wasn't only funny; she was intelligent and sexy.

"I can fill up a mop bucket if you don't mind the Lysol aftertaste."

He grinned. "You expect me to believe you baristas clean this place?"

"Get over here, smart ass," the woman said. She turned away as Carter approached the counter.

He studied her figure as she floated toward the coffee brewers. The gap between her tight black jeans and the short New Lou Café tee shirt drew his attention. The word HOPE adorned her lower back. When she turned to deliver the order, the tattoos on her hand showed a *Fleur De Lis* near her thumb and a pale blue cross at her wrist. Of course, he hadn't broached the subject—he didn't need to—but the crucifix obscured a horizontal scar carved into her wrist. His gaze followed the green vine and small hummingbird figure etched into her arm to a peace sign near her shoulder.

He reached into his pocket to get cash and said, "Thank you, Hope. How's school going?"

She shrugged. "Education is a wise investment, right?"

Carter laughed. "I guess it depends on what you do with your degree. Aren't you studying to be an Insect Poop Detective or something?"

She laughed. "How many times do I have to tell you I'm majoring in Forensic Entomology?"

"Now I remember," Carter said as he sipped his coffee. The black liquid scalded his lip and tongue.

"Funny guy," Hope said. "Do you have any Friday night plans?"

"Not unless you have something in mind."

She placed her elbow on the counter and leaned her chin against her fist. "Carter, you know I'm attached. My girlfriend might take offense to your obnoxious flirting." She wiggled her ring finger to highlight the faded gold band between her knuckles.

"Oh yeah. I forgot about your partner, too." A wicked smile.

He watched Hope Leto's nose wrinkle and her eyes, brown as wrens, fly upward. She kept her impossibly disheveled black hair clipped short, and three small diamonds lined the outside of each ear. She worked mornings, so he saw her often before work. He had learned she was eleven years younger than him and had returned to school after a divorce. Soon after, she recognized she was a Lesbian—neither her youth nor identity quenched Carter's desire.

"Why are you here so early? Did they call elementary school off or something?"

"I am meeting a police officer for coffee," he said. "I have to ask for some help."

"Does it involve your clash with protestors yesterday?"

It was Carter's turn to roll his eyes. "You've watched it? Does the camera make my butt look fat?"

"Yes indeed, it does," she said before turning serious. "I have to admit, it isn't your most shining moment, my friend."

"I haven't seen it," Carter said. "I'd give up anything, except coffee, of course, to avoid the attention." He took another small sip from the paper cup.

Hope said, "Don't. It's apparent someone edited it to make you look bad." She reached to touch his hand, but he pulled it away without thinking. Her brow raised, and she glanced past him.

"You didn't say your officer friend was so hot." Hope nodded toward the café's windows.

Officer Mona Ridge walked across the parking lot toward the door.

***

"So, this isn't a social call, I guess?" Mona smiled and shook her head.

"Are you kidding? Seeing you is the best thing to happen this week. But I do have something to discuss," Carter said. He smiled and added, "But first, it's been a challenging few days, hasn't it?"

"That's understating it, Carter. Officers and civilians end up in the hospital, and the city tries to destroy itself from the inside because a dimwitted, scared cop who shouldn't even be on the streets kills a teenager. It feels like a zombie movie has broken out in downtown Louisville."

"I understand," Carter said. "I know it's difficult for first responders, but I'm fortunate."

"What?"

"My life has always been chaos trapped in a barrel, and I'm sure I'd survive a Zombie Apocalypse."

She raised her paper coffee cup. "Now, that sounds like a social call discussion we should have."

Her smile and emerald green eyes mesmerized Carter. Despite the stripes decorating her uniform, Mona resembled an actress playing a cop. Her natural coppery hair glistened like new pennies in a fountain. Today, unlike other times they'd spoken at school, her smile was more authentic and less restrained by her badge. Makeup hid what some might consider her only physical flaw.

Carter banished any thoughts that she might be attracted to him. He was a third-tier participant in a world where only two levels existed—and she was top-tier beautiful. When they first met, Carter thought the tiny dots on her face were freckles but soon realized they were speck-shaped scars. The makeup covered them, but he wished they were still visible. Those minor imperfections made her more accessible to him, somehow.

I've got scars, too.

Nonetheless, her smile brightened as she stared back. It wasn't typical eye contact. Mona's eyes were kind but also impatient, as though she'd heard everything before, so Carter figured he should spill it and not waste her time. He cleared his throat and straightened his shoulders.

"I want to relay some information to you."

"Oh," she said. Her smile dimmed.

"Sometimes, I hear a story or rumor about families. You remember how I helped you with the drug dealer whose first-grade daughter brought weed to school?"

"That's not the only time you provided good intel, Carter," Mona said. "You helped us solve several issues that probably saved kids' lives. I still marvel at how you read the Russell boy's stance and recognized that his dad abused him. I called you "The Kid Whisperer" back at the station.

Carter nodded in appreciation but changed the subject. "Are you searching for a missing teenage girl?"

Mona laughed and reached out to touch his hand. "Is that a joke?"

He withdrew his hand and leaned away as he always did when he needed more distance from someone.

"You are serious," Mona said. "Haven't you read the newspapers?"

"I guess I haven't," he said. "I'm a sports page and classified ads kind of guy."

"I guess the Wagers boy will take the headlines now, but until the protests, the big story was three missing girls. The latest is a kid named Zara Turner," Mona said. "She's a seventeen-year-old honor student at St. Augustine Academy in the East End. Zara's parents thought she attended a Teen Leadership Conference in Indianapolis, but she didn't show up on Tuesday, and no one realized she was missing until Thursday night."

Mona shook her head. "Over the past four years, seven young women have disappeared. I'm not talking about runaways or teenagers with records. Not that it makes a difference, but these girls have intact families, good grades, friends, and are leaders at school and church."

Images filled Carter's head—the girl's bound hands, Babydoll's reflection, Honeyboy's ponytail. "How do you know if they are connected?"

"We don't," she said. "The guy has only left two bodies for us to find—one in Kentucky and the other in Southern Indiana. However, we have footage of a similar-looking guy abducting two other girls, but we can't be sure. Over three years, numerous affluent girls have disappeared. The further back we go, the more we find."

"Yes," Carter said, embarrassed by his ignorance. "The Good Girl Killer, as the press calls him."

Mona shook her head. "That name shows how lame our media is," she said. "I can't tell you much for obvious reasons, especially since it isn't my case. But I can discuss what is in the papers. The assailant gets the girls in parking lots of upscale shopping centers like Magnolia and Fig or Westport Village. We have limited surveillance video because he's so clever. Somehow, he talks these bright girls into his car."

Carter's heart shrunk inside his chest. He shuddered and stared at Mona for too long without speaking. The café's coffee grinder filled the brief silence.

When the quiet grew too loud, and Mona's expression changed, he asked, "How long does he keep the girls?"

"We don't have enough evidence to guess, but he isn't as regular as the paperboy, that's for sure. The two bodies we recovered suggest ten days or so."

The officer's brow raised, and she paused as though she needed to think before continuing. "What is this about, Carter? Please don't tell me you are a true crime podcast fanatic pumping me for information."

"I may have received some information about one of the girls."

"May have?" Mona leaned closer and cocked her head. "Which one? Did you call the station immediately?"

"I wanted to talk to you first. I don't have a name, but it sounds like your guy," he said.

"Okay, spit it out. What do you think you know?" Her impatient glare intensified.

"I overheard kids talking about an abducted high school girl. The man is holding her captive. She's Black. I don't know much except the man has a ponytail and has her in a house or apartment somewhere."

"A white guy with a ponytail and an apartment? That describes most hipsters living in the entire trendy neighborhood around this coffee shop. I bet he listens to Mumford and Son's, too."

"I don't know," Carter said, ignoring her snark.

Mona leaned back again, and the left corner of her lip rose.

"How did you come by this information?"

"Just kids talking at school."

"Really? How about you give me those kids' names so I can chat with them?" She opened her cell phone and positioned her thumbs. "I'm ready when you are."

Carter pursed his lips and took a deliberate, deep breath. *I didn't think this through*. He smiled. "I couldn't determine who said it," he said. "The hallway was full, and the kids darted by me. It was the day the protests started, so I didn't have time to follow up."

Even Carter realized how lame he sounded.

"How about any descriptions of the house, or at least a general part of town or the county where it might be? Do you have any idea?"

"I don't know the address, but the kidnapper has a girlfriend or wife who used to strip at Banger's. I think she still does. Her name is Idaho, and she lives with him in the house."

Carter stopped when Mona rested the phone beside her coffee cup and interlaced her fingers. She stared at him, her eyes more like sour green apples than jewels. "That is specific, considering you don't have any other information. Is there anything you want to tell me, Mr. Sykes?"

"I'm Carter, remember?" He smiled and held up his school identification card to lighten the moment.

She didn't respond. Instead, she stared at Carter without blinking or changing her expression. A storm was brewing.

"Are you connected to this guy or his girlfriend somehow?"

"No," Carter said, perhaps more quickly than he preferred. "I don't have much, but I figured any information might help."

"So, you're telling me a pony-tailed guy you don't know has kidnapped a teenager you can't name. You believe his stripper girlfriend, "I-da-ho" (she formed air quotes as she sounded out the syllables), lives with him in a house or apartment you can't describe and can't even offer a general location for. Does that sum it up?"

Carter glanced around the café. A man in workout shorts and a matching blue Kentucky Wildcats tank top sat in the far corner, devouring a scone. A young woman, earbuds visible, tapped a MacBook keyboard while staring at a three-ring binder. Two men in another corner argued about President Biden's Afghanistan debacle. Three tables over, a man and woman lamented inflation and the cost of avocados. Hope stood behind the bar, her phone against her ear. *At least no one's hearing this humiliating conversation.*

Mona unlocked her fingers and leaned closer. The wooden chair scraped against the floor. "Carter, I'm sorry. I appreciate your intent, but I can't run to the lead detective without more than this. Besides, it makes you sound..." She aborted the sentence and glanced down at her cup.

Carter lifted his coffee and took a long swig, leaving a brown smear on the lid where his lips touched the plastic. "I understand," he said. "I like to pass along information as soon as possible and..."

"I thought I'd bring you a refresh—on the house, of course," Hope said. She stood next to the table, holding a carafe. She smiled at Mona and then at Carter. He'd never seen Hope perform this service in all his visits to the café.

Mona glanced at her and said, "Thank you, but I've had enough. I'd better hit the streets and start protecting and serving." She stood and retrieved her phone from the tabletop. "Carter, thank you for the coffee and the conversation. If you find more to share, contact me."

"I hope I didn't waste your time today, Mona." He stood beside his chair. "I will get in touch if I get some details, okay?"

"Of course," Mona said. She smiled at Hope and strode toward the door. Her cup remained on the table.

***

"Talk about an intense conversation," Hope said. Steam rose from the glass container on the table between them. Her eyes sparkled like she witnessed a spectacular bike accident at the park.

"I'm surprised you could hear it," Carter said.

"I didn't hear much. Did the officer agree to help you with the thing?"

Carter paused, thought, and realized something monumental. "It's not that she won't help. She wants more information before she takes over." His stomach twisted at the statement. He heard Becca's words in his mind. "...watch like a creepy voyeur, then pass the responsibility on so someone else can solve the problem."

After a Trap, Carter always played the passive role. He remained anonymous, a helpful ghost floating in the background, watching, his secrets secure.

"The officer's body language suggested she has," Hope's lower lip protruded as if she offered terrible news, "or maybe I should say she *had* a big crush on you."

"It wasn't like that," Carter said. "It never is with me." *If good fences make good neighbors, I'm the master fence builder.*

"She still hopes you'll call Carter." Hope's smile widened. "Speaking of calls, I contacted Lenora."

"Lenora?"

"She's my partner, silly. I called and raved about what a funny, cute, and sexy guy you are. Even though I made that crap up," her eyes sparkled again, "she fell for it."

"What do you mean?" Carter said.

"For someone so smart, you're as bright as a broken lamp, Carter." She cocked her head and puckered. The young woman leaned closer. "Let me explain it in a way those rogue second-graders would understand. Both Lenora and I are very flexible in our sexuality. Remember, I was married to a man, and Lenora always loves it when we find a safe and discreet older guy. Maybe you visit our place tomorrow night?"

Safe and discreet. That's me, Carter thought. He cleared his throat and glanced at his cup. He hadn't passed the Trap to Mona, so the images still foamed in his mind. *Hand the problem to a better person, silence the Trap, and return to my cave—that's my plan.* But Carter feared if he accomplished anything today, he'd convinced Mona he was involved with the abductions.

A dark-haired girl, no more than six, walked past the table, her tiny white dress covered with sunflowers. She stopped behind Hope's chair and turned toward him. Becca's voice echoed inside his head.

"Oh, Cartie, we know you can't save anybody, right? Don't pretend you'll save that poor girl. Not when you have a chance to sin like this." She wagged her finger at him and shuffled away.

Carter leaned back in his seat and closed his eyes. Becca's words, as always, caused guilt and shame to swell inside him. He needed to find out more information about the abducted girl and give it to the police before his life could return to its normal abnormality. He didn't have time to indulge in diversions.

When he gazed at Hope again, the familiar tug of war commenced. The possibility of meaningless intimacy nudged against the better angels of his nature. Carter strained to resist the urge rising inside him. The urgent, persuasive demon spoke to him. It whispered to his deep-seated addiction, its hot breath brushing against his neck and ear. *Just this once,* it said. *There's no harm. They don't even know you. You deserve to feel something other than the bitter circumstances of your life, don't you? Give yourself a reprieve from this responsibility you never asked the world to give you. A respite to soothe your aching life. Just this once.*

Carter's willpower, in some instances, held like an indestructible wall, insurmountable. But not now. Not when it came to his medicine.

"Lenora," he said. "That's a pretty name."

CHAPTER 4

"I'll alert the media," Vickie said, smiling. "Carter Sykes arrived at school after sunrise."

It was 8:15 a.m., well before school started at WLES. He would handle his cafeteria duty.

"I told you, all I needed was a few hours of sleep," Carter said. He nodded at her and edged toward his office.

Vickie raised an eyebrow to express her skepticism. "Your girlfriend, Dr. Wallace, called to say she would drop by at 11:00 a.m., so clear an hour for her."

"Crap," he said after checking to see if anyone else was in the front office. "Did the good doctor give a hint?"

"Nope," Vickie said, "but she poured plenty of sugar, so it can't be good."

"Okay, I want to meet the buses and check on kids, then go to the cafeteria," he said. "Pull up an attendance report as soon as the teachers take roll. Judging by the damage to downtown and the incidents of violence last night, we might be the only ones here today."

"At least it's Friday, so maybe this will blow over this Memorial Day weekend, and the city will settle down by Tuesday."

"I don't think so, Vickie," Carter said. "Anger is spreading across Louisville. Some justified and some unwarranted. Whenever a police officer kills a kid, it will lead to chaos—and perhaps it should."

"People are too eager to get themselves killed or kill someone these days," Vickie said. She stood and straightened her light green jacket and immaculate matching slacks.

Carter surveyed the personal photos on the shelf behind her desk. Vickie, her husband Denzel, and their three kids resembled a toothpaste advertisement in a women's magazine. The parents sat on chairs, the kids posing behind them. A Bible rested on the table between the parents. Carter attempted to form a picture of his mom sitting in a chair while he and Becca hovered near her, but the image faltered like a computer monitor plagued by a virus.

***

Priscilla Wallace, Ph. D., stormed into rooms like a tornado, intending to uproot and dismantle anything in her way. The twister was most apparent whenever she entered Carter's office.

In mid-June 2018, Superintendent Coles hired Priscilla as one of his four assistant superintendents. As usual, the superintendent performed wink-wink-nudge-nudge trades with the Louisville Teachers' Association president Ronnie Haggerty. Wallace was Haggerty's close friend from Chicago who'd never been a principal but possessed an administrator's certification and a doctorate. Haggerty tried several times to find her a high-paying school district job but failed. However, the union leader and Coles each possessed something the other wanted. Haggarty would pull the board members' strings to secure a pay increase for Coles. In return, the superintendent would hire Wallace as an assistant superintendent.

In early August 2019, after ten years of teaching fourth and fifth grades in the Louisville Public Schools, the school hiring committee chose Carter as the principal at West Louisville Elementary. They did this despite Dr. Wallace's insistence that they select a different candidate. Since that moment, Wallace has described Carter's performance as underwhelming.

Dr. Wallace was an intelligent and savvy politician. Carter knew he should focus on her latest assault, but his brain buzzed with urgency. The Traps percolated inside his head while he completed his morning tasks. The girl's image, the playground dancers, and even Shandi's fear-filled touch caused his leg to bounce like a jackhammer beneath his desk. Nonetheless, he would hide his anxiety.

"The last thing I need today is a visit from her," Carter whispered to his empty office.

The moment he mumbled the words, his desk phone rang.

"Yes, Vickie," he said.

"Dr. Wallace is here."

***

"I'm doing well," Carter said, directing Dr. Wallace to the chair before his desk. He thought she'd commandeer his seat if he didn't mark the territory. She placed her Louis Vuitton handbag on Carter's desk. The brown bag, LV embroidered on the side, matched her expensive designer business suit and shoes. Although a few years older than Carter, she displayed a statuesque posture and a poise that made her appear younger than her years. Her turquoise glasses, golden bracelets, and diamond rings trumpeted wealth and style.

When Wallace opened her monogrammed black leather portfolio and removed a personalized pen, Carter leaned back, increasing the distance between them. He pushed his hand through his short black hair. Although Carter was over six feet tall and maintained a lean, muscular build, Wallace viewed him as a stickman or a scarecrow. She didn't pretend to like him, which he admired because too many people were phony friends or even pseudo-parents. It was better to know animosity than have it hide in open sight. Carter realized Wallace's transparent superiority triggered his poor sense of worth.

"So, Mr. Sykes, you think you're doing well?"

"Yesterday was tough, but we got our kids home without incident, thanks to my assistant principal, Lamar, Vickie, my teachers, and the bus drivers."

"No incidents?" She retrieved her phone from the purse while maintaining eye contact. "What do you call this?" Her long fingers danced across the screen like a tall ballerina. She turned the device so Carter could see a video.

It commenced with the protest leader's amplified voice. "The boss wants to explain it to us because we're too stupid to understand." The picture cut to Carter, his arms braced against the fence as if he wanted to vault across. Another quick edit returned to the protesters marching along 39th Street, fists raised—then to Carter again, his face stern, saying, "You do not have the right..." Another fast edit showed Carter rolling his sleeves as the marchers continued down the street. Then it displayed Carter, his face tense and his hands grasping Neon Red's collar. The video zoomed out as if Quinton Tarantino had directed the action scene depicting Carter shoving the protester onto the collapsed fence.

The final edit presented the leader speaking to the camera—her name and title stretched across the lower part of the screen—"Amara Turner, Activist." With her high cheeks, ebony eyes, and brilliant smile, she resembled a reality television star rather than a protest leader.

"We have dealt with people like that man throughout the march," she said into the camera. "They aren't worried about kids like K'juan Wagers, a little boy murdered by a brutal police officer. People like that principal don't have to worry about being shot because of his skin color. Thousands of times a year, black men and boys are dying due to racist cops. He's more interested in silencing us than ending the police department's executions."Dr. Wallace shut the phone case as if her closing statement was complete. However, it wasn't.

"I call that an incident, Mr. Sykes," Wallace said. "And honestly, I'm befuddled as to why you would dismiss it as if it's no big deal."

"If you want to be honest, Dr. Wallace, you might consider whether the video is an accurate..."

"Are you claiming that's not you all puffed up like a mall security guard?" Wallace slid back and smiled, proud of her quip as though the evil of mall security guards was self-evident. "Or is that someone pretending to be you?"

I'm always pretending to be me, Carter thought.

"I guess 'resistance is futile,'" he said. When Wallace didn't get the Star Trek reference, Carter inhaled and turned his palms up as if surrendering. Mounting a defense didn't feel like a worthwhile endeavor.

"Take my word for it, Mr. Sykes. The superintendent isn't happy your video has gone viral. He threw a fit when he saw you acting all Proud Boys."

"Viral?"

"Over 80,000 views and counting," Wallace said. "Do you even know who the young man you attacked is?"

Carter didn't respond.

"That's Kyle Waterson," she said. Her tone implied his identity should be as self-evident as the security guard's inherent evil. Carter stared at her. "As in Martin Waterson, the owner of the Louisville Tribune?" She shook her head.

The head shakes jabbed against Carter's temper like a cattle prod.

"It's funny, Dr. Wallace. Sixty-seven thousand of our students can't read on grade level, and bullies attack kids and teachers daily, but I have never heard Dr. Coles throw a fit about those things."

Wallace glared over her designer frames. Her disdain washed toward him as if he were gutter trash during a torrential downpour.

"I will let the superintendent know you oppose our social justice efforts, Mr. Sykes."

"Social justice? What about plain justice and truth? Appearances are not reality," Carter said. "For example, it appears you don't like me very much."

"Perception is reality, Mr. Sykes." She bounced from her chair. For a flash, he feared she'd stretch over his desk and rake her nails across his face.

"No, it isn't. That's why we call it per..."

"Tammy and Chuck at Public Relations expect you in their studio on Wednesday. You will film a short video for local media outlets. It will be a full and sincere apology for your insensitivity to yesterday's protestors and the community."

Carter's anger churned, but as usual, it was deep inside him in the swamp of drowned thoughts, floating regrets, and dirty deeds. His face remained stoic.

Wallace continued. "Dr. Coles and PR agree with me. A humble apology is in order. Community leaders have called for it." Wallace searched her bag, withdrew an envelope, and slid it across the desk. "Tammy wrote this script for you to study. It contains the required points for the apology."

Carter crossed his arms and stewed for a moment. "What if I ignore perception and live in reality instead of agreeing to kneel?"

"You don't listen between the lines, do you, Sykes?" Wallace's eyes bulged, and her lips drew a thin line.

Carter wanted to defend himself, but his mind tricked him. Instead of a retort, the abducted girl from his Trap reappeared—her agonized expression and the dirty cloth gag stuffed into her mouth. Her tiny moans crushed him. He pictured the oversized white tee shirt engulfing her body and the bonds securing her to the headboard. The only lines he memorized tethered her wrists to the headboard.

"If you don't follow directives, then so be it. My suspicions will be confirmed," Wallace said. "Something ain't right with you, as the kids say. I'm sure there's an occupation more suited for your skill set and unique personality."

Once, a foster dad suggested Carter work a crash test dummy at the Ford plant or a mannequin for a department store. "It suits your personality," he'd said.

Dr. Wallace strutted toward the door. "You're lucky Monday is Memorial Day. On Tuesday, you apologize or face the consequences." She swung her bag around and slid the strap on her shoulder. After pausing to collect herself and recapture her smile, Dr. Wallace turned and exited into the narrow hallway.

"Apologize?" Carter said to the empty office. "I've been sorry my entire life."

CHAPTER 5

Stephanie cried as the man wrapped his tattooed arms around her. His gentle touch raised goosebumps on her shoulders, and his goatee scratched her temple as she folded into his embrace. Her chin rested against the cartoon figure of a man holding a wrench above the "Kevin" embroidered on his work shirt.

"I do it all for you, Babydoll," he said. "You remember when I found you seven years ago, don't you?"

The question was so familiar that it was more a ritual than a conversation. Kevin's words toppled the first domino, starting an inevitable sequence—her defenses falling and ending with her full compliance.

"Yes," she said between whimpers. She gritted her teeth and braced herself against the kitchen counter in their Preston Highway Apartment. The fluorescent light fixture above the counter buzzed like cicadas, and the smell of burned toast and cannabis hung in the air.

"It's our compromise, Steph," he said. He pulled away, but his thick hands clenched her arms. He gazed into her brown eyes, and Stephanie convinced herself she saw kindness. "Right and wrong don't mean nothing to us. We create the right and the wrong together. We balance what we want with what we need, right?"

She raised her hand, palm up, and used the heel to wipe her nose. "I know, Kevin," Stephanie said, sniffling. "You and Kelsey are the only two people in this world I love."

Kevin's nose twitched as if she had given him a paper cut.

"But, Kevin, you said that church girl would be the last one. You've kept this one for days now. Can't you let her go back to her family?"

"Stop it." He raised his deep voice and gripped her shoulders tighter. She winced as his fingernails, lined with axel grease and oil, indented her pale skin. "Just because you saw her, you act like it's different. You know I got good intentions. I'll teach this little rich girl a lesson and send her on her way wiser. That's what matters. I can't help who I am, Stephanie."

"I just..."

"If you want me different, you want somebody else. Then, it'll only be a minute before you're on the street, giving up that sweet ass for nothing or, worse, for some pimp who'll kill you when you can't earn. Is that what you want?"

Stephanie lowered her head, and strands of brown and maroon hair fell like a frayed rope around her face.

The man released her shoulder, lifted her chin, and used his long fingers to push aside the hair obscuring her face. His fingers smelled like gasoline and cigarettes. "It's you and me, Babydoll. Nobody loves you like I do. Nobody. I choose little rich divas to make them pay for how you got treated back in the day."

She averted her gaze toward the bedroom door.

"Look at me," he said, closing the distance between their faces. His volume and tone changed. "You be Idaho, and I'll do what I need to do. These are the same kinda bitches who hurt you in school. They live in big houses with their rich daddies and mommies thinkin' they all that, but they ain't."

Stephanie inhaled and stood taller. Her gray t-shirt proclaimed, "Resist!" She sniffed and said, "I know, Kevin, but I thought..."

"Everything's not about you, Stephanie." His lip quivered, but his blue eyes were dry. "I'm hurting, sweetheart. Can't you see what they've done to me? It made me what I am. Hell, you know that better than anybody." He turned his back but didn't step away.

"I'm sorry," she said. "I know you can't help it."

He pivoted, causing her heart to skip a beat.

"My baby, my baby," he said, pulling her to his chest again until her nose mashed against the "Kevin" on his work shirt. "I'm here for you no matter what I do with her. It breaks my heart to picture you on the streets again. You make me better. Look at how I have slowed down. That's your doin', baby. Who knows what I'd do without you in my life? I might kill these girls instead of releasing them. You're saving lives by being with me. Let me teach these privileged girls, and you keep earning until the garage starts makin' bank again."

Stephanie sniffed, and her shoulders relaxed as she slipped deeper into his muscular body. Again, she glanced over Honeyboy's shoulder, imagining the girl's dark, tear-stained face, a mask of pain and fear.

CHAPTER 6

The vibrant red bricks and the landscaping made the two-story duplex appear newer than the other buildings on Central Street. The other houses presented faded facades, the mortar stained with blotches of black mold painting the exteriors. The barren flower beds stretched toward the oak trees lining the sidewalk. Only the most ardent spring weeds sprouted beneath the awnings. The mud, stirred by the torrential spring rains the week before, splashed across the brick paths that led to each door. A kinder landlord owned this two-family structure, Carter guessed.

An old Lucinda Williams song lilted from the Toyota's CD Player. The words proclaimed how the singer envied the wind blowing across her lover's face. Carter didn't covet the wind or even the beauty of Lucinda's voice. He envied people who connected with others free from fear and doubt. Carter was jealous of those who found solace in the secure arms of loved ones rather than a stranger's dangerous embrace. He envied her lover because anyone could touch him.

"Where are we, Carter?"

He glanced at Becca through the rearview mirror, sitting on her knees in the backseat. His sister was much younger than earlier, but her appearance didn't surprise him—she visited him in different stages of her life, if you could call it that. Now, she was the same age as the third graders at his school. Her light brown hair fell onto her shoulders, and her white and yellow dress seemed fresh like the sunflowers were new blooms. She cradled the damaged doll he had given her long ago. The kid-sized, red, heart-shaped sunglasses he bought her at the flea market rested low on her nose; the dark plastic lenses reflected the lights lining the street.

"Nowhere, Becca," Carter said, gazing at Hope and Lenora's house. He realized visiting Hope and Lenora was a mistake.

"This is stupid," Carter said aloud.

"It sure is, Cartie," Becca said. She shook her head and hugged the cloth doll to her chest. "You got bigger stuff to do than sneaking around with them girls. You gotta keep your job and help that girl the scary man's got tied up." She wagged her tiny finger.

His life felt like the end of a David Lynch movie—disjointed, confused, and filled with explosive emotional fireworks rather than resolutions.

The late afternoon sun rested on the horizon, and the distant roar of cars on the expressway replaced Lucinda's song after he shut off the engine.

"Cartie, Cartie, Cartie," Becca said in her most disappointed voice. "You are being bad again. Momma told you not to be bad, or she'd whoop your ass."

***

The ceiling light was off, and the dim lamps colored the darkness rather than cutting through it. Lenora and Hope melded together as shadows cuddled on the sofa. Lenora was younger than Hope. Her long blonde hair concealed her face and hung across her breasts like thick strands of golden fabric. Her arms were thinner, shorter versions of Hope's, not sleeved but adorned by one large mermaid tattoo and a line of poetry barely legible on her pale arm.

"For though she be fair and fairer, She is not so fair as In my heart."

Hope whispered in Lenora's ear, causing her to chuckle and gaze at Carter. Shadows concealed his blush.

The two women kissed. Hope's lips lingered on Lenora's, gentle like her whisper. When they parted, Lenora and Hope turned toward Carter.

"This is Lenora, Carter," Hope said. Carter's breath became shallow upon hearing his name spoken. He preferred nameless encounters. Anonymity and sex mated in his mind long ago because anonymous partners meant no commitments. Commitments were no more than opportunities to be hurt by others, no more than guarantees of disappointment and inevitable loss.

The two women stood. Lenora reached for him while Hope stepped to his side. Carter let Lenora's hand hang in the air before touching it. Hope rested her palm on his shoulder and pulled him closer to kiss his cheek.

He anticipated a Trap—perhaps the circumstances behind the crosses tattooed on her wrist. However, the Trap never happened. Instead, Hope's hand traveled down his back and stopped on his backside. She guided him toward an unlit hallway.

Lenora slid in front before returning her hand to tug his shirt. He saw her perfect bare shoulder peeking through the long hair cascading along her back. He estimated Lenora was five feet and one inch, several inches shorter, and much younger than Hope. She floated in the darkness like a ghost, drawing him forward. She left lavender and honey in her wake.

Third-grade Becca's voice echoed in his head. *"Shame on you, Carter. You are being bad, but you can't stop yourself."*

He shivered and recited his mantra. *"Just this once, and that's it."*

An image flashed across his memory. He heard his mother's moans and the rhythm of the headboard rocking against the thin drywall like a bird colliding over and over again with its reflection in a pane of glass.

Still, *"Just this once."*

Hope pressed her breasts against his arm, the fabric of her long black night shirt rubbing his sleeve. Carter raised his hand to trace her slender neck. Her warm skin and the smell of sandalwood, vanilla, and jasmine made him dizzy.

However, the farther they advanced into the house, the more the Traps haunted him. *I shouldn't do this. Guilt tastes like mud.*

Carter considered an exit: a fast explanation and an even quicker departure.

"You're nasty, Cartie." Becca's little girl voice chastised him. He imagined her fingers rubbing together like sticks. *"You're gonna ignore that scar on Hope's wrist? Shame, shame on you."*

"You're right. I shouldn't." His own voice joined the chorus inside his head.

However, within moments, his Boss, the inner voice that owned him, echoed harsh instructions. *"Don't stop."*

When Lenora opened the bedroom door, light spilled into the hallway. Hope, still resting against Carter's shoulder, turned his head toward her with her delicate fingers. She kissed him, her tongue darting past his lips. Electricity flowed through his body, and his knees grew weak. But still, there was no Trap. Hope led him through the doorway as Lenora drifted to the queen-sized bed. The sheets, lit by the bedside lamps, were whiter than Lenora's pale skin. *Heaven-lit*, he thought. *Like a cloud bathed in sunlight. Like the Middle Eastern horizon burning during the war.*

Hope slithered into Lenora's arms as Carter stood at attention. She whispered in Lenora's ear again. Lenora did not reply, but Hope laughed.

"She wants you solo first," Hope said. Lenora reclined beside her, wearing her shy smile and nothing else. The two women locked their gaze on Carter as they kissed again. Hope left the bed and stepped toward him for an embrace. "Have fun, Mr. Principal," she said, glancing over her shoulder at Lenora. "Be gentle with this one, Babe. He's special."

Lenora's fingertips traced down his bare chest toward his stomach. That gentle touch triggered a Trap.

***

Tears race down the older woman's cheeks as she screams inches from Lenora's face. A thick vein protrudes from the woman's forehead, and her eyes balloon with rage.

"I want you gone, Lenora. If you love your independence more than family, take it and get out." Lenora's heartbeat, and therefore his own, drums and sputters, the words shrapnel piercing her chest.

"No, Mama, no," the girl cries as she reaches for the older woman. Two suitcases sit on the floor, forming a border between them.

The woman pivots away, her eyes, the same blue as Lenora's, filled with tears, her contorted face a hybrid of anger and pain.

Lenora's knees quiver as if they might fold. Carter expects her to drop to her knees and beg for forgiveness. Instead, she straightens her posture, retrieves the luggage, and staggers through the open front door. Carter sees the yellow taxi in front of the tiny house and hears Lenora's staccato breaths and animal-like moans deep inside her throat as though they were his own.

CHAPTER 7

Mona Ridge sipped water from a silver container and stared at the duplex's storm door. As Carter Sykes ascended the steps and knocked on the glass, she closed the lid and frowned.

"What are you into, Mr. Sykes?" Her voice sounded curt and blunt against the police cruiser's windshield. When the storm door opened and the barista from the coffee shop appeared, Mona added, "Now that's five-star customer service."

The barista's unruly black hair spiked in all directions, and a black, form-fitting night shirt twisted down her body like a mystery. *She's a little young for you, Carter, isn't she?* Then Mona saw the other woman—a young blonde. "She's too young for you, boy-oh."

Is that why you haven't pursued me, Carter Sykes? I'm thirty-five years old.

The principal stepped across the threshold within seconds, and the red front door closed behind him.

"So, they were expecting you," Mona said. "Carter Sykes, you're something else."

She first met him on a dispatcher call to the elementary school, where two men fought over who had arrived first at the car rider pickup line. Carter helped her de-escalate the situation. Unlike many others she had encountered on such calls, the principal kept his cool and didn't hesitate to respond. Sykes even made her laugh when he claimed that the same thing had happened with fourth graders at the water fountain earlier, so he scheduled after-school detention if the angry fathers needed a time-out.

A single guy with a good sense of humor and a good job? Borderline handsome with thick black hair, kind brown eyes, and a lean, muscular build? The scar above his left eye made him appear rough yet vulnerable, and his smile was just wide enough to be genuine. Until the coffee shop chat, she considered him a unicorn in the wild dating world. However, when he shared his muddy information about a mysterious abducted girl, it made her suspicious. She didn't mention the Good Girl Killer's signature, hoping he'd slip up and reveal a detail the police withheld from the public.

However, Mona acknowledged that the latest missing kid was indeed African American and fit the profile of the other girls. She was between fourteen and twenty-five years old, high-achieving in her elite private school, and came from an affluent family. So, Sykes didn't sound crazy. Still, his tangled, specific, vague details didn't jive, leaving her with more questions than actionable information.

Mona was most troubled by what Carter did not say. She sensed he had omitted something important, so after she left the coffee shop, she pulled up his address and started following him hours later, in case her instincts were right. Seeing him at the barista's door didn't relieve her distrust.

Carter is hiding something. I hope it isn't what I'm afraid it is. She shook her head in frustration.

Criminals insert themselves into investigations for the notoriety or to disrupt the case with false information. *This guy must be a thrill-seeker and a player,* she thought. *He is safe enough to get young girls to trust him and physically fit enough to subdue them. Here he is, visiting two young women early in the evening.*

Then again, perhaps he'd acted odd because he had a date with the barista and didn't want to screw it up? Mona could only hope for that outcome.

No matter what she hoped, she couldn't ignore her instincts—she needed to discover what Sykes was hiding.

Then again, she could be an overworked police officer amid a city-wide revolt, wasting her time confusing an awkward, well-intentioned, but horny guy with the next Ted Bundy.

CHAPTER 8

Carter leaned toward the front door, left hand in the pocket of his jeans. His messy hair and untucked Goodwill, long-sleeved Reebok shirt suggested he had rolled out of someone's bed. He had. Although it was still early by his nocturnal habits, three hours of fun with Lenora and Hope sufficed.

"That was wilder than I expected," Hope said. "You're impressive, Carter."

Carter's face turned crimson, and he gazed at the floor. "I'm more lucky than impressive, Hope." He glanced at Lenora and noted she acted as awkward as he felt. She shuffled her feet and didn't make eye contact. He realized she was younger than he first thought, which explained why she was more reserved than Hope had been in the bedroom. Hope was uninhibited and loud. Her moans and talk echoed in his ears. Lenora was passionate but also reticent at times.

"Maybe we should make this a regular thing?" Hope said. She stepped closer to Carter and kissed him on the cheek, much like when he first arrived. Lenora pushed Hope on the shoulder as if to silence her.

"Sure," he replied. "Should" and "regular thing" sounded too much like a commitment to Carter. His shoulders tightened, and his mind flipped to when his foster mother turned as she left his tiny basement bedroom and said, "If you are a good boy, we can do that again and again."

Lenora floated toward him, hesitant and reserved. She extended her hand as she frowned at her partner.

A handshake? Carter hesitated, then grasped her warm hand. The Trap he experienced with Lenora hung in his memory—her mother refused to accept Lenora's life—the very life her mom had given her. Her reluctant hold indicated Lenora might be as averse to making a connection as he was.

"Keep the coffee hot for me at the cafe, Hope," he said. He nodded toward Lenora and added, "I've got an early Sunday morning."

"Don't tell me you're going to church," Hope said. She smiled but rescinded it when she realized Carter might attend a service. "I don't mean to judge."

"The Jefferson County Family Shelter," Carter said. "I volunteer there two Sundays a month."

Why would I tell her that? Was I ashamed she thought I might go to church?

Lenora backed away as though Carter's words stung her. She glared at Hope. Carter interpreted her reaction as regret.

"Philanderer and philanthropist," Hope said, unfazed by her girl-friend's reaction. "So many surprises from you, Carter."

Carter pointed his shoulder toward the exit, "I think I need some rest, so..."

"Thanks for the good time," Hope said.

Carter nodded and exited, happy to wear the darkness of Old Louisville's streets like a veil.

CHAPTER 9

"Did you enjoy yourself, Cartie?" Becca filled his rearview mirror again, only now she was a short-haired teenager, her eyes blazing with anger, as though Carter had left her in the Walmart parking lot too long. The white and yellow sunflower dress slipped down her shoulder, revealing two tattoos—tiny, red handprints, side by side, as if a child dipped her palms in paint and placed them on her chest.

She glared for several seconds before her face softened, and she leaned forward into the front seat. She touched his cheek. "What's sad is you know the right thing, but you have sex with two lesbians." She smiled and shook her head as if amazed by his boneheaded moves. "That can't be bad, right?"

Carter held his breath for a moment, then exhaled. "I'm going to do what I..."

"You're like Noah's Ark, taking them two at a time now," Becca said. "Who knows? At that rate, you might fill up the big hole inside you, whatever it is."

He stared at the holes in her body. Becca's words were tangled knots in a shoestring. Sure, he could slip the shoes onto his feet, but he would continue stumbling until he stopped and untangled everything.

Becca was right, of course. Carter retreated toward strangers and ever-increasing danger with little regard for the consequences. The pain and guilt escalated after each encounter, but he failed to resist. Whenever he succumbed to the habit, the regret returned tenfold.

"Damn right, it comes back," Becca said. "You're such a fool, big brother. You don't even control what you can; then you wonder why the uncontrollable world ignores you when you try to do what's right. It's pathetic. You're repeating the same old tricks and constantly crying about the consequences. Grow a pair, please." A loud bubble gum pop punctuated her words.

Carter pressed the accelerator and headed toward home. He redirected his mind to the abducted girl trapped in Honeyboy's bedroom. Except now, the young woman tied to the bed was a girl with short black hair, pale skin, and baby hand prints over her heart. He blinked and rattled his head, hoping to erase the image and dislodge the heavy guilt crushing his brain.

"You are like those smart bombs you saw during the war, Carter," Becca said. "You explode and take a bunch of innocents with you. Why aren't you searching for the girl instead of leaving her in the castle, so to speak?"

The words pierced him all the way through.

***

As he drove, anger consumed the city around him. Firetrucks and police cars blocked traffic as two cars burned near UofL's campus.

When he finally reached the ramp, he merged onto I-65 to avoid the protestors, blockades, and rogue brick throwers. The elevation showed the city from a different vantage point. Smoke gathered in the night sky, swirling in the spring winds. The gray mist dimmed the artificial lights, obscuring landmarks like Slugger Field and the clusters of people still on the streets. When he finally exited, protesters blocked Broadway, forcing him to detour through Cave Hill Cemetery and Phoenix Hill.

Carter often compared Louisville to an avocado. The hull had softened over time as people moved from the downtown into the outer shell of the county. As the edges ripened, inner-city Louisville became a hardened core.

He poked the radio knob, and the car filled with disagreement. Two anger-laced voices struggled for control.

"The police don't care if they shoot a black child in the streets," one said. "They'd like to eradicate all of them if they could. You know..."

"That's a blatant lie," the responder countered. "Race and poverty aren't factors in this. The streets are so dangerous officers fear for their lives. That's why they shoot."

"Then why aren't white kids catching bullets on their way to the..."

"K'Juan Wagers was out at 1:30 in the morning on a school night. Why did his parents..."

"Read a damn history book, and you'll understand."

Carter turned off the radio. *Radio hosts are more like sports announcers, advocating for their hometown teams and ignoring complex truths and answers,* he thought.

After his mother died, the state placed Carter in four consecutive foster homes before he aged out at eighteen years old. Each place Carter landed, he confronted a different definition of the truth.

Carter was the only child placed with the Bergers, his first foster parents. Owen, the father, viewed Carter as a broken toy soldier. He and Renee expected to fix him and place the poor boy on the mantle for all to see. However, the repairs weren't as easy as the couple antic-ipated. They decided the effort required outweighed the benefits of a virtue-signaling fireplace. Their initial promise of "a better life" melted like ice spears hanging from a tin roof. By spring, they had boxed him up like an unacceptable collectible and shipped him back to the store.

Social Services placed him with the Welch family in Loveland, Ohio. The transition was challenging, and he slipped into profound sadness. However, despite his depression, Carter found happiness with the Welches. Their kindness persuaded him to trust them. He'd found a home—at least until the family played Cornhole in the backyard.

Mrs. Welch gave him a high five and hugged him for an excellent, game-winning bag toss. Carter hadn't felt such love and belonging since his time with Becca.

He hugged his foster mom back. "I'm sorry those boys hurt you in that truck after the concert," Carter said.

She stared at him, bewildered and then humiliated. Her eyes widened, and her mouth gaped as if he'd recited a magic spell and turned into a frog. After that exchange, she never looked into his eyes, and by the time he turned fourteen, Mr. Welch, sounding like an assistant manager at Kroger, explained to him, "It isn't working out."

Days later, Carter moved in with the Zellers in Florence, Kentucky.

When Carter arrived, the Zellers already cared for two foster kids, Selina and Jewel. They were twins, three years older than he was, but had been with the Zellers since turning seven. Carter had learned to keep his Traps to himself, so he was even more careful and cloistered as he tried to fit into the family.

However, his time at the Zellers also taught him to keep other secrets. Mr. Zeller worked as a construction supervisor, traveling the country building department stores. On the nights Mr. Zeller traveled, Mrs. Zeller visited Carter's room in the finished basement. It started as a kiss on the cheek and a "Goodnight, Carter." However, it evolved into a secret she said he must never reveal. Her name was Leslie. She entered his room with a wine glass and locked the door. She was in her late thirties, with blonde, wavy hair and blue eyes that she closed when she kissed him. Her soft hands traveled along his body in ways he had never experienced, temporarily easing his pain and guilt. Carter felt released from his childhood and valued.

However, soon after his sixteenth birthday, a social worker whisked Carter away without allowing him to say goodbye. Later, he concluded that Selina and Jewel had pieced together what was happening and confronted Leslie about it. It didn't surprise him, especially since his foster siblings had touched him, Trapping him in their trauma. Their drug-addicted biological mother and her boyfriend abandoned them at a fire station when they were five years old. Although they would soon leave the Zeller's custody, they couldn't bear losing their mother to trash like him again.

Carter cringed when he realized he'd arrived home. He gripped the steering wheel and wondered where the last five minutes had gone. His watch read 10:32 p.m. Becca's face was no longer visible in the mirror, leaving only his shame-filled eyes staring back.

CHAPTER 10

Kevin rotated his wrist and squinted at his father's watch. It was 10:32 p.m., which left plenty of time with Zara. Stephanie's shift at Banger's ended at 3:00 a.m.

As Kevin entered the shadowy bedroom, he sang her name, "Za-aara, Zaaara." The tune was from an old Jefferson Starship song from the 1980s that his mother enjoyed in the car, although the song serenaded "Sarah," which was his mother's name.

Zara screamed through the bile-soaked gag shoved into her mouth. She knew what she intended to tell him, but her muffled words translated into a shriek and further saturated the cloth with spit. When he switched on the bedside lamp, the seventeen-year-old's eyes widened and filled with tears. The bed springs creaked as he sat beside her.

"Beautiful," Kevin said, lifting a thick strand of matted black hair from her cheek. He drew closer and inhaled the fragrance of her shampoo. Zara trembled and leaned away from his touch as though his hands were lava.

Those moments, the horrified retreat and the fearful gasps, excited Kevin more than her perfect skin and her breasts pushing against the white tee shirt he'd forced over her head. Her fear stoked the powerful fire inside him. It had always been that way for him. Whether it was his neighbor's cat, the random chicks he picked up on the street when he was just a teenager, or the little straight-A, go-to-church-every-Sunday-better-than-every-one-else-young-women he played with now—they all died with fear in their eyes, consumed by the heat in his heart.

Zara would be no exception.

"I'm gonna let you go if you make me happy, Zara," Kevin said. "Do what I tell you, and you'll be all right." He traced his dirty fingernails along her arm's smooth, dark skin, pausing to check the brown extension cord securing her wrist to the bed before caressing her palm and long fingers.

Zara's breathing came in short bursts. Kevin feared she might hyperventilate or vomit.

"You're not as confident as you were in the parking lot, Zara," he said. "People like you think danger will never darken your door. Your daddy makes lots of money at the university, and your momma is a bigwig attorney in town, so you're invincible, right?"

When Kevin mentioned her parents, Zara wiggled her butt against the spotted sheet on the bed. He recognized "please" among the muffled words shouted into the cloth in her mouth.

"You don't understand what it means to lose, do you?" he said as he slid closer to her on the bed. Sweat rolled from her hairline, mixing with her tears. "Of course you don't. Maybe you should think about how lucky you have always been, Zara. Being rich leads to high standing. It's easy to forget the faces you've kicked as you climbed up there."

She shuddered and turned away.

Kevin touched Zara's cheek as if admiring a souvenir in a collection. He tilted her head to one side and then the other, humming a kid's song imprinted on his brain. She tried to identify the tune but failed. Without warning, Kevin jerked the girl's face forward and leaned so close they were nose to nose. He moved even closer to rake his tongue on her cheekbone. Her tears and sweat tasted like warm ocean water.

Zara gagged. Kevin swore he could see the bile rising in her throat like magma inside a volcano. She was the lava now. He retrieved a box cutter from his pocket. The silver blade glinted in the light from the lamp.

Kevin thought it would be interesting to see what happened when the hot bile reached her obstructed mouth. He pictured a carburetor unable to suck in air due to a blocked bottleneck. Choking. Flooding. Dying. He raised the triangular blade to Zara's throat. Her eyes pleaded with him to stop. While it would be entertaining as hell to see her choke, he decided there was much more to do with Zara.

Kevin slipped the blade beneath the gag and severed it near her cheek.

Zara coughed as vomit, spit, and tears covered the white sheet and her white shirt.

"Don't worry, Zara," Kevin said. "I'll get you another gag. In the meantime, let's get to know each other better."

CHAPTER 11

Carter inhaled before lifting a stack of black, folding chairs. He carried them to the middle of the room and placed them around a rectangular cafeteria table and a card table. Soon, the homeless shelter would serve brunch to about sixty men, women, and children. Many of the kids were his students at West Louisville Elementary who stayed at the facility with their mothers. Several men had served in Iraq and Afghanistan, just as he had done. They often joked that the Gulf Wars were the pipeline to the shelter.

He stood tall after arranging the seats and examined the room. He saw the silver serving bins, steam rising from the water beneath the pans of pancakes, scrambled eggs, and plump pork sausages. To his right, the recreation room doorway allowed the gospel music on the television to drift into the dining room.

He'd denied the church when Hope asked him, but this homeless shelter served as his church in many ways. It supported his repentance and atonement, and although he'd only gone to church for the last few years as a foster child, he'd grown fond of kindness to his fellow man, although the religious principles hadn't stuck.

His foster father had insisted he attend services. Over twenty years later, Carter found himself listening to gospel music, standing in a room with crosses and a faded replica of The Last Supper hanging on the wall. He would serve out of the goodness in his heart. God wasn't the answer. He'd hoarded enough guilt and shame to do him a lifetime, so he didn't need religion to spoon him a second helping.

Carter half expected a version of Becca to rise from the steaming pans, pointing out that he'd slept with two women the night before. She didn't, probably because he already acknowledged his grand hypocrisy.

Carter stared out the window and saw the men gathered outside. He hoped to see Chester Price among those waiting, but his friend wasn't there.

Chester used to set up camp near WLE, beneath the US 64 overpass. Several parents voiced concern about "that homeless guy" accosting their children as they walked home from school.

Although the underpass wasn't on the route of students walking to and from school, Carter responded. He contacted Officer Ridge and met her at the tunnel to confront the villain. Instead of a criminal, they discovered a soft-spoken war veteran suffering from alcoholism and mental health issues.

"I don't blame you," Chester said. "The government tracks me because I tell the truth. I'm known to partake in spirits and even steal a Hershey bar or two, but politicians and bureaucrats threaten children more than I ever would."

After that meeting, Carter and Mona Ridge helped him get support at this shelter, and Carter signed up as a volunteer.

"Carter, can you give me a hand?" David Burton, a social worker who acted as the shelter director, carried a large serving pan filled with scrambled eggs.

Carter turned, smiled, and slow-clapped. He stepped toward the tall, dark-skinned man in jeans and a Blessings in a Backpack t-shirt. David's wild and wiry black hair and wisdom reminded Carter of Thomas Sowell, a writer whose words about education connected to Carter's experiences.

"Very clever, Carter," David said as he passed the pan to his friend. "It will be even funnier when we're mopping up all these eggs."

"You have a strong grip, David," Carter said. He trusted no one as much as David except Vickie. Both were exceptional professionals. Just as Vickie knew everything at the school, David understood the streets and neighborhoods. "I wasn't worried about you dropping the ball... or the eggs."

"My friend," David said, "are you as tired as you appear?" He wiped his dark hands on a kitchen towel hanging from his belt. Although David grew up in Louisville, his voice sounded like a Harvard professor speaking at a lecture.

"I'm fresh and full of energy," Carter said as he carried the pan to the serving table and placed it on the stained white tablecloth.

"You're full of something, Carter," he said. "I saw the viral video. Please be careful. Most people who march like that are concerned and want to see change; however, some do it to make themselves feel powerful and vital. That can make them dangerous."

Carter noted a smudge of white flour on the director's dark cheek. "You have something white on your face, David."

The man laughed and stirred the eggs with a large spatula. "You do, too, Carter. You're a white devil."

Carter laughed. David's sharp humor and willingness to help others drew Carter to him. Often, Carter referred families and individuals to David for assistance, just as he had Chester when he met him at the underpass. The social worker never disappointed him. Unlike many activists and advocates, David measured his worth in outcomes for his clients rather than accolades or social media hits.

"You can change the subject like a weatherman spins colors. I'm just saying, be careful. If you're tired, head home. We've got help today," David said.

Carter changed the weather again. "Have you seen Chester this morning?"

"No, but he was here last night," David said. "I know you two are buddies. It's one of the reasons I like you, Carter. You treat everyone you meet with dignity and respect. Usually, I would not say anything, but you might want to chat with Chester."

"Has he gotten into trouble?"

"No, but speaking on his behalf is not my place. You can ask him yourself," David said as he rotated the sausage pan. "He's outside now."

Carter turned and saw Chester through the handprints and grit dotting the front window. People greeted Chester with fist bumps and hugs. He wore a heavy brown coat with a fur-lined hood resting on his shoulders. Although they were about the same height and age, Chester's face and the specks of gray in his tangled hair made the African-American man older and shorter. His shoulders slumped, and he appeared more lopsided than Carter remembered when he last saw him two weeks earlier. Smoke rolled upward from the cigarette held between his fingers. However, even from that distance and through the dingy glass, Carter recognized the sharpness in his eyes and his unwavering grin.

Carter pushed more chairs under a table and met Chester at the door.

"There's the mayor of 39th Street," Chester said as Carter approached.

Carter shook the man's hand. He'd experienced Chester's trauma when they first met under the bridge years earlier. He'd seen the woman and the little girl telling Chester goodbye as he boarded a Greyhound bus in Oakland, California. His heartbreak and fear of never seeing the little girl again caused his heart to pound like the cool rain striking the bus roof. He had made a mistake, which the Trap didn't reveal, that uprooted his life even more than the Middle East.

"I've been watching for you, Chester," Carter said. "I was afraid we'd run out of pancakes."

"I'd join them protests if that happened," Chester said. The grin flashed across his narrow face and protruding jaw.

They both laughed, and Carter surveyed his friend from up close. Chester was thinner, and his always weary face carried more weariness than two weeks earlier. He resembled an actor who had shed pounds for a movie role. He wore that heavy coat year-round, but now it resembled a brown cocoon more than clothing. His dark, gaunt face rested on his bones like a detachable appendage. Nonetheless, Chester was fully engaged, which meant he wasn't drinking as much.

"What's going on, my friend?" Carter said.

***

"I've been dying since the day they dropped me in that hellhole," Chester said.

Carter lowered his head and placed his hands on the card table. He contemplated what Chester had told him before gazing up again and staring at his friend.

"Can't the doctors at the VA do anything?"

"Carter, the government sent me to Iraq and ordered me to the burn pits," he said. "I haven't trusted them since and won't trust them now. Besides, I'm living on borrowed time anyway."

"What does that mean, Chester?"

"It means the doctors don't know when I'll depart, but there's a ticket waiting at the gate. The good Lord gives us justice when it's all said and done, Carter," Chester said. "I came back filled with the poison that floated in the air. The US Army used me and threw me back into the world like time stood still. But I wasn't that sweet eighteen-year-old black kid when I returned to the streets. The fire and smoke in my lungs soaked into my soul, and I regret the anger and what I did when I came home."

Carter had hated the war but loved the order. He excelled as a soldier because the chaos mirrored his life. That's what Carter knew—danger, uncertainty, losing people you counted on and who counted on you. When the second battle of Fallujah raged, Carter stayed calm because he'd stood toe to toe with that rage. Drill sergeants yelled at him, but they couldn't make him flinch. Bullets pelted Iraqi sand at his feet, yet he didn't overreact. Carter's greatest fears resided inside him, not externally.

Best of all, firearms meant no one touched him.

Carter might have stayed in the Marines had it not been for a single incident. One day, an IED exploded near a main road near Bagdad. It wounded Carter and four other soldiers, but that wasn't what led to him not re-enlisting. The explosive killed a little black-haired boy who stood watching the long line of vehicles and Americans. After helping his unit, Carter limped to his tiny body, twisted, broken, and serenaded by the cries of injured soldiers and a heartbroken mother. It dug another grave in Carter's mind that he could never close. It reminded him that he'd been helpless in the past.

Carter said, "Chester, so many people returned with missing parts and a life of pain. Whatever you did is a consequence of sending kids to fight meaningless wars."

David waved at Carter from the other side of the makeshift cafeteria to get the principal's attention. Carter waved back and raised one finger to signal he would be there in a minute.

Chester leaned across the table, closer to Carter. His eyes were wide, and his lip trembled. Cracks and lines creased his brow and around his eyes like broken asphalt. The homeless man scanned the room as if he planned to say something no one should overhear. His voice was deep but small as if it emanated from the plastic tube Carter had used to talk to Becca when they were kids. The man's chest rattled as the people entered the cafeteria. He said, "My name is not Chester."

***

Carter remained silent. Over the three years he had known Chester, his friend claimed many dubious things—the government trained rats to spy on people with tiny cameras; the military planned to clone WW2 veterans so the best generation could fight in the next great war; every president since Carter worked for China. However, Chester's conviction and tone made this particular tale ring true.

"But you didn't pull the trigger, Chester," Carter said. "You were there, that's all."

"It was a robbery. I helped to plan it, and I stood there as it happened. That meant the police might charge me, or, as a black man in 2007, I should say they'd convict me."

Carter nodded. "So, all this time, you've been hiding?"

"I was so screwed up, man. I disappeared into the streets," he said. "The drugs and alcohol kept me on the brink, but I never fit into the world. My baby's mama, Alice, knew what to do. She took me to a local cemetery. We found a gravestone of a baby who died a year before I was born. His name was Chester Price. I stole his name like I robbed that Circle K. Alice worked at the courthouse and got me a license and a birth certificate. I moved from Oakland to Louisville and have lived the nightmare ever since."

Carter had experienced Chester's Trap when they first met under the overpass. He recalled it well—Chester holding a little girl in his arms, unable to let go, as he cried and told her goodbye. The war, the return home, and the robbery were powerful experiences for his friend. But being forced to leave behind his daughter had been the most traumatic.

"So that's why you're on the streets?"

"Hell no," Chester said. "I'm an alcoholic, buddy. I'm not trying to explain myself. I figure I don't have much time left, so I'm trying to escape the lies I've been livin' before I go. There are two important things to me right now. I want to hug my daughter again before I leave this world and be honest with my friends. That's the good thing about dying—it's like you're on a barge hustling down the river. All the meaningless shit behind you gets smaller as you float away."

Carter pictured himself standing on the deck of a large boat cutting through the brown waters of the Ohio River. Although the sky was dark, there were no stars.

CHAPTER 12

Carter passed fifty bucks to the gray-haired lady behind a glass partition. Over her shoulder, a sign listed the cost to enter. Single men paid fifty, married couples spent twenty, and single ladies always received free admission to the Dirty Mint Julep.

The gray fox gazed at him, her drawn-on eyebrows raised as he lowered the Bellarmine University baseball cap to shield more of his face. "Have fun," she said. It sounded more like a dry judgment than a greeting. However, Carter nodded and ignored her tone. He was there for one reason—to persuade Idaho to lead him to Honeyboy so he could provide Mona with what she needed to save the girl.

"Easy peasy," he said aloud.

Three steps later, he stood inside a room with tall ceilings and brown paneling adorning the walls. The swingers called it the "Meet and Greet Room." When Carter's eyes adjusted to the dark corners and dim lights, he veered to an empty table and dragged a tall metal chair behind it.

Once seated, he scanned the booths, sofas, and people filling the space around him. Tom Petty's "Free Fallin" played in stereo. Laughter and whispers crackled like fire at a campground. The shadows clung to the huddled groups lounging around the room. Most of the illumination emanated from television monitors attached to the walls and corners. Perfume, beer, and stale cigarette smoke from an era lost to city regulators hung in the air.

A petite woman, black silk hair draped across her bare shoulders, approached him. Her see-through white blouse billowed at the sides and put her beautiful body on display while giving her the aura of a seductive angel. Their eyes met before Carter lowered his chin, concealing his face behind his baseball cap again. She stopped, peered under the hat's bill to ensure he returned her smile, and then continued toward the doorways leading to the back rooms. She turned a few steps away, said, "They call me Khloe. I'll be around in case you get interested later," and floated away on her angel wings.

The Dirty Mint Julep was closer to Satan than most clubs. The owner, Allan, was a British transplant who had opened it beneath his gentlemen's club, Bangers. Banger's owners were transparent about its purpose, with a giant neon sign sporting a large sausage and a glowing, bikini-clad cartoon dancer, her right hand covering her mouth in awe of the smiling pork product.

But the Dirty Mint Julep was much more exclusive and low-key. Allan persuaded—meaning bribed—the county government to provide the building's basement with a different address than the club upstairs, establishing it as a separate entity with an independent entrance.

Upstairs, Banger's Gentlemen's Club followed all the rules necessary for Allan to retain his liquor license, keeping him prosperous, out of jail, and surrounded by women. Each night of the week until 3:00 a.m., women danced around a silver pole in sync with the deejays blaring music and the audience's adoration. Their bare bodies glittered and writhed in the stage lights.

But the Dirty Mint offered something different below ground level. It was a Swinger's Club catering to adventurous folks who participated in "the Lifestyle." The establishment hadn't changed since his visits last summer and in December during winter vacation. Louisville had a long tradition of sex clubs. In 2012, eleven years earlier, a construction crew working two floors below East Main Street discovered the remnants of a 1970s-1990s sex club. Known as LATEX—Louisville Area Trust eXchange—the underground club catered to those seeking alternative lifestyles. The crew found erotic art, wooden racks, chains, and even lamps to signal when the different sex rooms were in use.

The Dirty Mint Julep offered six rooms, not including the showers or the "Meet and Greet" area where Carter sat. Each room showcased a different theme. The Jungle Room, for example, provided leopard skin sheets covering a king-sized bed with artificial vines hanging from the ceiling, fake lion and tiger heads attached to the wall, and a large portrait of Elvis above the headboard. Carter had visited all the rooms except the Hot4Teacher Room. Allan furnished it like a classroom with a sturdy padded desk, chalkboards, and abundant rulers and paddles, making it too creepy for Carter to consider.

The Dirty Mint wasn't where any school principal or teacher should spend time, but it attracted Carter like a wild coyote to rabbits. Every time he visited, he became immersed in the artificial intimacy as though he had shed his true self at the door.

Nonetheless, Carter resolved not to visit the back rooms tonight and prided himself on his restraint with Khloe. Years ago, he'd worked with a teacher who tried to overcome the bottle through will and the church. Despite his family, job, and religion, alcohol won out in the end. Carter seldom resisted the ever-escalating parade of sexual experiences that defined his secret life. It was a small victory that he ignored Khloe.

The open area contained tables and chairs, lockers for valuables, sofas for comfort, and a television mounted in each corner. The monitors rotated every five minutes, allowing viewers to watch what happened live in the six rooms. The sofas allowed people to sit, talk, or do whatever they wanted. He pried his gaze from the corners, but each flickering change drew his attention back to the screens. *Like the voyeur you are.*

Sets of couples laughed and flirted without limits. Strangers, ready to be intimate yet remain strangers, leaned close, their laughter rising above the murmurs and music.

Dancers from Banger's often ventured into the basement and performed for the couch crowd. Their lap dances weren't limited since the Dirty Mint didn't serve alcohol or pay the performers in any way except for free admission. If the strippers performed any acts, there was no requirement to pay, although the dancers accepted "donations" without hesitation.

One such volunteer entertained a party of five, three women and two men, on a worn gray sofa across the way. Carter watched as the red-haired woman, wearing only a thong, straddled one of the women while caressing the face of another sitting next to her. The men talked like strangers who shared the same favorite NFL team, only glancing at their partners with passing interest.

Nearby, a tall blonde flowed across a man's lap like water. When she returned Carter's stare, he averted his gaze, adjusted the bill of his cap, and surveyed other sofas around the room.

Where was she? He recalled meeting the dancing protester one night during the previous summer. She had stood out because of her smile and long legs, and the aggressive way she approached him had made an impression.

"Shy boys get me hotter than a red poker," she had said after darting across the room where Carter sat alone. She reached for his hand and settled for his arm. She tugged at his shirt until he stood up. "Come over, and let's get comfortable, handsome." She towed him by the sleeve until they sat next to another man being attended to by a heavy-set Latino woman wearing red lingerie.

Carter recalled how Idaho hovered over him, dipping her writhing body onto his chest as her face came so close he could smell her bubblegum breath. He placed his hands on her sides before she touched his skin, and she wriggled away, her palms resting on his thighs. Her body glided over his, still not touching but allowing her electricity to leap across the small chasm between them. Whenever he touched her, she reacted with a short, rapid breath and wafted away like steam.

Idaho. Idaho. Idaho. Where are you?

Carter snapped into the present and scoured the room, searching for the girl. He didn't see her, but he sighted the next best option. Carter stood and walked toward another young woman seated with a couple across the room. Carter gazed away as he approached so the threesome didn't realize they were his target.

Carter stopped as if he had just noticed her and said, "Hello, Kelsey."

She appeared puzzled at first, but then a spark of recognition crossed her face. "Look who it is—the man from 39th Street." She stared at Carter and smiled. "Where's your shirt and tie, Mister? You slumming?"

Carter said, "I'm looking for your friend, Idaho. You seen her?"

"Idaho sure got your attention at the march, didn't she?" Kelsey glanced at the couple. The man was forty-five or so. His perfect line of brown hair plugs reminded Carter of the carpet at his second foster home. The man's puffy face sagged toward his cleft chin, sunglass-

es dangled from his tropical shirt pocket, the yellow and green ba-
nanas and leaves glowing in the fluorescent lights. The man's left arm
wrapped around his blonde partner's shoulders. She was a few years
younger than he was, and her blue eyes and silicone implants were
impressive.

"Kelsey, aren't you gonna introduce your handsome friend?" The
woman leaned forward, offering Carter her hand and a generous peek
at her ample cleavage. He carefully delayed the handshake and patted
her on the covered shoulder before taking her hand. Her skin felt
smooth and warm in his palm.

"I'm Jen, and this is my husband, Larry," she said, nodding toward
the man without breaking contact with Carter. Her eyes widened, and
she traced her upper lip with her tongue.

"You three are cozy over here," Carter said. "I hope I'm not intrud-
ing. I'll go as soon as Kelsey helps me."

"You can intrude on me anytime you want," Jen said. She wetted her
lips again and giggled to punctuate her offer.

Kelsey laughed and patted Jen on the arm. "Back in your cage,
cougar," she said. "I think our friend here has a crush on my girl, Idaho.
Don't you, big boy? Did our little show at the school leave you wanting
a repeat performance?"

Carter cleared his throat. "Something like that," he said. "Is Idaho
working upstairs tonight?"

"She's not here tonight, Mr. 39th Street. I haven't talked to her since
Thursday after the march. Besides, I wouldn't tell you anyway. For all
I know, you're a creep stalking her." She cocked her head and offered a
half-smile.

"Shoot," Jen said. "You better leave the young ones alone and come
spend some time with us."

"It is cool, man," Larry interjected. "I'll stay out of your way and tip our Kelsey here." He pointed toward the dancer. Her eyes sparkled like on 39th Street, and she tilted her chin. She was so petite. Carter thought she wanted to appear taller.

Carter's gaze traveled between Jen and Kelsey. They smiled like temptation always did—confident, alluring, probing his brain, searching for the upright lever that opens the gate.

Of course, Carter planned to resist. He was forty-one years old and, in some ways, a public figure with too much to lose to continue taking these risks. Only fools jeopardize their life with such reckless abandon. He wasted too much time counting bricks on whore house walls and sinning inside dark dens like this sex club. He acted in his own worst interest, which wasn't Dr. Wallace's doing. It was time to overcome, abstain, and delay base gratifications with strangers. More significant issues demanded his attention, including someone who needed him and deciding how to save his job.

Besides, so soon after Hope and Lenora? What's wrong with me? No way.

Moments later, with Jen and Kelsey holding an arm, Carter watched a video monitor mounted on the wall. Naked figures tangled, rising and falling like undulating vines made of flesh.

In unison, the threesome followed Larry into the Jungle Room beneath the watchful eyes of The King.

CHAPTER 13

Mona considered Captain Anderson a leader to watch closely. She didn't possess the skills required to attain a high rank in the LMPD like he held. The captain had proven himself able to ignore the big picture and take care of minute, meaningless issues associated with special interests and political expediency. Anderson demonstrated the courage to speak one way to officers yet another way to Chief Sylvia C. Rhodes, the Metro Council, and the Mayor's Office. When the proverbial crap rolled downhill toward him, he exhibited the moral agility to dodge the brown boulder and redirect it onto the officers doing the work. The captain sure had their backs, and the knives to stick in them. Indeed, Anderson was the perfect model for how not to lead others.

Anderson didn't glance at her until she said, "My point is, I don't have any hard evidence, but this guy may know something about the Good Girl Killer."

The captain looked up from his paperwork—using bureaucracy as a roadblock to progress was another leadership skill he possessed in abundance—and wrinkled his brow as he surveyed Mona. His black hair, gray clouds spotting the sides, immaculate white uniform shirt, and numerous stripes gave him an air of distinction and authority. It indicated his great wisdom, yessiree.

"Hellfire, Ridge, that's not your case to worry about," Captain Anderson said. "Detective Vincent's on point." Anderson's expression hardened, but a demeaning smile snaked across his thin lips. "He's a detective, and you're a grunt riding shotgun in the Wild West."

Heat rose from her neck to her cheeks. "I know, Captain, but this might be a..."

"You need to hit the streets, keeping order as yahoos burn the city down, not playing detective by talking to some stupid school teacher."

You dumb, self-promoting, arrogant, ass-kissing waste of a badge, she thought. The words tried to kick open her lips to gallop into the world, but her brain yanked the reins.

"Yes, indeed, sir," she said. "I knew you'd provide guidance. It's classy. Many leaders would get involved on the outside chance they'd crack the case. If this stupid teacher is wrong, we'll keep it to ourselves, but if he did know something or even turned out to be the perp, you'd steal a high-profile career changer from Homicide and Vincent."

The captain's smile faded, and his lips tightened.

Mona's face remained stoic, but she stared at Anderson without blinking. She heard his brain working—creaking and grinding as he weighed the potential opportunity to add another rise in the ranks. She imagined he saw himself at the podium, announcing how he'd assigned a female officer (for diversity's sake) to observe a person of interest who turned out, as he predicted, to be the Good Girl Killer.

Mona shoved him harder to break the silence and unclog Anderson's mental constipation. "But I understand, sir. I have special access to this guy, and he's already demonstrated suspicious behavior, but you're right. The west end is a mess, and we must do more to protect the people of color and poor white people there. Thank goodness you are the only person I have told about this guy—no reason for you to try and outshine your detectives. Vincent's a superstar, I know. And the press, sheesh, they'd have a fit if you solved this case before Homicide did."

"Don't be so jumpy, Ridge." Captain Anderson leaned forward. His face reminded her of a kid at a comic book store staring through the glass. "You're too quick to give up on our instincts. I'm giving you an assignment. Watch this guy. If you get any evidence, call me first and only."

Mona smothered a laugh. *Our instincts?* She brought her best serious face forward and said, "Yes, sir. I will follow through and not do anything without consulting you."

Mona stood and exited the room, pleased to have achieved her goal, before he realized she'd played him.

However, once she stood beneath the harsh fluorescent lights of the police station, she inhaled and confronted the real question.

Carter Sykes, who are you, really?

She glanced at the newly waxed white and gray tile floor, straightened her uniform, and followed the fluorescent glare toward the exit sign and the answer.

CHAPTER 14

Memorial Day wasn't Carter's favorite holiday. He admired the veterans who lost their lives in wars or after they returned home, and being a veteran brought him some sense of belonging, although many others, like Chester, didn't share that feeling.

The holiday reminded Carter that had he died in Iraq twenty years earlier, only two people would have visited his grave—his last foster parents. His life, and all the traumatic Traps he'd experienced before, would have been buried with him in Arlington.

If he died today, there still wouldn't be a stampede of mourners trampling his graveside. Sure, Vickie, David, and Chester might attend, but who else?

"Becca?" he said. The complex insanity of the statement caused him to laugh.

Nonetheless, this Memorial Day allowed Carter to recover from the rigorous weekend activities. He slept until noon before heading to Louisville Fitness Plus for a workout to clear his mind. His body felt better, even his knee, but it didn't ease his thoughts. He spent forty-five minutes on the treadmill, considering a plan to find Idaho, Honeyboy, and the girl.

What if he took his information to a police station or called the Crime Hotline and shared what he knew? He'd played that scenario in his head several times. Each replay ended with him trying to answer tough questions and the police shoving him into the spotlight as a witness or suspect. He'd kept his head down and his abilities a secret for years. Despite her response, he trusted only Mona Ridge to protect him.

***

The next day at work, the Turner girl's predicament distracted him. It was so intense that Vickie's words startled him.

"This one looks personal, so I'll let you open it," Vickie said as she placed the yellow envelope on Carter's desk. She often cornered him in his office and insisted he read his mail and return it for her to respond, file, or discard. He preferred to toss the entire stack into the third pile.

"Also, a quick reminder about your appointment with Public Relations this afternoon," she said as she made a U-turn and hurried into the hallway.

Carter nodded, then flipped the yellow envelope over. "Confidential: For Carter Sykes ONLY." He pried open the sealed flap and removed the folded paper inside. The text was a combination of words and letters clipped from a magazine and glued to white notebook paper.

Dear Principal,

Don't ignore this letter. U sure like to b on camera. We have a video of u in a very compromising situation with a

YOUNG lady. You received plenty of likes when u pushed down a protester. The news stations would love to add this sexy movie of u sexing a young woman, don't you think? Your bosses won't like this movie?

On Friday at 1:00 p.m., u must hang a white plastic garbage bag filled with $40,000 on the Witches Tree at South 6th Street and Park Avenue. U know it? If not, then Google it. Place the bag at eye level and make it easy. On the outside, write in red marker, "Witches Rule." You MUST leave the area by 1:05 p.m., or we'll email your sex tape to all the local stations/newspapers/schools. If you thought the violent video with the protester went viral, wait until people see this action!

Maybe u believe this is a prank? Check out the close-up photo of the cute horseshoe-shaped scar on your left butt cheek. Ouch. That's you, CS.

We r not playing. B there with $$$ or see yourself on the screen.

Carter wiggled in his desk chair as his face reddened and his shoulders tightened. He searched the envelope, finding a close-up of his bare rear with a red circle highlighting a scar he had received during the war. Shrapnel from an IED explosion had torn through his fatigues and dug into his flesh. He struggled to sit for several weeks but felt fortunate it was his only wound. Too many others were not so lucky. Then, he pictured the Jungle Room at the Dirty Mint Julep. As Kelsey, Jen, and he played on the leopard skin bed, Larry, Jen's husband, leered from a chair in the corner. Carter recalled Larry placing his cell phone on his lap. It all came together in his mind.

Anger coursed through Carter. He brought the heels of his palms to his face, covering his eyes, and then placed his elbows on his desktop.

Then he laughed. *That's what I deserve. Instead of insisting Kelsey tell me how to find Idaho so the police could save the girl, I ended up screwing two women at once while someone watched and took pictures—Becca's right. I am a smart bomb.*

He released his face and leaned back. The office chair whined. What aspect of his life worked? School? Relationships? His inner life? The past? The present? The future? He shook his head and laughed again. Life was a tennis ball machine pelting him with 150 mph serves—leaving him with few options beyond laughter and luck.

Now, he had two reasons to revisit Banger's and The Dirty Mint: finding Idaho, wringing out information for Mona, and wringing Kelsey's neck for extortion.

CHAPTER 15

"You forgot, didn't you?" Vickie stood in his office doorway yet again.

"Me, forget? You know better than that." He paused before adding, "What's your name again?"

"I saw you pondering life like a skinny Buddha. It tells me you don't remember the home visit you scheduled with David from Social Services."

Carter closed his eyes. Of course. He'd scheduled a visit to Shandi's home at a Family Support meeting. He had seen the trauma in Shandi's Trap and had planned this visit to connect the family with Social Services. At that time, he hadn't anticipated a blackmail letter falling on his desk the same morning. Nor had he considered his viral video apology date would sneak up on him so soon.

"David is out there right now waiting for the always punctual Mr. Sykes," she said, tapping her watch with an index finger. "And you're expected at the Public Relations office at 4:15 p.m. today to film a video for the district's social media pages. Did that slip your mind, too?"

Carter paused and stared at his hands for a moment.

"You look like trouble is your only friend, Carter. What's up?" Vickie's tone shifted from playful to concerned.

Carter looked at her and smiled.

"Tell David I'm on my way," he said. "I need five minutes."

***

Carter leaned forward and glanced at the worn thrift shop briefcase he'd purchased on Frankfort Avenue. Its slender black outer shell was dented and scarred, and the combination rollers' numbers faded. The blackmail letter was inside the case, along with the "I deeply regret my actions with the protestors" monologue he'd ignored since Dr. Wallace's directive to memorize it.

Carter rolled his shoulders counterclockwise and closed his eyes again. Dr. Wallace's stern face lodged in his memory like a splinter. Her venomous words foretold consequences he did not want. Carter's work was the fulcrum between his darkness and his light; to lose his job might break the lever forever, and he wasn't sure which side would prevail.

Carter's body tingled. He recalled Shandi's Trap on the playground—the little girl held tight, the fear rising as her mother's tears fell onto her daughter's thin jacket. Carter had felt the mother's arms wrapped around Shandi's shoulders and the rise and fall of the mother's chest against the little girl's face. Frigid winds abused them as they huddled together on the sidewalk, leaning against the building wall. The dark sky served as the background for the glowing street lights. The frozen walkway caused the little girl's bottom to grow numb, and her empty stomach twisted inside her like a bully's fist. In the distance, a siren whined. To Shandi, the world offered suffering and uncertainty in such large gusts that not even her mom's arms could shield her.

The principal opened his briefcase and stared at the blackmail note and the apology letter. Both texts rang with all the passion of AI-produced poetry, with even less subtlety and truth. He searched the apology script's footer and found the Public Relations Department's phone number, then punched it into his desk phone.

"Tell Tammy and Chuck I won't be coming by to do the video today," Carter said. He listened to the receptionist on the other line.

"Oh, believe me, I've heard about it. Consequences." He closed the case without considering the blackmail note.

***

David knocked on the apartment door while Carter examined their surroundings. The pungent odor of raw sewage and cigarette smoke permeated the air. The building's exterior reminded him of damaged Iraqi homes during the war—pieces of siding hung like lifeless, broken arms from various sections of the two-story complex. Sharp-edged pieces of concrete pointed upward like a shark's bottom teeth. Rotted tendrils of roots snaked beneath the dying trees in the yard, and cigarette butts, food wrappers, and beer cans littered the few tufts of grass straining toward the sun.

Two doors down, a 2019 Mazda 3 shined in the parking lot. Its oversized custom chrome rims and immaculate black exterior absorbed the May sunlight. The tinted windows were so dark Carter couldn't see the interior. Nearby, a 1993 Chevy pickup truck, its pale red body marked by holes and rust, sat on cinderblocks where the front tires should have been.

Overhead, loud voices rolled from an open second-floor window. A deep male voice said, "Can't you just shut up a minute?" An angry yell, a crash, and a baby's cries answered the man's question.

"Who is it?" someone said from behind the door.

"It's David Burton and Mr. Sykes," David said. "We're from the school."

Carter understood why David stretched the truth by claiming to be from the school; however, the woman's reply confirmed the need to fib.

"You ain't from the school," she said. "My baby girl is fine, and I'm takin' good care of her. She's got a cold. That's why I didn't send her to school today."

Carter intervened. "Ms. Gibson? It's Mr. Sykes. We met at the open house earlier this year at West Louisville Elementary. I know you're doing right by Shandi. She's very good at school in every way and is one of my best students."

Silence. The deadbolt turned—followed by another latch—then the door opened a few inches until the rusted chain pulled tight.

Carter heard Shandi's tiny voice. "He not a stranger, Mommy. He my Mr. Principal." Her right eye and half of her beautiful smile were visible in the door's gap. He returned the smile.

"I'm here to offer help if you need any," David said when Shandi's mom appeared again above Shandi. The social worker's tone was so soft Carter saw Ms. Gibson's face relax.

"Understand this," she said in a less defensive tone. "Nobody takes my baby. Nobody. You understand?"

David nodded.

The door closed, the chain rattled like a broken chime, and the door reopened.

A third face leaned into the doorway. Taller than Ms. Gibson and Shandi, she smiled and waved her arm as if guiding them into the small apartment. Carter blinked hard and didn't speak to Kitchen Becca, but she greeted him with a smile.

"You see, Cartie? It isn't all that difficult to let someone in."

***

"We lived with my cousin for a while, but her boyfriend..." Ms. Gibson paused, glanced at Shandi leaning against Carter on the sofa, and continued. "I didn't like how he acted around the kids if you know what I mean. So, we walked to a friend's house, but her husband wouldn't let us spend the night when we got there. Said he wasn't running no St. Catherine's charity."

Carter envisioned Shandi wrapped in her mother's arms, both propped against the side of a building downtown. He considered asking how long they lived on the streets but realized he couldn't explain how he knew they were homeless.

"It was a rough few weeks, just getting by however we could." She sat cross-legged on the linoleum floor while David sat in an old vinyl-covered kitchen chair. She reached over and caressed Shandi's cheek. Carter watched her bone-thin brown arm and followed it to her dark face and worried eyes. He figured she was twenty-three or twenty-four, but those eyes carried decades of pain.

"So, how'd you get to this place in the south end?" David asked. Carter had seen it many times before today. David focused on a client at the shelter—his body language, questions, and eye contact indicated he was fully committed to them and hearing what they said and didn't say.

"Shandi and me weren't doing so well. Then I remembered what my friend's husband said about not being a charity like St. Catherine's," she said. "So, I spent my last three dollars on a bus to St. Catherine's Church. We slept on a bench outside the church until we saw a nun."

"Sister Shaughnessy," Shandi said.

"That's right," Ms. Gibson said. "The Sister helped us get money for this apartment, and they provided some furniture and got me hired cleaning an office building in the evenings. It don't pay much, but it keeps us off the streets. What's the best thing, Shandi?"

"The bus takes me to my school," Shandi said. She smiled at Sykes as she raised her hands above her head.

Carter nodded, but he feared Shandi spent evenings alone while her mom worked.

"What's it cost a month here, Ms. Gibson?" David pulled out his phone to take notes.

Ms. Gibson's voice faltered. "Too much," she said. "We have to find someplace else that's cheaper 'cause the rent's going up next month, and these apartments are the same as the west end places."

"Then we can help you," David said. His thumbs bounced on his phone's screen.

Shandi stared at Carter's face. "Just like you told me," she said. "Everything be alright, Mr. Principal."

CHAPTER 16

They left Ms. Gibson's apartment too late for Carter to return to school. David accomplished much, securing a placement at the shelter and starting the welfare assistance process for Shandi and her mother.

Only two school days remained until summer break, and Carter had created a solid plan for those last days. He phoned Vickie to ensure the afternoon had ended without incident and to check for phone messages.

"You already know who called, so why ask?" Vickie said.

"How did she sound?"

"Dr. Wallace seemed as jovial as if she'd picked a longshot at Churchill Downs, and it proved her right."

"She wants this thoroughbred sent to the glue factory pronto," Carter said. "She might get her wish."

"Don't break my heart, Carter. Work this out."

Carter held the phone closer to his ear. "Truth isn't always something you fix, Vick. I've fought the truth my entire life, and I've come to respect it now. It's not something you work on or repair—it comes wholly imperfect and inconvenient, but it's like an element. It is what it is."

Vickie exhaled into the phone and said, "When you talk all philosophical like that, Carter, it makes me nervous. You're telling Wallace to go to hell. Am I right?"

"If she calls again, tell her I will be available tomorrow," he said. "Thanks for all you do, Vickie. I haven't said that enough during these years."

"Yes, you have," she said. Carter detected a rare sadness in her tone as though she expected the worst for the first time in a long while. "You've kept many secrets, Carter, but that's not one of them."

"I'm like a dog, Vickie. I bury bones in my backyard and leave them alone."

"My dear friend," Vickie said, "people who care about you recognize holes in the yard. Everyone has them. They won't think less of you if you're imperfect. Our pastor says it best: Don't be afraid of the past because nothing is covered that shall not be revealed, and nothing hid that shall not be known."

Carter's past clawed his heart like a cat inside a cardboard box.

CHAPTER 17

The tinted glass doors at Banger's Gentlemen's Club reminded Carter of the Mazda he'd seen earlier. He checked his watch—almost seven o'clock, at least an hour from a late May sunset. He'd never been here so early before. His reflection, no more than an inky faceless outline, filled the door frame before bending when he yanked the handle outward.

Carter paid the twenty-dollar cover charge to the broad-shouldered bouncer sitting on a bar stool. The man wore a blue blazer over a white tee shirt and a patch covering his left eye. A tuft of his long brown hair created a hook on his forehead. His unpatched eye followed Carter like an ominous portrait in a horror movie scene. Carter imagined no one told this guy an off-color pirate joke and lived to tell another.

He crossed the white tile floor to a short, carpeted staircase. The multi-colored lights flashing from the ceiling made the stairs roll like a slot machine's reel. When his sight adjusted, Carter realized another six-foot-six behemoth stood beside him. The man's bald head and chiseled jawline resembled a computer-generated re-creation of an ancient species. Although only four inches shorter, Carter imagined himself as a tiny satellite floating beside a planet.

The landing overlooked the shadowy figures hovering at the tables scattered around the room. Three separate and illuminated stages served as the focal points. The stage lights lit the prancing dancers, accentuating their bodies' contours and sparse clothing. On one, a young woman, her blonde hair loose and hanging over her eyes, writhed in rhythm with the music. On another, a woman older than the first kneeled, talking to two men flanking the stage. Her short black hair and tattooed skin reminded Carter of Hope. Finally, a young woman who appeared too young to be in the club, let alone nearly naked on the stage, leaned her back against the silver pole. Her spiked hair glowed red in the lights as she stretched her thin leg toward several adoring audience members.

Carter knew where to search. To preserve his anonymity, he always kept his distance from others, covering his face with his hand or a beer bottle whenever someone came near him. But he remembered the setting well.

Several women fluttered through the darkness from table to table, whispering to the men and sitting down whether they received an invitation or not. The fake laughs rose above the music and the chatter.

Carter recognized Kelsey as one of the whispering butterflies. She spoke with several men at a table near the center stage, sipping a watered-down drink and throwing back her head as she had in the dimly lit Jungle Room.

Despite his urge to charge toward her, he waited for her to stand and leave the table before he descended the four stairs. With each step down into the inferno, his anger rose. This stupid girl and her friends jeopardized his professional life beyond his own risky behavior. She and Jen had seemed genuine at the Dirty Mint—at least as authentic as anonymous, no-strings-attached sex could be. He huffed. Blackmailing him crossed a line already far past society's accepted moral guideposts. For an instant, Carter recognized the stupidity of his reasoning—but only for a moment as he melted into the shadows and the glowing lights of the stages.

***

"We have to talk," he said, his tone harsh and commanding. Kelsey stopped and turned to face him. Her wide smile surprised Carter. He stepped close enough to smell her floral perfume and see the mascara outlining her eyes.

"I'm working now, but we could go downstairs later," she said, not bothering with a greeting. "Who knows, Jen and Larry might stumble..."

Carter leaned into her space, his anger percolating. "You think I'm stupid? Is that it?"

Confusion. Then Kelsey's lips pursed. "What bit you on the ass?"

"Really?" He inched closer to her. "You're gonna play it innocent and ignorant?"

It was her turn to lean away. She glanced around the dark room, probably searching for Captain Hook or Mr. Planet.

"I treated you well, even though you didn't give me what I wanted," Carter said. "Then you scam me for money?"

"Are you on crack?" She glared at him. "I treated you right the other night. You didn't get scammed; you, Jen, and Larry got what you wanted from me. It's what I do. You got more than two hundred dollars worth of..."

"I wanted you to connect me with Idaho," Carter said.

"And I told you no. What's the big deal? You had more fun..."

"I got your little note, so stop it," Carter said. "Have you, Jen, and Larry blackmailed other people?"

Kelsey reacted as though he'd asked for an organ transplant. Her green eyes expanded, and she pushed a tendril of hair behind her ear. Carter expected her heavily caked makeup to crumble like a dry creek bed. Her right arm dropped to her hip as she raised her left hand, index finger extended toward his nose. "Now you're acting stupid," she said. Her face tightened even more. "I didn't know you were married, so who'd I tell?"

"I don't have a wife," Carter said. "Are you accusing Jen and..."

"Hell no," she said. "I've known those swingers for a long time. Larry's got so much money, I'd blackmail him, not you, if I wanted cash. Jen works in Frankfort, earning more money than some piss-poor West End school principal, I bet." Her shoulders rose as she spoke, and she waved her finger.

Her indignation shoved Carter back on his heels. He wasn't always the best at reading people, but her denial rang true. If she was lying, Kelsey belonged on the stage at Actor's Theatre, not Banger's.

She edged closer, her finger cocked and loaded. Before Carter could react, Kelsey poked the uncovered skin on his lower neck.

***

The reflection in the dresser mirror reveals Kelsey is a teenager. Her jeans, boots, and an orange and black tee shirt appear typical, but the ring on her finger flashes like new coins in the lamplight. She reaches to touch the man's arm but stops as though his frail bones would not survive gentle contact. The man beneath the bed sheets seems to be around

Carter's age or a little older, although his skin is gaunt and gray, and his bald head resembles an Easter egg against the white pillow. His ash-colored arm rises an inch before returning to the mattress. His pale blue gown swallows his thin body, covering him like a man's shirt worn by a delicate child. A framed family photograph adorns the wall—a smiling man with thick red hair rests his hand on a small girl's shoulders.

Next to the bed, pill bottles and wadded tissues cover the nightstand like sparse patches of winter snow. A transparent plastic bag dangles from the vertical IV pole—another silver pole—connecting the clear tube and the port piercing the man's body.

The young girl pulls her hand away from the man's skin, reminding Carter how he responds when someone wants to touch him. She twists the ring around her finger to release the helplessness and pain consuming her.

"Daddy," she said. "Please."

The man's weak eyes narrow, and his brow furrows as though her unspecified request harmed him. His moan sounds sharper than a newly whetted blade; he inhales as though his lungs are metal cans filled with pebbles. Kelsey's father tilts his head and rasps, "You would if you loved me."

The words slice through her heart, weakening her knees.

Carter's heart bled, as well.

Kelsey cries as she kisses the older man's cheek. The man manages a feeble smile as she reaches across him, grasps a pillow, and lifts it above his face. His cloudy eyes spark with gratitude.

"Oh, Daddy," she sobs. Carter felt desperation and despair. He experiences the agony that spirals through her body as she folds the white pillow over his face.

Kelsey presses it downward with the weight of her thin body and the heavy suffering of her severed heart.

***

The Trap left Carter off balance. He swayed. The anger toward Kelsey morphed into empathy. Instead of wringing her neck for blackmail, he should kick himself for that night at the Dirty Mint. That teenage girl, hurt and confused, still resided inside this woman. No matter how clever and carefree she acted, that moment spawned ripples across the surface of her life. Carter floated beneath those tiny waves, unable to rise for several moments after the Trap let him go.

"What did you do with the ring?" he said, his voice so weak he cleared his throat to reset it. The Trap depleted his oxygen, leaving him dizzy.

After a confused expression, Kelsey's posture stiffened, and her lips parted in awe.

"What?" Her hand moved to her bare neck as if covering a hole.

"People do what they have to," Carter said, his tone so soft the loud music made it indecipherable for anyone besides Kelsey. "You were a kid. Your father shouldn't have asked you to do that."

"Stop it," Kelsey said, stumbling backward. "Just shut up. I don't talk about..."

"Please tell me where I can find Idaho," Carter said, his words still gentle. "I can help someone else if you do. A girl the age you were when... you know."

Kelsey trembled.

"Leave me alone," she said. "She'll work a party at the Dirty Mint tonight at 11:00 p.m. That's all I will say, so stay away from me, freak."

Carter stepped closer. He wanted to make her understand.

"Kelsey, I'm sorry."

"You don't know what sorry is," a deep British voice announced behind him, "but you will if you don't step away from the lady."

Carter turned. The Pirate and the Planet grabbed his arms and muscled him toward the stairs and the building's exit. He glanced over his shoulder at Kelsey. Her hand covered her eyes like she had stumbled upon something she didn't want to see.

"I shouldn't have..." he yelled, but she had already turned away.

CHAPTER 18

Kelsey scrambled to retrieve her phone while the bouncers shoved Carter toward the stairs. She brought the phone to life and gnawed on her fingernails while she waited for someone to answer.

"Stephanie," she said. Tears formed in her eyes. "I had to get him away from me. Forgive me."

Stephanie chuckled. "Calm down, Kel. Who and for what?"

"That principal on 39th Street," she replied after a quick sniffle. "He came to the club looking for you. He's scary, Steph. He knows things and wouldn't quit until I talked to him."

Stephanie's tone changed. "What'd you tell him?"

"I told him you'd be at the Dirty Mint tonight," Kelsey said. "I'm sorry. He had me cornered."

Stephanie took a deep breath. "It's okay, girl," she said. "I can handle that guy. Lots of customers crush on me. You're my best friend. I know you wouldn't do me wrong."

"I know," Kelsey said, "but this guy has something going on. He talked crazy like he might be losing it. He accused Jen and me of trying to blackmail him."

"You need to take care of yourself, Kelsey. I'm not alone like you are. I got Kevin watching my back. You know, he was a boxer when he was a kid. He's here now. Besides, that dude might be good for some cash along the way."

Kelsey didn't respond. Steph often prodded her about having someone to keep her safe, but it was easy to ignore her jabs as long as Kevin was Stephanie's protector. Instead, Kelsey wondered if Kevin made her friend safer or placed her in greater danger. Kevin was danger. Kelsey felt it. Sometimes, he stared at her when Steph wasn't paying attention, and Kelsey felt like prey.

"What's that, Honey?" Stephanie said, her voice projected away from the phone. "I will find out."

"Kevin has seen the principal on the video," she said, returning her attention to Kelsey. "He wants to know if he's still at the club."

"Allan's boys are dragging him out right now."

"Okay," Stephanie said. She turned from the phone again. "He's still there, Kevin. They are kicking his ass out this very minute."

Kelsey heard Kevin's voice in the background but couldn't discern what he said.

"Look, Kevin shouldn't hurt this guy," Kelsey said. She paused and took a breath. "The principal freaked me out but didn't try to hurt me. He knows something and wants to talk to you about it. He's crazy, but I don't think he'd harm you."

"I'll try to catch Kevin and tell him to go easy. You know how Kevin gets when someone tries to mess with me."

Kelsey chewed her nails as she considered how to slow this runaway train. She blinked her heavily mascaraed eyes and glanced at the bloody cuticle of her ring finger before telling Stephanie goodbye.

CHAPTER 19

Carter's rage rekindled as he drove away from the club. Images of Kelsey's trauma crowded out the death grips of the Banger's bouncers and the paw-shaped bruises inevitable on his arms. However, even the Trap faded as he realized the source of the blackmail letter.

He had nearly three hours before Idaho would arrive at the Dirty Mint—more than enough time to reach his destination. His goal wasn't to hurt anyone but to remove yet another distraction and find the abducted girl before it was too late. The clock was ticking.

"It's my fault," he said as he merged with the traffic. "Why can't I resist the temptations and do what's right?"

A stifled pop rang throughout the car. Carter shook his head and peered into the rearview mirror again. An expanding globe of bubble gum concealed Teenage Becca's face. After she deflated the bubble and sucked it into her mouth, she smacked her lips and commenced chewing.

"It's all my fault," Becca said, her voice imitating Carter's. "I'm li'l ol' sad Carter Sykes, and everything happens because of poor little me."

Her lower lip extended, and she scrunched her face until she resembled a bulldog.

"I've been distracted."

"Oh yes, you have, big brother," she said, reclaiming her sixteen-year-old voice. "Between work, beating up protesters, taking care of me, trying to help rugrats in need, and trips to the gym, you barely have enough time to hook up with whores two at a time. You better give up all this crazy 'trying to do the right thing' stuff and focus on tenderizing your meat. Am I right?"

As he drove, Carter twisted his mirror to the side so he didn't see Becca's image. He stared straight ahead at the street, concentrating on his destination.

When he arrived, he pushed the car door open, allowing the momentum to carry him from the seat onto the sidewalk. He stomped along the path and up the steps. Without hesitation, he struck the door with his knuckles. Within seconds, he repeated the knocks with even more urgency. The sound reminded him of his mother's bed knocking against the wall between her bedroom and where he and Becca slept as children.

The heavy door opened without any urgency. Lenora stared through the partial opening, her mouth ajar like the door. Although pulled into a tight bun, her hair made her appear even younger than when he last saw her. Her blue eyes widened, and panic formed like a web across her face.

"Lenora, what did I ever do to you?" Carter held his hands palms up.

Lenora provided a weak response. "I don't know what you're talking about, Carter."

"Is that right?" He reached into his shirt pocket and retrieved a piece of paper. Although subtle, his movement caused her to flinch.

He unfolded the blackmail letter and shoved it against the glass storm door.

She lowered her gaze.

"Do you and Hope want to ruin me?" Carter said, straightening the wrinkles on the paper as he held it against the glass. "Maybe it's only you?"

Lenora clenched her jaws. Her thin shoulders rose.

"I didn't... I mean, I don't feel good about any of this." To her credit, she opened the red wooden door wider, enabling Carter to see she wore a forest green polo with the word "Denny's" embroidered near the shoulder. Her black polyester work slacks and matching Converse low-cut shoes caused his anger and guilt to jockey for position in his stomach.

He slid the letter across the glass to her eye level. "I love the arts and crafts approach you've taken with the note, Lenora. It takes me back to first grade." His tone had softened.

Lenora's lip trembled, and she wrapped her arms around herself. For a moment, Carter thought she would cry. Her waitress shirt wrinkled at the chest behind her sharp, white elbows. However, she didn't weep at all.

"You're a stupid, stupid, rude man," she said. A sad laugh escaped her lips.

"So, you're offended?" He removed the letter from the glass to see her better. He folded the paper and shoved it into the pocket of his khaki pants. "I'm so sorry I've hurt your feelings, Princess. Maybe it's because you and your girlfriend are blackmailing me?" He thrust his face closer to the glass.

"Maybe you should consider who you sleep with before you get all self-righteous and holy. Hope told me you were a puppy lapping at the water bowl when she invited you here."

Carter ran his hand through his dark hair as he stared toward the early evening sky. He took two deep breaths to gain control. Lenora was right. As always, his urges led to this moment. He was at the mercy of his vices and his trauma—and neither had granted him much compassion. *"Just this once."*

"I trusted you and..."

"No, you didn't, Carter," she said. "You used us. Hope called you "some guy at the coffee shop." All she knew was that you flirt with her, and you're a school principal. Hell, I knew half that from watching one video online. You're like the man searching for his keys under a street lamp. He lost them across the street but says the light is better on this side. You're searching for something, but it's not where you think it is, and it sure isn't in bed with a lesbian couple."

"Maybe I'm what you say, Lenora, but at least I am not trying to ruin you. Why are you doing this?" He placed his hand against the glass.

"Hope is desperate," Lenora said. "She needs money now."

"Everyone needs money, Lenora."

"They're going to kick her out of school."

Carter shook his head. "Money? That's it? You can tell her she won't get a penny from me. I've got bigger problems than bankrolling her tuition." He banged his hand against the glass door and stomped toward the sidewalk. His mind was a blender mixing his various problems into a stew he couldn't stomach.

He heard the door slam behind him but refused to look back.

"I built this life," he said under his breath, "so I can't act puzzled when it's falling around me."

CHAPTER 20

It's never easy being the most intelligent guy in the room. Although Kevin often marveled at his superior intellect and ability to bend the world and its people to his needs and wants, he recognized the injustice of a world where people like this idiot earned the big bucks and looked down on everyone else.

He shook his head in disgust as Sykes stomped along the sidewalk to the duplex door like the Big Bad Wolf building up steam to blow the house down.

Kevin shifted in his seat and flicked his cigarette ashes out the window, careful not to burn the interior of his Lincoln Towncar. It was the one thing he'd kept of his father's, besides the last behemoth auto repair shop. Why keep driving a twelve-year-old Lincoln? The impressive trunk, of course.

He observed Carter's interaction with the tiny blonde chick. It pleased Kevin.

"I'll show Mr. Bigshot who's the Big Bad Wolf," he said. "It's almost too easy."

Kevin started the Lincoln and punched the power button on the customized Rockford Fosgate sound system he had installed himself. He tapped the buttons until Warren Zevon's Werewolves of London filled the entire car, including the trunk. Kevin liked to share his favorite tunes with all his good-girl friends.

CHAPTER 21

Carter parked across the alley from the Dirty Mint. It was only 9:20 p.m., but he didn't want to miss Idaho when she arrived. The cobalt sky, dotted with pinholes and light, offered cover, but to see better, he exited his car and leaned against the abandoned metal building on the fringe of the lot. His khakis, sneakers, and gray Louisville Bats Baseball tee shirt blended into the darkness and charcoal siding.

With only two days of school remaining before summer break, he refused to take the day off, so he hoped to get the information he needed from Idaho and make it an early night.

Humming commenced beside him. It sounded like the Rolling Stone's "Beast of Burden." He raised his index finger to his lips and spat a long "Shhhhhhhh."

Becca giggled and stepped so close her breath tickled his ear. "Thought you'd like some Jagger, my brother. Do you remember how we danced in the living room when the Rolling Stones were on the radio? What happened to that, Cartie?"

Beneath the metallic shadows, Carter stared at his sister, an adult again, standing beside him in her white and yellow dress with her black hair tumbling onto her shoulders. The silver moon filled her eyes with glimmering coins. Her grin was one part affection, one part mischief, and one part pity.

"I don't have time," Carter whispered.

"You sure don't, mister," Becca said. "You've got trouble snapping at your heels like our neighbor's Doberman chasing the mailman. You remember that, don't you? The dog's name was Rocky, and poor Mr. Eddie couldn't hold him back."

"Yes," he said. "You were afraid for the mailman, so I told you the post office gave them dog-resistant pants."

"That's right." She tossed her head back, causing her dark hair to bounce. "It's funny, the lies we tell the people we love. You ever have an animal you can't control on a leash, Cartie?"

Carter closed his eyes tight to reset his vision. He turned his back to Becca and craned his neck to watch the Dirty Mint's entrance across the alley and club parking lot. Two couples approached the door; their heads were down, and their pace quickened with each step. A man rose from his vintage Monte Carlo and took long strides toward the building. Other cars rolled in, and the parking lot became more crowded.

Becca had left, Carter assumed, until he heard her voice again. "You know the only thing funnier than those lies we tell to protect those we love, Cartie?" She paused as if awaiting his response.

He fought to focus on the club and finding Idaho. "I will keep it on a leash when I go in this time, Becca," he said.

"It's those lies we tell ourselves. It's our way of trying to control a world as vicious and wild as Rocky, the Doberman," she said.

***

Idaho stepped toward him, leaning close to his face. Even in her stiletto heels, she stood several inches shorter than Carter. She was so close that Carter smelled the cherry bubblegum mixed with her pungent perfume and the cigarette she had discarded in the parking lot moments earlier.

"I hoped to find you here tonight," Carter said, careful to quell any hint of threat. The patrons continued about their business in the Meet and Greet room. Laughter and whispers floated beneath the Cardi B and Meagan Thee Stallion song, vibrating the speakers. The television monitors displayed pornography or live streaming of the various rooms.

"Is that right? You want time with me?" she asked. Her red velvet hair didn't seem real to Carter, and her low-cut silver top sparkled in The Dirty Mint's fluorescent lights. The thick lipstick resembled red velvet frosting, matching her hair, and a thin eyeliner stretched to form an arrow from her eyes to her temples.

Idaho reached for his hand, but Carter pulled away. He had already suffered her Trap, so he didn't need to risk experiencing another more recent trauma. He figured she had an abundance of pain to share.

She nodded but beckoned him with her index finger toward a door labeled "Employee's Only." Carter figured it served as a shortcut to the themed sex rooms in the back. She maneuvered around a tall table like a serpent and said, "Let's go where we can talk and get to know each other again."

Carter followed despite the goosebumps warning him. He'd press her to provide information about the girl, relay the information to Mona, refocus on his job, and confront Hope's blackmail scheme. *You can't make this stuff up,* he thought.

Idaho stretched her arm back and clutched the doorknob without breaking eye contact with Carter. Carter followed her through a short hallway into a dark passage, larger than he expected. Light drifted from a door to his left. He believed it led to the box office and the older woman taking money. Tired LED lights lined the ceiling and the floor. The glow provided enough light for Carter to see Idaho's devilish smile and the seductive way she motioned for him to trail her. They passed two doors, both back entrances to rooms.

Idaho leaned against the third door and made eye contact with Carter while slipping her hand into her bra. She pulled a key from the cup and held it up for Carter to see. Her exaggerated purr put Carter on edge, but he remained silent as she turned, unlocked the door, and entered the doorway. She extended her hand from the darkness, grasped his shirt near the waist, and jerked him into the room. He touched her hand to ensure first contact.

Once inside, Idaho wrapped her arms around him and shaped her body to the contours of his frame. She closed the door, and they shuffled into the shadows.

"We've been hoping to see you, too, man," she said.

"We?" Carter said.

Before Carter could turn, a firm hand gripped his right shoulder and spun him. He raised his right arm in time to block a punch, but before he recognized what was happening, a heavy object struck his left temple, and darkness swirled and tilted, discarding him onto the floor.

CHAPTER 22

His mother's voice, distinctive as it was anyway, sounded differ-ent than a few hours earlier. Then, she moaned and whispered as the headboard drummed a steady beat throughout their small house in Mansfield, Ohio. Only thin drywall formed the barrier between her bedroom and the room he and Becca shared. Now, she stood outside the door and barked the command to her oldest child.

"Carter, you better watch out for your sister, you hear?"

Although only ten years old, Carter understood the chaos and was already hovering near his little sister's bed. When the first loud bangs on the front door woke him, he had rolled off his mattress on the floor like a soldier during a sneak attack. Staying low, Carter had crawled across the room and shook Becca's shoulder.

Her sunflower dress draped across an old kitchen chair beside her bed.

Carter said, "Get dressed," as he helped pull the outfit over her head. "Let's put it on over your jammies, okay?"

She nodded and rubbed her eyes, and a yawn pried open her mouth. "What's happening, Cartie? Who's knockin' so hard."

He knew but didn't answer. "Don't worry," he said. "We'll watch Scooby Doo in a little while once it's quiet." She wrapped her arms around his neck and whispered, "Can we have Cocoa Pebbles? With milk this time? I'll be quiet." She leaned back and held her tiny four-year-old index finger to her pursed lips to assure him she'd shush.

He held her and said in the calmest voice he could muster, "Let's put you in the castle until I can come back and save you, okay?"

"As long as I get Pebbles and Bam-Bam," she said.

Carter lifted her and hurried toward the closet door. Beneath the sparse clothes hanging from a metal bar, he had placed two pieces of cardboard and a discarded white comforter on the floor. A flashlight, several books, and a small paper crown rested in the folds of the bedding. A red-haired rag doll rested on the sofa pillow he'd positioned on one end. The doll's left eye hung against the doll's cheek by a single red thread. The stuffing had breached the outer fabric. He'd promised to fix it last week but never did.

He placed Becca on the closet floor as though returning a fallen baby bird to the nest.

Angry voices sang from the living room. Becca's eyes grew big. Carter kissed her forehead and said, "You stay put, Princess Rebecca. I will be back very soon."

Those wide eyes stared back at him as he stood.

"Cartie," she said. "Don't forget me."

"I promise," he said, pushing the slender closet door until the latch clicked shut.

CHAPTER 23

Carter thought he was underwater—the ocean of darkness pushing against his dream and the ache spreading inside his head like a blood stain on a white shirt. He tried to rub his face with his right hand, but the nylon electrical cord wrapped around his wrist prevented him. He raised his left hand and swiped his palm across his forehead and down to his chin. The sweat and blood retreated down his cheek.

"Honey," Idaho said, "you didn't kill him." She stood a safe distance away, bent over, and examined Carter with a child's curiosity at the Louisville Zoo. Her breasts and her thick hair hung toward the floor.

Carter cleared his throat and shook his head to upset the fog. He saw a large desk with a thick rubber surface, a chalkboard with crude drawings of breasts, a penis, and lips doodled across it, and several smaller student desks scattered near the large desk. Paddles hung from the wall to his left. When he realized he was in the Dirty Mint's Hot4Teacher room, Carter searched for the cameras near the ceiling and above the doors. He found them, but black electrical tape obscured each lens.

He yanked on the cord again, attempting to break free from the iron radiator attached to the wall. The abrupt stop tightened the loop and bruised his wrist even more.

When he turned, Honeyboy had joined Idaho to watch the caged animal. However, he resembled a predator outside the cage rather than a curious kid at the zoo.

"Dude, you ain't going anywhere," Honeyboy said, reaching his steel-toed work boot to tap Carter's running shoe. Carter didn't react. Honeyboy was broader than he appeared in the Trap, and his height equaled Carter's six-foot-two frame.

Honeyboy added, "It's funny. You seemed a helluva lot tougher when you pushed that kid on his ass in the video."

Carter sniffed. "You can't believe everything you see on the internet." His voice sounded drier than the chalk on the blackboard.

Honeyboy slapped his knee and laughed. "You're right about that one, old man."

"Quit playing around, Kevin," Idaho said. "At least give the guy a drink of water."

Kevin. His name's Kevin. The cartoon figure adorning his work shirt confirmed it, as well. It portrayed a wild-haired man holding a wrench. The pale red lettering read Nally's Auto Repair. The white thread below confirmed his name—"Kevin."

Honeyboy smiled, leaned closer to Idaho, and kissed her. Their mouths attached for several seconds before they unlocked. "Sure, Babydoll," he said. He lifted a backpack from a student-desk and removed a plastic water bottle.

"No thanks," Carter said as Honeyboy handed the Aquafina bottle to Idaho. Carter's mouth was parched, but he risked being drugged or worse.

"You are a suspicious one, aren't you?" Honeyboy reached into his front pocket and retrieved Carter's wallet. He opened it like a tiny book and turned it over in his hand. "Mr. Carter Sykes, who lives over on Swan near downtown."

"It's not poison," Idaho said as she raised the bottle. "Look, it's never been opened." She turned the cap, and it cracked—brand new.

"Still not convinced?" Honeyboy shook his head. "How about this? Honey, I'm thirsty." He bent his body, remaining steady like a mesmerized snake. Idaho smiled and poured water into his mouth. The liquid dribbled down his chin as he gulped to keep up with the heavy stream. Carter's stomach churned as the water saturated Honeyboy's goatee and rolled onto his bearded neck. Kevin's obscene sideways glance caused Carter to avert his eyes.

When Kevin straightened, he ran his sleeve across his mouth to wipe away the water. "See there, Mr. Sykes," he said, "it's as clean as a nun's daydreams." He took the bottle from Idaho's hand, tightened the lid, and hurled it toward Carter's head.

Carter snatched the bottle from the air with his free hand without breaking eye contact with his captor.

Kevin laughed and patted Idaho on her bare shoulder. "See, Stephanie, this guy will cooperate. He's not as crazy as Kelsey claimed."

Carter sat straighter and stared at the cord tethering him to the radiator. Now adjusted to the darkness, his vision enabled him to see the various costumes hanging on a rolling rack on the opposite wall. Several boxes labeled "Cleaning Supplys" balanced on a slim folding table beside Idaho, or as Kevin called her, Stephanie. Various brooms and mops leaned in the corner like canes, and the floor's warped hardwood made the room roll.

"What do you want from me," Carter said. He continued to stare at his abductors.

"Just like you fat cats," the man replied, lifting his shoulders toward his ears. "You hide in the shadows hawking my woman, and now you demand to know what I want."

"It's probably some of this, Honey," Stephanie said. She traced her hands along her body like a game show model presenting a prize.

Kevin sidestepped toward Carter and bent over him. It seemed he planned to ask if Carter required medical attention.

"Is that what you want, Sykes? To steal my girl. Maybe you'd hurt her real good?" The wide grin returned to Kevin's face. "You can rent my Idaho for a while, but you can't take her, Desk Jockey. That's how these transactions work."

Carter glanced at Stephanie standing behind his captor. Although her face remained stoic, he read the uncomfortable reaction to Kevin's words on her slumped shoulders and the slight shuffle of her feet. He sensed she didn't want Kevin to harm him.

Kevin's right hand shot out like a snake's bite, slapping Carter's left cheek and rocking his head backward against the metal radiator. The pain rippled through Carter's face and echoed inside his head. Bile rose into his throat, and he heard Idaho yelp.

"My God, Kevin, there's no need to..." Her voice faded as if she had fallen or drifted away on a boat floating on the Ohio River.

Something more ominous than a slap gathered like a storm in Carter's brain and body.

***

The woman throws the whiskey bottle at his head, but Kevin ducks and rolls from the chair onto the cheap linoleum floor. Carter sees it, too, and experiences the boy's fear-induced adrenaline rush.

The woman doesn't stop. She staggers toward Little Honeyboy, her hands outstretched. She is younger than old, but her crimson eyes, thick matted lipstick, and the uneven streaks in her rouge make her appear older than young. Alcohol and cigarettes taint her breath, unabated by the scent of her expensive perfume. Carter hopes Little Kevin can avoid her hands, but he cannot.

The woman grabs his sloped, bare shoulders with impressive long fingers, and her sharp, manicured nails sink into the skin like talons.

"Kevin, you're just like your father—a loser," she says.

He tries to wiggle away, but her nails dig deeper, causing blood to streak down his back like the makeup lines on her face.

Kevin howls.

She drags him to the floor, pinning his back to a blue throw rug. Now, she sinks her claws into his cheek and throat, turning his head to the right to whisper into his left ear.

"I don't come from white trash like your daddy, Kevin," she says. Her putrid spittle dampens Kevin's face. "When I married him, your father had standing and money, but he shit it all away. Now look at us. Look at me." She weeps and thrusts her weight on the boy's pale chest.

As his breath escapes, Kevin rasps, "Dad."

She stops crying and raises her body from his. Her jaws clench, and her eyes narrow. Kevin's body trembles as she glares at him.

"You want your father?" she says. She chokes up again, but the cruelest smile Carter ever witnessed accompanied those tears. "I think that's a great idea."

She stands, swaying over the child.

Kevin sits up to catch his breath. Again, the talons extend and pierce the boy's skin—sinking into his arms. Carter realizes Kevin is no stranger to those nails. Scars, shaped like quarter moons, mar his arms and shoulders.

She yanks the boy to his feet and pushes him toward the stairs and the second floor.

Kevin scrambles up the steps, creating distance between him and his mother. Without hesitating, he turns onto the worn green carpet in the hallway. At the end of the hall, he bangs against the door and turns the silver doorknob. The door flies open and slams against the bedroom wall.

Kevin stops breathing. So Carter stops breathing.

His mother staggers into the room and grips little Kevin's shoulders again—nails first, of course.

"You want your precious father, Kevin?" she said. "You can have him." She extracts her claws, turns, and exits, closing the door behind her. The door latch clicks and locks.

Kevin stares at the queen-sized bed against the back wall. Its blankets tumble onto the floor like a landslide in progress. Alcohol and pill bottles litter the nightstands. A hammer rests on the pillow, and chunks of ceiling drywall cover the pea-colored carpet and the white sheet.

As the boy raises his head, Carter sees the man's purple feet and ashen legs. He sees the white underwear, the man's blanched skin sagging on his naked torso. His broken neck stretches, a cruel twist, and his head tilts to the side. Then Kevin observes the thick, brown extension cord connecting the man's corpse to a rafter visible in the damaged ceiling.

The hanging man's face, white as a bleached cloth, sags toward his chin, drawing the skin away from his bulging eyes.

Kevin stumbles backward as he reaches for the doorknob. However, when he tries to turn the knob, it refuses to move. Carter hopes Kevin can escape, but the mirror on the door indicates Honeyboy is no more than eleven or twelve years old. No matter how hard he tries, he won't generate enough force to break the lock.

Carter's Traps, even the most traumatic ones, lasted through the host's initial confusion and shock before releasing Carter back into the world. However, this Trap, like Mom's fingernails, didn't let go. Kevin remained with his father's dead body—trapping Carter as well. Carter lived the boy's pain, fear, hunger, confusion, and agony, albeit concentrated into mere moments until the Trap released him.

Kevin sat on the cold floor and rocked. For hours, the little boy hummed an old children's song Carter had heard teachers and kids sing in the classroom.

Carter inhaled the stench—rotting beef and feces—and listened to the boy's melancholy hum.

***

Carter returned to the Hot4Teacher room. It had only been a few moments, but he carried twelve hours of anguish with him. *Quiet, Carter, quiet. Keep that big mouth closed.* Sometimes, when he escaped a tremendous Trap, his disorientation and shared sadness caused him to blurt out words he regretted. *Please, don't let me slip and reveal the Trap.*

"She's lovely," he said, nodding toward Stephanie. His ear rang, and his cheek drew tight with numbness.

Kevin raised his hand again as if to strike but pulled up short, holding his hand still. After a short pause, he laughed. "Did you hear that, Steph? This guy's funny as hell." He stood up and nudged Carter with his boot. "You remind me of my old man, Sykes. Always tryin' to be a clown."

The image of Kevin's father—the bulging eyes and tongue lolling—flashed into Carter's mind. The smell permeated his nostrils.

"You see your daddy often?" Carter watched the younger man's face for a response. His brow lowered, and he double-blinked like a gnat flew into his eye.

"I'm more a mama's boy," Kevin said.

"Me, too," Carter said. His wrist ached, and his head stung, the slap still echoing inside him. "What are you going to do with me?"

"Do with you or do to you?" Kevin laughed again.

Stephanie slithered beside her Honeyboy. "You're gonna leave me and Kelsey alone 'cause the next time you bother us, I'll let Kevin kill your ass. You hear me?"

"Sure thing," Carter said. "You aren't as lovely as I thought."

"Screw you, principal." She turned away and walked toward the teacher's desk, picked up her tiny pink change purse, and swayed her hips as her heels clicked toward the door.

"Stephanie, you go on. I'll take care of this guy." Kevin lingered in front of Carter, waiting for her to leave.

"Remember what I said, Honey," she said over her shoulder. "He ain't gonna hurt us."

"I know," he said. "I'll talk to him and cut him loose."

The moment the door slammed shut, the Good Girl Killer's smile and cold eyes told Carter that Kevin didn't intend to keep his word. Instead, he retrieved a roll of duct tape and a cloth from the "cleening" table. Kevin whistled the same children's tune from the Trap and danced back, stopping long enough to kick Carter in the ribs. As Carter tried to catch his breath, he heard the rip of the duct tape.

CHAPTER 24

The blade raked against Carter's cheek, and the blindfold lifted like a stage curtain. The knife rose toward his face again—his fluttering eyelids turned the movement into an old 8 mm film. Bile rose into his throat while his reflexes evaded the blade.

"Quit wiggling," a soft voice said. Carter lifted his palm to his face. "We only have a few minutes before he gets back."

Kelsey crouched beside him. She sawed the line around his wrist with a kitchen knife and glanced over her shoulder.

"You get your ass in gear and leave this place," she said, her breathing keeping pace with the rapid back and forth of the knife. "Kevin will kill you, no matter what Stephanie says."

"Honeyboy," Carter mumbled as he revived his brain.

"What?" Kelsey's body was so close that Carter recalled the night with her and Jen.

"I'm sorry I accused you of blackmailing."

"Shhhh," she said. "It doesn't matter now. Leave this place and never come back." She severed the cord and bounced to her feet. She leaned down and gripped Carter's hands to help him stand. She handed him the kitchen knife. "You need this more than I do."

Carter's vision had returned, though he rocked toe to heel and toe to heel before gaining balance.

"Thank you," he said. "He's dangerous, Kelsey. He's the..."

"We don't have time to chat," Kelsey said, shoving him toward the door. "Turn left in the hallway and leave through the back exit. Kevin and Stephanie live at Preston Apartments right down the street, so don't go in that direction." Sweat traveled down her face, and her shoulders trembled.

"He's killing girls, Kelsey," Carter said as he rubbed his wrist and straightened his shirt.

"I pawned it," she said.

Carter wrinkled his brow and shook his head. "I don't under..."

"My momma's ring," she said. Her face twisted in pain. "I pawned it to pay a debt. It was the moment I cut the cord to everything I was. I don't understand how you knew about my dad, but..." She trembled, and her shoulders dropped.

"It wasn't your fault, Kelsey," Carter said as he stepped closer. "Parents manage to love us and hurt us at the same time, and often both things happen unintentionally."

Kelsey moaned and pushed him back. "Take the back exit, Sykes. It's your only chance."

He swayed again and staggered toward the doorway leading into the hall.

CHAPTER 25

Kevin crept behind Stephanie and wrapped his arms around her bare shoulders. He kissed the butterfly tattoo on her neck. "I sent your Romeo on his way. He said he wouldn't bug you anymore. Dude hinted he's leaving town."

She turned around and hugged him. "Thank you, Honey, my big protector," she said, touching his biceps. "Isn't that better than hurting him any more than we already did?"

"Don't push it, Steph," Kevin said. You know my nature." He glanced around the dark Dirty Mint's meet-and-greet room. The laughter and moans reminded him these sheeple were beneath him. The fools couldn't control their base needs, while he exhibited the willpower to refrain from cutting them into pieces. He held sway over their lives like a hunter does a deer—he decided when to pull the trigger and field dress his prey.

Soon, when he'd finished his fun, he'd end the stuck-up little rich girl and present her to the world. He wished the media recognized his talents, including his signature move. He'd better work faster if he wanted this city's respect. Eleven years earlier, they'd caught Sammy Little, the most prolific killer ever in downtown Louisville.

Kevin inhaled and was sure he smelled his mother's perfume.

A woman's throaty laughter rose above the noise.

"How'd a goat get in here?" he said.

"The only way Randa's like a goat is she's horny," Stephanie said, half smiling as she gauged his response to her joke. When Kevin didn't laugh, Stephanie said, "Hey, don't pout. Kelsey asked us not to hurt him too bad."

Kevin leaned away and ran his fingers through his goatee. He searched the crowd for Kelsey. "Steph, where's Kelsey? I saw her earlier."

"I don't know," she said. "She's around here, somewhere."

"I'd better get back there and clean up," he said. Stephanie hugged him again, but he didn't respond. As soon as she released him, Kevin hurried toward the Hot4Teacher Room as if he were late for class.

CHAPTER 26

C arter heard Vickie's chair roll and creak as she stood to follow him to his office. He veered left and entered the office work-room instead. He entered his code into the copy machine keypad.

He had arrived home by 5:00 a.m., in time to shower, shave, bandage his head, and apply ice packs to his swollen cheek. Carter refused to miss the last school day with his students and teachers. He couldn't imagine life without them, or at least, he had never tried.

Vickie closed the door behind her as he leaned down and shuffled the clear white paper in the paper catcher.

"So, did a horse or an angry girlfriend kick you in the head?" Vickie assumed her usual pose—hands on hips and her chin held high.

"Let's just say never try to take an extra chocolate milk when Liz the Lunch Lady is on duty. She packs a punch." He hoped the joke might persuade Vickie he was fine.

"With those eyes and your wrist rubbed raw, you could audition for The Walking Dead as a zombie, even without makeup," Vickie said. She refused to ignore the obvious. "You're trying to shove me into my grave earlier than I want, right?"

"It's a regular last day, Vickie. We remind our kids what we expect this summer, hug each child, and load them up with books and information for their moms and grandparents."

"It's a regular day, but your swollen noggin looks more irregular than usual." She raised her hand to gesture. "Please, tell me what's happening, Carter. Your Lone Ranger routine isn't necessary. I can help you."

"You're the best, Vickie, but you can't solve my problems." He dropped the papers on a cart beside the copier. *Apparently, neither can I,* he thought.

"I can't believe knocking a protestor on his butt has led to so much disruption, Carter," she said. "I know you don't want to apologize, but can't you—"

"I've made mistakes, Vickie. Other things that I can't talk about with anyone. Not even someone I trust, like you."

"Denzel and I consider you family, Carter. You can tell us anything, and we'll help," she said. "Is it money or something illegal? Denzel is a great investor. We do well..."

"You know I'm a cheapskate, Vick," he said, smiling. "I don't have any debts. At least, not the kind you pay back with money. I'm dealing with conflicts that are more important than my job."

She frowned. "It must be bad. The only thing you seem to care about is the work. It bothers me that you don't mention family. Your only hobby I know about is buying broken stuff at flea markets and antique stores."

Carter concealed so much from the people who cared about him. His chest rose and fell like an ocean tide. *At least try*, he thought.

"I've told you about Colonel Scott, right?" He glanced away from Vickie toward a demotivational poster someone had tacked to the wall. Beneath an image of five women in construction hats on a worksite were the words, "There's No "I" in TEAM!" Printed below those words in smaller script, it said, "Remember, you can always be replaced." Someone had placed it there during Carter's first few months as the Principal. He figured it was to test his sense of humor. He left it there, and it seemed he had passed the test.

Vickie's brow wrinkled as she probed her memory. "Your last foster home near Fort Knox? You've mentioned him once in all these years."

"Yes," Carter said. "When the State placed me with him and Kris, I thought I might not survive. In my other homes, especially the worst ones, they pitied me. They expected nothing, so I saw myself as a victim of my circumstances. Victims have little to lose."

Vickie stepped closer. Carter realized it was because his tone had shifted. He resisted jokes or intentional diversions to avoid the conversation. She leaned into his words as if watching racehorses sprinting down the stretch.

His heart beat faster. *So, this is being vulnerable? I'm not fond of it.*

"The Colonel practiced a different approach," Carter said. "His expectations were clear at the start. I was a sophomore in high school making poor grades—and he didn't accept it. 'You're too smart to be so stupid, Carter.'" His voice deepened to imitate the Colonel.

"He sounds like Denzel with our kids," Vickie said.

"Colonel Scott explained it wasn't my circumstances that would define me, but my character." Carter's voice wavered, so he cleared his throat. "The Colonel didn't let me be less and showed me what more looked like."

"I bet it was hard to change, wasn't it?"

"It was. We'd talk in the garage as Scott taught me woodworking. He told me a story once while we fixed and finished a table for a woman at the church. As a soldier, his unit had spent six weeks taking a mountain climbing course. The instructor ordered one man to climb a mountain face while everyone else watched. The guy, called Knoxville because of his hometown, was the best climber in the unit. He set his ropes and scurried up the rock like a lizard. However, after about 250 feet, he stopped."

"I'm afraid of heights, so I'd stop, too," Vickie said.

"I thought the same thing, but Knoxville wasn't afraid. He was stuck. The instructor informed us climbers called it being 'Frozen to the Face.' A climber couldn't ascend or descend—he just hung there, stuck."

Vickie waited, her breathing soft.

"Colonel Scott told me there was only one solution when you're Frozen to the Face. You have to let go. The instructor directed Knoxville through the walkie-talkie to push away from the path he was on and swing to another part of the mountain. It's scary but necessary if you want to advance."

Vickie said, "Did you understand what he meant?"

"I was seventeen and not very bright, Vick," Carter said. "I just thought it was a cool story at first. But as I've grown older, the ice melts."

"Change is hard for all of us," she said.

"Yes," Carter said. "Especially when you're poor and don't know much. I had developed some bad habits to cope with the gunk in my brain— harmful habits I still use to forget painful memories—but the Colonel gave me dreams when I didn't have any of my own."

"Is he still around?"

"He is why I went to the service and came out ready for college," Carter said, unconsciously tugging his red tie. "But no, he died while I was in the Middle East. He never saw me come home or graduate from UofL."

"I'm sorry, Carter," Vickie said.

"Me, too, Vickie." Carter leaned against the copier. "It pushed me back into my old ways of thinking and created new habits."

"You're a good man, Carter," Vickie said. "I don't know what those memories and habits are—you're too good at hiding them behind your work. But I do know you're a good person."

Lamar, the assistant principal, knocked before opening the workroom door.

"I'm sorry to interrupt, Carter," he said. He stood inside the doorway behind Vickie, his broad shoulders pushing tight against his tailored shirt. His brown face harbored worry. "Dr. Wallace is here and wants to speak with you before school starts."

CHAPTER 27

D r. Wallace's smile reminded Carter of his Drill Sergeant's grin in Boot Camp. Sergeant Doogan walked down the line, examining each soldier with a devious delight written on his lips. In his Alabama drawl, he'd say, "If y'all knew what I got planned for you today, you'd turn around, pack your duffel, and slip town slick as an otter's pecker."

Dr. Wallace sat at Carter's desk, staring at her phone. She wore a purple power suit with a white blouse under the jacket. Her flawless nails matched the outfit even more closely than her smile mirrored Sergeant Doogan's.

For a moment, Carter recalled Kevin's mom and her sharp talons.

"Every time I talk to your secretary, she describes the long hours you work and your great relationships with families, kids, and staff," she said. "It's funny how good people like her can be wrong sometimes, isn't it, Mr. Sykes?"

Carter stood beside his desk but didn't reply. His location and stance communicated that he expected her to relinquish his seat.

"I hope you don't mind me making myself at home," Dr. Wallace said. "I didn't want my back to the door." She gathered her phone and exquisite leather bag before standing. Her rose oil perfume lingered after she passed Carter.

Carter didn't move until she sat in the seat facing the desk. Then, without breaking eye contact, he eased into his chair.

"What can I do for you today, Dr. Wallace?"

Her smile reappeared.

"I'm here on official business today, Mr. Sykes," she said, as though she often visited to hang out as friends. "I have some news to deliver." She removed an envelope from her bag and slid it across the desk.

"What's this?"

"I so hoped you would ask," she said. Genuine glee oozed from her spirit. "That's a two-week suspension from work issued by Dr. Coles and Human Resources. I offered to hand-deliver it on the superintendent's behalf."

Carter pushed against the anger swelling inside him.

He cleared his throat. "For missing an appointment with Public Relations?"

Dr. Wallace laughed. "Are you joking?"

Carter's eyes narrowed. He rested his elbows on the desk and intertwined his fingers.

"You ignored a directive from a supervisor," she said. "Insubordination is the quickest route to a new home."

Carter remembered his struggles with the Bergers, his first foster home. *Not being what they wanted was the quickest route to a new home.* He glanced at the suspension letter on the desk.

"This isn't unemployment; it's a suspension."

Wallace laughed. "It's a suspension now," she said. "However, the investigation conducted in those two weeks will determine you failed to uphold the district's commitment to diversity and equity. That means the next time you misstep—an inappropriate word during a meeting, an absence without the proper paperwork, or even a parent complaint..."

"I protected the school grounds," he said. "Isn't school safety a commitment?"

"People watch what we do, Sykes," she said, shifting to a less gleeful, more professional tone. "You sent the wrong message and then refused to apologize, so..."

"Apologize?" Now Carter laughed. "We both know that formula. Minor incidents plus apologies equal a confession more egregious than the initial act. You must pay once you confess to doing wrong, even if you didn't do anything wrong."

"Pushing the Watterson kid sealed your fate. Don't you get that? You're dead wood, Sykes. Someone may make you a footstool or toss you into their garden to rot, but you'll never be of real value again in our school system."

Carter pictured Hope's blackmail letter. The devil invented phones with cameras.

"But you get one advantage, Mr. Sykes," Wallace said. "You don't have to be here when the kids go wild at the end of the day."

"What do you mean? It's the last day," he said, "I need to say..."

"Goodbye?" She held up her phone and stabbed it with one of her long nails.

Within seconds, Carter heard Vickie yell in the front office, "Wait. What's happening?"

Two school district safety officers appeared at Carter's office door. The male officer, a thin man with origami shoulders and a bright orange vest strutted into the room. A stocky African-American woman wearing an identical vest followed him, her gaze lowered toward the dull gray carpet.

"Mr. Sykes," the man said, "we're here to escort you off the school grounds. Please come with us."

Carter stared at Dr. Wallace. Despite her apparent disdain for him, he had never hated her until now. Carter's self-loathing had long kept his hatred too occupied for hatred. Was it her partial smile and evident pleasure at suspending him that seared his heart with a branding iron? He did not have time for a diagnosis. "I'm talking to you, sir," Thin Man said. "Pick up your keys and any personal items, and come with me."

Carter glared at the security officer.

Wallace chuckled. "I'm sensing some anger, Mr. Sykes," she said. "If you didn't want this, you should've apologized like I told you. We discussed consequences."

"You act like justice is a rock you get to throw at people, Dr. Wallace," Carter said. "It's just a word if there's no truth behind it."

"I'll let Dr. Coles know you think the murder of a kid on the streets of our city is akin to hurt feelings."

Thin Man started to speak, but Carter silenced him with a wave.

"You're so confident I've had a soft life, Dr. Wallace," Carter said. "A few years back, you told the principals your father has a Ph.D. from Stanford, didn't you? Isn't your mother a school superintendent in Colorado?"

Dr. Wallace glared at him, her eyes like burning coals. Only today could acknowledging parental success spark anger.

Carter started to say more, but the security team stepped between them. "It's time to go, Mr. Sykes." The female officer's voice was so gentle everyone stilled.

Carter picked up his keys on the desk and his briefcase from the floor. He glanced at the officer's name badge. It read, Salima.

The officers herded Carter toward the front office. Vickie met them in the short hallway.

"Mr. Sykes?" she said. Carter forced a smile to reassure her.

Lamar stood beside Vickie, staring at the security guards.

"Don't worry, Vickie," Carter said. "Lamar, you're in charge. I won't be able to return for a few weeks, but you can phone me whenever you need me. I have great confidence in your leadership. Plus, you've got Vickie's support."

After they exited the building, Carter sped up, leaving the guards in his wake. He squinted at the morning sky as he veered toward his Toyota in the parking lot. He hadn't expected the last day of school to be this way.

The heat trapped inside his car caused Carter to sweat when he slid into the driver's seat. He turned the ignition and cranked up the air conditioning. The air streaming toward his face reminded him of the small fan in the castle—the one that rustled Becca's hair. He leaned forward against the steering wheel and closed his eyes.

When Carter straightened, Becca stared at him from the front passenger's seat. Her silky hair appeared darker, contrasting her pale skin and dress—the sunflowers were now the color of egg yolks.

"You don't understand, do you?" Her smile was gentle.

"Understand what?" Carter recognized that this version of Becca was five years younger than he was now.

"The Wallace woman kindles hate in you for a reason, Cartie."

"Yeah, she's out to get me," he said.

"It's not that simple, my brother," Becca said. "Your hatred comes from the inside. Our bodies know where we bury our pain and shame. When things go wrong, our guilt and doubts dig up those sharp, jagged bones and stab us with them. We fight back but end up with more hurt and regrets."

"Stop it, Becca," Carter said aloud. He squeezed the steering wheel until his knuckles turned white and pink.

"This fight ends when you dig up those bones and examine them like an archeologist," Becca said. "You'll understand you hate her because she's stealing your atonement."

Carter faced the windshield and reclined his seat a few inches. Exhaustion enveloped him, crushing his ability to forget.

"Dig deep and brush off the past, Carter," Becca said. "You can't change if you don't. You can't smother the pain until you quit cutting yourself with the jagged remains."

CHAPTER 28

The boy crept toward the living room. His mom's open bedroom door lit the way. When he arrived, Carter crawled behind their worn gray sofa. Three shadow puppets performed on the wall behind him, their hands and arms gesturing as if controlled by tight, invisible strings. The shadows overacted like slapstick comedians, but the words suggested the play was a tragedy.

His mother screamed and said, "What the hell, Andy? Have you lost your mind?"

"You better put that down, buddy," Brent, his mom's latest boyfriend, said. Carter heard his fear but didn't raise his head until he heard Andy rack his Remington 12 Gauge. Carter recognized the gun's command—the pumping action made an unmistakable sound—and recalled its weight and kick from the picnic months earlier, where Andy showed him how to use it.

"Linda," Andy said, his voice a rant and a sob, "You wouldn't listen. We coulda made each other happy."

Carter rose from behind the couch like an actor entering stage left. His unkempt hair cast spikes and valleys as he hit his mark.

Andy, his mother's ex-boyfriend, had been kind to Carter. Even after Linda ended their relationship, Andy brought gifts to the house and appeared at the Buckeye Motel, where Linda cleaned rooms. Carter was in the car when Andy blocked his mom's old Plymouth in a parking lot, refusing to let her leave until they reconciled—which his mom refused. As the big man begged her from outside the car window, Linda told him, "Grow up, Andy. I'm moving on, and you should, too."

Andy didn't move on. Instead, three days later, he loaded his shotgun and tucked a black-handled revolver into his belt before driving his pickup truck to their small rented house on Poplar Flat Road.

Carter stared past the adult triangle into the dark streets. He wished he and Becca could fly away from Mansfield, Ohio. He imagined holding his sister's hand as they ascended into the sky toward a real castle, a farm, or even an island.

However, only Andy's shotgun barrel flew upward.

Andy's face, a perverse blend of pain and resolve, froze behind the trigger as if his head rested a spike.

As he steadied the shotgun, Carter darted into view and said, "Mr. Andy, don't."

All three adults stared at the boy beside the tattered sofa. Carter pleaded for this performance to end but knew it would not. He tasted the familiar and inevitable sadness so common in his ten-year-old life.

"Hey, little man," Andy said as he shifted the butt of the shotgun against his shoulder. "Always protecting your mama and sister. You're a good boy, Carter."

Carter wanted to beg Andy to lower the gun. Maybe they might talk it out. But the words clung to his throat. The best he mustered was a gasp.

The first blast rocked the entire house. Carter stumbled backward as a storm cloud of gunpowder and fire filled the small living room. The slug tore through Brent's chest and shredded the thin drywall to Carter's left. Brent's shadow danced, his arms flailing, as the shot flung him to the rickety coffee table, the marionette strings severed.

Carter whimpered, and his throat tightened as if the moment held him in a chokehold. His bare chest and shoulders heaved to escape. Bitter. Inevitable.

Like a robot, Andy rotated until the gun pointed at Linda.

Carter's mother raised her hands and retreated several steps until she couldn't move farther. "Don't," she said.

Andy slid the shotgun's forearm back and forth with such power and speed that Carter's mind struggled to register the move. Nonetheless, the boy broke his paralysis and stumbled toward the shooter.

The second explosion sounded louder than the first because Carter was closer—so close the gunpowder settled on him like a delicate, bitter mist falling from an angry sky. He turned his head in time to see the slug splatter his mother's blood on the ceiling, the wall, and the floor. Her body contorted, and she dropped to the floor, limp, her eyes wide like Becca's rag doll.

Carter also felt his chest crack open, leaving his heart as vast and tattered as the bare drywall behind his mother. He shattered but couldn't stop his feet from driving forward.

Carter's momentum carried him into Andy. Unlike the slug striking the wall, Carter flattened against the large man's hip and slid to the floor onto his butt.

Andy glanced at him. The man's wet eyes and tortured expression confused Carter, causing him to scuttle away like a crab.

Andy walked with Carter for several steps before tossing the shotgun onto the couch.

Carter stopped yet kept his hands and feet on the floor beneath him, his face and stomach toward the ceiling, and his butt elevated. He resembled a human table.

"Carter," Andy said. "You're a good boy, so it hurts me to do this." The man removed the revolver from his belt.

Carter shivered and said, "Please, Becca needs me."

Andy appeared perplexed. He dropped to his knees. "I'm not an evil man, Carter," he said as he peered at Linda. "I loved her too much to let her go."

When Andy raised the gun and stretched his hand outward, Carter winced and crab-walked farther away.

"You will understand, Carter," Andy said, looking down at him. "Tell Becca I am sorry."

He placed the handgun barrel in his mouth and pulled the trigger without hesitation. Carter watched the fountain of blood and brain matter rise toward the yellow-spotted ceiling. The man leaned backward, his body kept upright by his thick knees planted on the living room floor.

Carter fell flat and rolled away. Andy clutched the gun even after his hand dropped to his side. The puppeteer had drawn a red velvet curtain on the ceiling above the man's contorted body.

***

After the bitter sulfur smell kicked his senses, Carter stood and staggered down the hallway. He hurried to catch Becca before she exited the closet and entered the living room. He didn't want her to see their mother's lifeless body.

"I'm right here, Becca," he said when he entered their bedroom. Carter paused to wipe his tears and rake his forearm across his wet, sticky nose. He smelled the gunpowder residue on his hand and arm; it burned his eyes but didn't burn away the image of his mother's fractured frame.

Carter cleared his throat once more before turning the knob.

"Hey, Princess Becca," he said. His voice sounded odd in his ears, hoarse and old. "Time to come down from the tower."

The small fan hummed as his eyes adjusted to the closet's darkness. The flashlight shined on the comforter's corner, casting light toward Becca's tiny hand.

"Rebecca Marie Sykes," Carter said, sounding like his mom whenever she struggled to get Becca's attention. He fought back tears, his new voice cracking. "Wake up. We have to go."

When Becca didn't answer, Carter's hands trembled. He kneeled and lifted the flashlight, trailing the beam along her arm to her shoulder and, then, her face. Carter was sure his blood reversed its flow, creating a pond inside his brain. His chest swelled as he tried to catch his breath, but his lungs were stones, unable to draw air.

He raised the flashlight to illuminate her entire body. The white dress with sunflowers he'd slipped over Becca's tiny head appeared stained and wet near her chest and shoulder. "Moon's Wish," a book Carter checked out for her at the public library, rested against her knee.

Carter sniffled as he leaned closer. Becca's head tilted to the left. The light revealed her face, peaceful eyes, and the tendrils of dark hair matted against her scalp and neck. A halo of blood encircled her head on the white comforter. He dropped the flashlight and bent over her as he cried so hard his every muscle strained toward failure.

He didn't see her hand twitch and fall against his arm, but he felt it. An electric shock and dizziness invaded his brain, while nausea stirred his stomach. He slipped and fell—for the first time—into something that would become more familiar to him than happiness. He'd call it a Trap.

***

The soft knock on the foggy glass startled Carter. He lowered his window.

"I'm sorry, officer," he said. "I'll exit the property."

Salima shook her head and leaned closer to him. "Don't worry, Mr. Sykes," the Security Officer said. "Take as much time as you need. That's not why I circled back to talk."

"Thank you, ma'am," Carter said. He paused, inviting her to speak.

"My nephew, Kenny Booker, went to West Louisville Elementary for your first three years as principal."

"I remember Kenny very well," Carter said. He smiled despite having just revisited his most traumatic moment.

"I thought you would," Salima said. She flashed a half smile and shook her head side-to-side. "That boy raised hell when he was little."

Carter nodded. "How is he doing in middle school?"

The officer sniffled. "That's why I needed to talk to you. He's doing great. His momma and I are so proud of him."

"I thought he would," Carter said. "He worked hard."

"Mr. Sykes, that's because of you and your teachers. He changed 'cause of the challenges you all made him meet right here." She waved her hand toward the school.

Carter lowered his eyes. "I think having a great mom and auntie had much to do with that, along with the teachers."

"Mr. Sykes," she said, "that's kind of you to say, but when anyone asks how he got so smart, he mentions you."

Carter's cheeks felt hot. "Thank you," he said.

"It's the truth. I figured with all this happening, whatever's going on, you needed to hear that," Salima said. She glanced around the parking lot. "When I heard we were heading here this morning, I studied this quote I keep on my desk to make sure I got it right. Frederick Douglass said it. 'It's easier to create strong children than to repair broken men.'"

Carter cleared his throat and attempted to respond, but the words stuck.

"Isn't that something?" Salima said.

Carter finally responded. "Yes, it is. Thank you."

Salima tapped the Toyota's roof twice and said, "Please take care, Mr. Sykes. I'll let you get going."

Carter thought about saving kids and fixing broken men as he shifted his car into gear and drove toward home. He was the fractured boy who became the broken man he'd never figured out how to fix.

CHAPTER 29

Kevin Nally rolled the Lincoln along Market Street, away from Banger's and the Dirty Mint Julep. Although it was almost 5:30 p.m., more protestors filled the street now than the day after the pig killed the Wagers kid.

"I'm a smart mother for hooking up those speakers in your boot, my Lincoln." He patted the dashboard with his hand. His cigarette smoke rose toward numerous pine tree air fresheners hanging from his rearview mirror.

He eased past the people roaming the streets and sidewalks, his speakers pumping out Slipknot. He didn't love the band so much; he needed loud music to mask any noises from his trunk.

But he did love the chaos of the streets. He spread more pain and fear with little worry. His music contributed to the disorder and enabled him to drive through the streets without getting accosted. Other cars were not so lucky. At the corner of Broadway and 7th Street, flames and smoke engulfed a burning police car. Some people partied as if UofL won the NCAA Men's Basketball Championship again. Others raised handmade signs demanding "Defund for De'juan." People shuffled along the sidewalks. Their ragged clothes, shopping carts, and slumping shoulders suggested they lived on the streets. The police treated the riots as an out-of-hand parade. He hoped they'd lose funding. Fewer cops would simplify his life, that's for sure.

One thing bothered Kevin. Not the protestors, of course. He'd marched with one of his former mechanics. They wore hoodies and masks to hide their identities so they could smash windows and take what they wanted. They tossed Molotov cocktails into businesses. Kevin had loved setting fires since his early teens, so it excited him to have an opportunity to do it in the open.

No, it pissed him off that the Louisville media outlets shifted focus to some idiot cop and a dead kid and away from the so-called Good Girl Killer. Damn.

"I guess I won't get the PR my old man did when he ruled Kentuckiana," he said. People call the Louisville, Kentucky, and Southern Indiana area Kentuckiana. Probably some rich marketing bitch came up with that name.

He turned onto 9th Street and found it so empty that he lowered the music and rolled up his windows. He heard muted cries and kicks against the trunk lid, so he pulled into an empty Fifth Third Bank parking lot.

"Same PR bitch named this bank, I bet."

Kevin parked beneath a Cherry Plum tree behind thick shrubbery and grabbed a tire iron from the passenger seat. He pulled his ski mask over his face and lifted his hoodie before exiting the car.

He walked to the Lincoln's rear fender and kneeled as if preparing to change a tire. He examined his surroundings as he held the tire iron against the hub cap. He'd used this spot before—there were no cars or lights, and the only cameras faced the front parking lot.

At first, Kevin worried about his plan—a rare thing for him. He was always prepared and organized in any risky venture, but Syke's escape from the Hot4Teacher room hurt. It injured his most precious possession, his pride. But after reflecting, he saw how jacked this plan was and figured he had considered this option long before it presented itself. He must have because he operated on a different level than the losers and the sheep.

Sure, Kevin knew the risks, but, as always, he would gamble and win. His only problem might be Stephanie, but he owned her. Hell, she allowed him to hunt and bring the prey home. She bent to his will like every girl he'd encountered over his thirty-one years—except his dear mom, who loved him.

Kevin whistled that kid's song again—the one embedded in his brain like a tick—as he strutted to the Lincoln's trunk. His keys jingled when he opened the lid. A female hand rose toward him, but he swatted it away. The plastic covering rustled when the girl attempted to retreat from him.

The Good Girl Killer raised the tire iron, its arc tall, and swung it downward, again and again, until strings of blood splashed onto the hot trunk lid with each new swing.

CHAPTER 30

C arter awoke like a vampire. After Security removed him from school at 7:50 a.m., his bed called him to it like a coffin, and he plummeted into a deep, dreamless sleep. His thrift store clock, its digits a dull red, now read 11:28 p.m. He'd slept nearly fourteen hours and might have snoozed longer if not for the laughter.

Carter sat up and searched the room. Besides the nightstands, he had a cherry-wood chest, its bottom drawer crooked and broken, and a dresser on the front wall. The dresser's mirror tilted to the left due to a missing brace he had yet to replace. The door to the main bathroom, if you could call it that, and the bedroom closet door stood to his left.

He rubbed sleep from his eyes and stood by the bed. He eased toward the closet, hesitating before opening a door.

Becca stared up at him, a grin on her face. "You know, this closet is the same size as the castle back in our old place, Cartie." She held the grin, then said, "Look how far you haven't come, my big brother."

It was Kitchen Becca again, her sunflower dress even more faded than the night before. She reclined against the side wall, his wardrobe dangling above her long legs.

Carter interlocked his hands behind his head. "Why tonight, Becca?"

"You know why, Cartie," she said. "We didn't finish our discussion this morning, did we?"

"As far as I'm con..."

"You're concerned?" she said, her voice as pointed as a thorn. "I'm the one who's concerned. You've forfeited so much these past few days, Carter, because you'd rather throw away your shoes than remove the pebble inside."

Carter tried to turn away, but his bare feet stuck to the floor outside the closet.

"I'm sure you remember the old joke Mr. Andy told when he took Momma, you, and me for pizza at Bearnos," Becca said as she leaned back and folded her hands behind her head.

Carter shivered upon hearing Mr. Andy's name. He swallowed against the thick wall of denial and resistance inside his chest.

"It's kinda ironic now, but you and Momma thought it was funny then," Becca said. "Of course, I didn't get it, but I laughed because my big brother did."

"I don't want to think about..."

"Don't blame you, Cartie," she said. "But that's the point I'm slamming into your fragmented mind. Mr. Andy told Momma he bought his ex-wife a birthday present she wouldn't use. When Momma asked what it was, he said, 'A cemetery plot.'"

Carter glared at Becca.

Her grin evaporated, and she stared back with toxic pity.

"It's about time you used the present I keep giving you," she said. "I'm telling you to face it all. Not some of it; all of it. Start by dropping the idea that what happened to me was your fault."

"But it was," he said. His heart pounded, and he shuddered.

"You believe that because you refuse to confront it and then let it go. You have to face that first Trap," Becca said. "Come into this castle, Cartie. If not for yourself, then do it for me."

***Carter crouched and lowered his body onto the closet floor. He smelled the sweat of an old pair of running sneakers wedged between the dress shoes and winter boots. A blade of light found the perfect angle between the bedroom curtains to stab into the castle, and the bedroom lamp illuminated the closet, so Carter closed the door with his foot. Still, light slipped beneath the door, allowing him to see his hands. He bent his knees toward his chest and hugged his legs.

Carter returned to Mansfield, Ohio. His bony knees ground into the closet floor, with Becca's tiny, fragile fingers resting against his bare skin—Trapping him.

***

Becca's arms flailed, and her feet, suspended above the shopping cart, kicked. Her head swiveled from right to left and back again like wiper blades. Carter never forgot how her panicked heartbeat scared him so much that he yelled for her to calm down. Of course, she could not hear him. In Traps, Carter was a silent passenger, unable to give directions or provide assistance—instead, he was as useless then, during the Trap, as now, recalling it.

A blue light, attached at the top of a sign, towered above the toilet paper and cleaning supplies. The sign read, "Attention, Kmart Shoppers!" Carter had hoped Becca would turn and find their mother; however, he realized the shopping cart wasn't moving, and his mother wasn't behind them.

His sister, no more than two years old, became more agitated. She stretched her hands over her head and leaned to the right and left. She kicked at a box of Saltines and a Jif Peanut Butter jar, but her legs were too short. Carter experienced her desperation and the escalating fear of abandonment flooding her petite body.

Why didn't someone respond? Why was Becca alone?

The little girl's cries transformed into loud shrieks and raw, primal screams.

Looking through Becca's eyes, Carter had seen his mother at the aisle's far end. The toddler recognized her, too, but continued to wail.

Linda panicked as though she had only now recognized that the baby was alone. She scrambled up the aisle. A pickle jar slipped from her hand and smashed against the white Kmart floor. However, she didn't turn to see it or slow down.

Serves her right, Carter thought, *leaving a baby alone in a Kmart*.

When Linda arrived, she lifted Becca from the shopping cart and maneuvered the baby's feet through the leg holes near the buggy's handle.

Still, Becca remained hysterical. Her small pale cheeks burned red, and her toothpick arms flailed as if she might drown in her tears.

Then Carter heard his sister say her first complete sentence.

"I want Cartie."

Carter hugged his knees and pressed them against his chest so hard it hurt. He pictured Becca crying at Kmart in their mother's arms—crying for her Cartie.

He relived the rest of his first Trap.

As his mother held Becca against her shoulder, the little girl's trauma expanded like a dark cloud from the Mill Creek smokestacks.

That's when the little boy rounded the corner and shuffled down the aisle. The boy appeared slight, his Louisville Cardinals tee shirt and tattered jeans revealing his thin arms and slight ankles. He held a silver plastic airplane above his shoulder, humming like an engine as if the plane flew beside him.

When Becca saw the boy, her crying lightened, and she reached for him. Her hands opened and closed to draw him nearer.

"My Cartie," she said.

Carter had sensed his sister's relief at seeing her five-year-old brother. Her heart slowed, and she wiggled, not from fear but because he was near.

However, their mother had a different response. As Carter approached, she pinned Becca to her right hip. Then she swung her left arm like a tightly hinged screen door, slamming her palm against his face. The fierce sting burned his right cheek and ear, and the airplane launched from his hand.

"I told you to watch your sister," she said. "What if somebody took her and we never saw her again? It'd be your damn fault, Carter. Can't I count on you to protect your sister?"

A shocked couple circumnavigated the scene, but they stared like gawkers at a car accident.

Carter remembered the humiliation more than the slap. But her words about somebody taking his sister produced the most enduring fear and shame.

In the Trap, the ten-year-old Carter heard the five-year-old Carter, tears welling in his eyes, say, "I'm sorry," a second before the Trap ended abruptly.

As forty-one-year-old Carter sat in the dark castle of his Shotgun house on Swan Street, he realized something for the first time: the abrupt escape from the Trap occurred when Rebecca's heart stopped beating.

CHAPTER 31

"Yes, sir," Mona said. She feared some monumental screw-up must have happened for Captain Anderson to call her three hours before her 7:00 a.m. shift started. She sat up and cleared sleep from her eyes.

"Ridge," Anderson said, "Dispatch contacted me. A male called the station, claiming he saw a guy shove a young woman into his car trunk a little after one a.m. this morning. It happened in an alley beside the Banger's Gentlemen's Club parking lot.

Mona woke up. "Who was the caller?"

"He wouldn't give his name," the captain said. "He didn't want his wife to find out he'd been to the club. But the desk said he sounded reliable."

"Okay," she said. *Sounded reliable?* "But, sir, if you provided information that might lead to apprehending a serial killer, wouldn't you want everyone to know your name? Everyone's heard about the reward, right?"

Anderson grunted as though Mona spouted foolishness. Without addressing her questions, he continued speaking. "I'm calling you because the caller said the man resembled the—let me quote: 'It was that principal dude from the playground video who knocked out the protestor. He forced a woman into the trunk of an old Toyota Camry. The plate started with KPE, but I didn't get the rest.'"

Mona paused. Now she understood why Anderson called her instead of multiple other on-duty units.

"I'll call Detective Vincent to inform him, but you'll check it out first. You know, since you and I suspected Sykes for a long time."

Mona rolled her eyes. Damn politicians and bureaucrats never ceased to amaze her. The "you and I" reference almost made her laugh. Anderson didn't hesitate to send her into harm's way to advance his career.

"I appreciate it, sir," she said, fighting her urge to demand he do it himself. "I will be on my way in five minutes."

"Remember who ordered you to investigate this lead," he said. Then, to be more explicit, he added, "Remember the conversation in my office. You were ready to forget about it, but I ordered you to follow up."

"Don't worry, Captain," Mona said, gritting her teeth. His calculating and passionless voice pained her. "I'll be careful."

Anderson paused to process her response. "Yes, that's what I mean," he said. "You better be careful." It sounded more like a threat than a concern.

Mona punched the button on her phone and rolled from the sheets. She had dreamed of this moment—a chance to save lives and get justice for the girls already killed by the psychopath. However, doubt spread inside her like spilled wine on a white napkin. Something felt off-target.

"An anonymous caller? Carter Sykes, a killer?" she said as she retrieved her gear.

The clock's red eyes blinked 3:48 a.m.

***

Carter stared into the crooked mirror attached to his bedroom dresser. He didn't avert his eyes. Its portrayal of his off-kilter inner self was accurate. Instead, he analyzed it like an art critic might consider an artist's final self-portrait.

His conclusion soon surfaced. Trauma resonates inside a person, like the soundwaves inside a bell. The shock forces the clapper to swing and strike the sound bow and the lip, producing an everlasting vibration. Some people believe every challenge is traumatic—an ice cream cone falling onto the sidewalk, being insulted or called an un-flattering name, or even being poor or different. However, the Traps taught Carter that real trauma is a cannon blast assaulting the bell, while pretend trauma is a squirt from a tiny, orange-tipped water gun splashing against the bell's husk.

With real trauma, the body carries the vibration. It hurts mentally and physically, but it also shakes the foundations, affecting the sufferer's balance, vision, and sense of belonging.

He had rolled onto his side in the closet and curled up, his body folded like a quarter-open pocketknife. He'd forced himself to recall the first Trap and relive it as a man rather than the little boy hovering over his dying sister. After a few moments, he'd crawled out of the castle to the bedroom floor, eventually standing as if for the first time.

Carter placed his hands against the dresser and leaned closer to the mirror.

"You falling in love with yourself, handsome?" Becca's reflection peered at him over his shoulder. However, he had never seen her like this before. Gray threads lined her dark hair; her glasses weren't cheap plastic sunglasses but authentic bifocals with an invisible wireless frame. They rested on her nose, causing her to resemble a therapist or librarian.

"You may be the only person who ever loved me, Becca," he said. "And I let you down. I let you die, and now, I'm about to let someone else die." His voice cracked and he trembled.

"Oh, Cartie, you'll always be my hero," she said, using her finger to push her glasses higher on her nose. Her sunflowers had lost their yellow, leaving long stems and thread outlines that favored wilting daisies. "Moments ago, you did the bravest thing you've ever done. You confronted our worst moment and survived it. See how strong we are?"

Carter's phone beeped on the nightstand.

When he turned, Becca wasn't behind him. The ancient clock radio on his nightstand read 4:20 a.m.

The loud knocking on his door downstairs rattled his nerves. He recalled Mr. Andy pounding on the door in Mansfield and the fate awaiting him as a boy. He shivered.

Nonetheless, he crossed the room, picked up his phone, and brought it to life as he trotted toward the stairs. A text from Mona Ridge greeted him. *Please see me out front.*

CHAPTER 32

C arter stood in his doorway and managed a smile. Somehow, Mona was still beautiful, even under Swan Avenue's dim street lights and the starless sky.

She stood several yards from the concrete steps leading to his front door, her face glowing as if reflecting the late May moonlight. She wore her full black LPD uniform and protective vest, but her hat did not hide her unruly hair and staggered defensive stance. Her hand rested on her belt near her holster.

"So, I guess this isn't a social call," Carter said, hoping she caught the reference to their coffee shop disaster.

Mona swallowed, pushed her chest forward, and straightened her posture as if she needed to appear more intimidating. *She thinks I'm a grizzly bear; she's afraid. Of me?*

"No, it isn't a social call, Mr. Sykes," Officer Ridge said, "Funny, though."

"I'm Carter, remember?"

She shook her head, ignoring the second reference to their last meeting. "The station received a call claiming you were involved in an incident earlier in the evening," she said. "Maybe that's how you bruised your face—an incident?"

Carter wondered if someone had witnessed what happened at the Dirty Mint. However, that was the previous day. Before he could respond, Mona continued.

"I'd like to check your car. Will you grant permission?" Her tone suggested this wasn't a request.

Carter stepped from the doorway onto the first step. The rough concrete felt cold against his bare feet.

Mona backstepped another yard from him toward his Toyota parked on the street. Her hand remained close to her firearm.

Carter raised his hands while lowering his shoulders to communicate he was more bunny than bear.

"I've been here since before noon, Mona," he said. "I don't care if you check my car or house—even without a search warrant."

"I appreciate that," she said, but her high-alert demeanor didn't change. Steadily, she backpedaled to the metal gate leading to the sidewalk. "The question is, do you have your keys?"

Her voice indicated that if he didn't have the keys, they were at a standoff. Carter surmised she wouldn't let him into the house to retrieve them—too dangerous. *Good for her*, he thought.

"They're in my pocket," he said.

He sensed the officer's relief.

"Come on down, then." She motioned for him to descend the steps and approach her.

"I'm a tenderfoot," he said as he approached her. He noted how each step forward prompted her to retreat an equal distance. Soon, they stood behind his car.

"Pop the trunk," she said as she drifted to the right.

Carter's keys rattled, and the lid rose like one side of a draw bridge. Without looking inside, he turned toward Mona and said, "See, I told you there's..."

Officer Ridge moved with such grace and speed that Carter froze in place. She slid backward, increasing her distance from him, while simultaneously pulling her sidearm from the holster. Carter pictured Alan Ladd in the old western movie *Shane* drawing his pistol with blazing speed to kill the evil gunslinger, Wilson.

"Hands up!" Mona shouted. "Move, and you're dead." Her voice rose a scale, but Carter saw the barrel of her weapon remain steady and pointed at his torso.

Carter inhaled a deep breath through his nose and lifted his hands, palms out, toward the night sky. He didn't panic, but Mr. Andy and the Marines trained him to expect the worst when firearms entered the scene. He held that breath and stood at attention.

Mona glared, keeping the gun aligned with his chest. She tilted her head and peered into the trunk again. Disappointment and disgust crossed her face. She brought her hand to the radio on her vest. With his hands still raised high, Carter followed her line of sight into the trunk.

The woman's eyes were open but devoid of life. Her scalp oozed blood, making her hair dark and wet. Her head tilted like Mona's when she prepared to speak into the radio mic. The dead woman's bare, broken shoulder reminded Carter of Becca's lost doll he promised to repair in Mansfield.

Carter exhaled, the breath a stutter as he capped his urge to yell. Someone had ripped open the woman's blouse and severed her red bra at the bridge between the cups. Her arms, bent with shards of bone emerging through the skin, resembled jagged, exposed roots—*bones buried in the backyard.*

The dead woman's white hands, spotted with defensive wounds and clotted blood, caused Carter to shiver. The killer had amputated her fingertips at the top knuckle beneath the nails, leaving behind the bloody stubs of her ringless fingers.

Shaking, Carter turned his full attention back to Mona and the gun.

"Her name is Kelsey," Carter said. "And she saved my life."

CHAPTER 33

C arter tasted the oil and tar soaking the pavement. A small stone dug into his right cheek, and when Officer Ridge forced his hands behind his back, his right shoulder tightened like a stressed rubber band.

He heard Mona's handcuffs clang behind him.

"Do not move a centimeter, Mr. Sykes," she said. Her voice growled as she kneeled behind him. She grabbed his left wrist and cuffed it first, then jerked the other hand closer and attached the cuff. She straddled his legs, pressing them into the street, and shifted to better control him.

"How could you, Carter?" she said. "I thought you were a good man, but I guess..." She stopped. He thought she might cry, but instead, she grabbed his bare wrists and yanked them to check the cuffs.

Carter wanted to respond, but he couldn't form the words. His rigid body was face down on the street; however, his mind existed elsewhere.

***

The little girl wiggles in the car's backseat. She doesn't like how the belt and car seat restrict her movement. She needs to bounce. She stares forward, allowing Carter to see the man driving the vehicle.

"Papaw," she says. "I'm bored."

Papaw chuckles. "Is that right, Mona Moonshine?"

"Papaw, don't make fun of me 'cause I like the moonshine. It's beautiful in the sky."

The man laughs and runs his tanned, white-spotted hand through his shale-colored hair. Carter sees multi-colored splotches beneath his nails and on his knuckles.

"Any ideas 'bout what might cure your boredom?"

The little girl sighs. "I don't know. It might be exterminal."

"Exterminal?" he says. "What in the world does that mean?"

"Papaawwww," she says, exasperated. "You know. Doctors can't make it better with medicine."

Papaw's broad shoulders rise and fall as he laughs even harder. After a moment, his deep voice fills the car. "I can't have my little Mona suffer with exterminable boredom, can I?"

"No-sir-eeeee," she says, wiggling in her seat again. They'd performed this ritual before. "Maybe some candy and pop might make me good again."

Carter sees the hillsides and hollers flow past the windows, the trees rising into the sky as gray and white as Papaw's hair. The shadows and clouds suggest dusk is near.

Papaw slows the car and pulls onto a vast turnaround space beside the blacktopped road. The gravel crunches and Mona's tiny sneakers dance back and forth as he turns the car toward the general store they passed a few miles earlier.

The girl stretches her arms upward and says, "Yayyyyy."

Carter feels the warmth in her heart when she sees Papaw in the rearview mirror. Little Mona watches the road flow beneath the car as her grandfather slows at each turn. The steep embankments pass by the window, and the engine's gentle hum sings her a lullaby.

Papaw recognizes it first. Carter follows within seconds. Between each flutter of Mona's eyelids, he sees the truck grow more prominent in the windshield as it swerves back and forth across the road's faded yellow lines.

Mona's grandfather says, "Mona Moonshine, this guy's drunk or..."

His words startle Mona right in time to see the large red pickup truck veer over the line and into their path. She and Carter watch it grow in the glass.

The collision catapults the truck driver from his vehicle and into Papaw's windshield. Sharp shards and blood hurl toward Mona in the backseat. Her body remains limp as the belts hold her firm against the seat despite the inertia. The driver's shoulders slam against the headrest of the front passenger seat. His crushed skull and decimated face stare at Mona as if preparing to ask a question.

Pain shoots through the little girl's shoulders, neck, and back. Glass pelts her bare legs and face. Fragments lodge in her cheeks and nose. Her shoe no longer dances—it flies from her foot and lands next to a bucket on the floorboard, leaving only her sock in place.

Carter prays she won't gaze at her grandfather, but she sees him.

Papaw slumps forward, his forehead and shoulders leaning against the steering wheel.

The sight wakes her again. She pushes aside the physical pain.

She says, "Papaw, come get me." Her hands open and close.

Carter pictures Becca in the shopping cart, calling his name.

Little Mona wills her legs to move as she asks her grandfather to embrace her as he has every day since her mom abandoned her. However, her limbs refuse to respond, as does her Papaw.

The gray and white sky turns charcoal before they find her. She is alone except for Carter. The car seat hugs her like her grandfather never would again.

CHAPTER 34

When the Trap released him, Carter snorted, inhaling dirt into his nose. He raised his head and attempted to blow it out, but Mona's knee on his back made it difficult. Even worse, she shoved his face into the pavement.

"Keep your head down, Sykes, or next time won't be as gentle." She twisted his arm to remind him the cuffs were locked, then stood over him.

Carter closed his eyes and rested his right ear against the street. He imagined Tonto listening for an approaching train or a gang of bandits on horseback.

"I knew she'd get you in handcuffs, bruh," a teenage voice said, "but I anticipated a much kinkier scenario."

Carter raised his face. Teenage Becca sat cross-legged on the sidewalk. She wore the sunflower dress, the fabric resting low on her shoulders, revealing the red baby-hands tattoo.

She smacked her gum as she chewed and smiled to celebrate her clever remark.

"Not now, Becca," Carter said.

"What's that? Who's Becca?" Mona said.

Becca's face became serious. "Now is the time to show someone who you are, Carter. You may not get another chance if you don't. Look what happened when you listened to me earlier. You survived it, didn't you?"

Carter heard Mona click her radio and turned his head to the right. His heartbeat quickened.

"Before you call this in, Mona, hear me out," Carter said. When he rotated his head to the left again, Becca was gone.

"Quiet, Sykes," Mona said. "You've been playing me since we first met at your school. At the coffee shop, you weren't telling me the whole story. I hoped this wasn't how your story ended, but I guess it is."

"I withheld information from you, Mona, but I didn't kill anyone," he said. "Especially not Kelsey. I told you she saved my life."

"Should I read you your rights? You have the right to remain silent. Anything you say or do..."

"Used against me, and I can get a lawyer. I know my rights," he said.

Mona paused, saying, "If you have anything to say, spill it now, Carter."

He realized she wanted him to confess or tell her about other missing girls. However, for the first time, Carter had nothing to lose.

"I'm cursed, Mona," he said.

She wrinkled her nose. "Is that right? You poor, poor man. If only you were as fortunate as the lucky girl in your trunk."

"When people touch me, I can see things. Their trauma. Their most devastating moment." The words rolled out faster than he intended. Since the Traps started when he was ten, he had never said those things to anyone except Becca.

"So, every time you bump into somebody, you see their scariest moment?" she said, her tone bordering on mockery. "That makes sense. You're the Good Girl Killer. You are their scariest moment."

"Not everybody or every time," he said. "Only when it is traumatic enough to affect their entire life. I live it with them."

"Well, I should touch you and see what you can dig up on my sordid past."

"You don't need to, Mona," he said. "You touched my wrist." Carter rattled the cuffs behind his back.

Mona's disgust registered on her face. She glanced up and down the silent street as if she might shoot him if no one watched.

"Shut up," she said. "I'm disappointed in myself for thinking..."

"Your Papaw was a good man, Mona," Carter said, his voice gentle. He waited for a reply.

The last vestiges of May blew around them. Spring would become summer, and summer would turn golden as autumn approached until, eventually, the trees would wear white shawls and diamonds on their arms and fingers. However, at this moment, Carter's time stopped. Only the dim street lights and porch lamps illuminated Swan Avenue.

"My God, you're evil scum," Mona said. "You must've researched me the first day after we met."

"I'm telling you," he said, "because I don't want to know things, but it won't stop. I learn about people when they touch me. I can't control it."

"I'm about to touch you hard," she warned. Carter winced at her threat.

"Your grandfather painted houses," Carter said, recalling the paint on Papaw's fingers. "Your mom left you with your grandparents and never returned."

"Did you call friends and neighbors in Paintsville?" she asked. "Is that what you did?" Doubt crept between her words for the first time. She clicked the radio mic and said, "This is Unit A21, Officer Mona Ridge. Please have Captain Anderson contact me via cell."

"You're the only one I've ever told," he said. "I know who did this. His name's Kevin, and his girlfriend is Stephanie."

Mona stepped beside him and planted her knee into his back. "I thought it was Idaho and the guy with the ponytail?"

Carter grunted. "That's who it is. Kevin and Stephanie," he said, the words pouring out. "He's a psychopath who manipulates her. She grabbed my wrist that day at the protest. I saw the kidnapped girl tied to a bed in the background at the end of the hallway. Kevin abducted the kid and had her in their apartment."

"So, you got all of this by touching people?" Mona said. Her disingenuous tone hurt more than her knee between his shoulders.

"No," he said. "They touch me."

"As you said, I touched you, so tell me my biggest trauma." She shifted, smiled, and said, "This should be good."

Carter swallowed. Little Mona's fear and pain lingered inside him. He preferred to let it evaporate like the dew departing the early morning grass, but he could not. He remembered the last time he revealed a Trap—how his foster mom stared at him as if watching a geek bite off a chicken's head at a carnival.

"That's what I thought," Officer Ridge said as she stood and laughed. "The only trauma you'll see is your own, Sykes... in prison."

"Mona Moonshine," Carter blurted out. "He called you his Mona Moonshine."

She stood and backed away two steps. Carter heard her holster snap, and when he lifted his chin to see her, Mona's gun barrel targeted him again.

"Shoot me if you want, Mona," he said. "But I'm your best chance to find the girl Kevin abducted, assuming she's still alive."

"How do you know he called me...that? Nobody knew except us."

"It's like we shared the same body, and I couldn't leave," he said. "I call it a Trap because I can't escape until it's over."

"No way. No one can do that."

Carter closed his eyes and relived the Trap. "You were in the car seat. On the way home, I think, you said you were bored and only candy and pop..."

"Stop it."

"...could cure it. Papaw laughed when you said 'exterminable.' Do you remember that?"

"No," she said.

Carter knew she remembered. Her voice, weaker now, coated in equal measures of doubt, fear, and surprise, suggested the moment was just as recent for her as it was for him.

"The man in the truck came through the windshield. His eyes stared at you. It reminded you..." Carter stopped speaking when Mona fell to her knees. She covered her face with her hand and trembled as the memory cascaded over the dam she had built around it.

Carter remained silent for a moment, unable to console her and persuade her at the same time.

"It's okay, Mona," he said. "We will both always remember how much he loved you."

***

Officer Ridge answered on the third ring.

"Yes, sir," she said.

Anderson sounded excited, but he talked in hushed tones. "What you got, Ridge?"

"As always, sir," she said, her stomach tightening, "you're right. I found Syke's car and discovered a young woman in the trunk."

"Good work, Ridge." Mona never imagined a person could be so pleased to hear about a murder. "Do you have body cam footage?"

"No, sir," she said. "My gear's at the station. I was sound asleep when you called."

"All right, give me details to relay to the chief." Mona heard the disappointment between his words.

"Okay, here goes. I did a visual check of the suspect's car. Nothing in the front, but the back lid appeared to be open. I glanced inside..."

"You opened it?" Panic.

"No, Captain, I didn't until after I saw a woman in the trunk."

"You sure you didn't screw this up?"

"Captain," Mona said. *Was she speaking to a child?* "We're good. I had reasonable cause. I believed the woman needed medical assistance, so I lifted the lid and checked vitals."

"Good. How'd the victim look?"

Just gorgeous, Anderson.

"Brutal attack, Captain. Head, shoulders, arms. Tire iron or a hammer would be my guess."

"Where?" Anderson was in a hurry. He wanted to be the first person to call the Chief and tell her how his brilliant plan broke the case."Swan Avenue near Barter and Broadway," she said. "In front of the suspect's house."

"Why don't you have him in custody?"

"I couldn't enter his house without a warrant, so I called you, called for a bus, and waited for your instructions."

"Do you think he is in the house or near the crime scene?"

"I'm sorry, Captain," she said. "Sykes is nowhere to be found."

CHAPTER 35

Carter wore a black hoodie, casting a shadow to hide his face, jeans, and an old pair of Saucony running shoes. He weaved through the alleys and side streets, mixing into the morning shift of protesters and pedestrians only when he had to. He swerved around a group of men walking toward the Alpha Mirror factory on Barter and drifted between two office buildings when a police car rolled down Broadway.

After emerging on the building's other side, he saw the sun rising in the east, its crimson blood staining the gray clouds hovering over Louisville, reminding him of Kelsey's bloody body and her ashen-colored skin.

Blood stained his hands, too. Kelsey's death happened because he didn't think ahead. His rush to abdicate responsibility gave Honeyboy Kevin the advantage and opportunity. *I'd be dead without Kelsey, but she would be alive without me. First Becca. Now Kelsey.*

Would Mona Ridge be the next victim of knowing Carter Sykes?

Mona had uncuffed him and allowed him to run into the house. "You get a head start," she'd said, her body shaking from the unbearable weight of setting him free. "But you better realize I'm risking my entire future. I will hunt you down and target your head if it's a lie. I swear on my grandparent's graves. My life's mission will be to find you. I won't miss. Now, get what you need from your house and disappear. You will know when we get your Kevin and Idaho."

He believed her but wondered, *"Isn't everything about me a lie?"*

Carter sprinted into the house, stopping to lock the door behind him. He took the stairs two at a time to his bedroom. After dressing, Carter grabbed his wallet from the nightstand, then dropped to his knees to open the dresser's bottom drawer. He emptied dress socks, cheap underwear, and several ragged tee shirts he'd hoarded since the Marines until he uncovered a black lockbox. The metal box, its handle brown, caused him to pause. He heard Dr. Wallace's voice: "Consequences, Sykes. Always consequences."

Consequences have much in common with vulnerability, he thought. Even when you don't face them now, they linger like blisters on your heels, hurting and making running away tricky. He wondered if his vulnerability and consequences might burst like blisters or become calluses, his skin so thick he might run forever.

Carter turned the dial on the lockbox to the right, the left, and the right again. When the latch clicked, he pulled the shackle until one side lifted from the lock's core, enabling him to raise the lid much as he had popped the car's trunk open earlier.

He stared at the contents as if he dreaded seeing them. First, he retrieved a large, stuffed yellow envelope, several smaller office-sized envelopes, and finally, a blue, faux leather checkbook. He bundled the envelopes together and slipped the checkbook into his back pocket. Then, he lifted a large stack of one-hundred-dollar bills. He folded the money, pushed it into his front pockets, and stuffed the envelopes inside his bulky black hoodie against his stomach and chest.

Several smaller items remained in the box. Carter picked up the framed photograph first. It depicted a teenager standing between a tall, bald man in a military uniform and a petite woman in a pale blue blazer, a white blouse, and blue pants. He recalled Kris worked as an administrator and professor at the college in Elizabethtown. The man's immaculate Army uniform had numerous medals pinned to the chest and stripes sewn into the shoulders. Colonel Scott trained and supported the soldiers at the Army base at Fort Knox.

Goosebumps prickled Carter's skin. These two people had invested so much in him. Already bounced from different homes and facilities, even Carter wondered if he was a worthwhile investment. However, they helped him build a future—a life better than he had ever conceived. When the Colonel passed away while Carter was in Iraq, and Kris followed soon after Carter returned home, Carter was alone again. Although his resolve to attend college and become a teacher survived, he resumed the habits that helped him forget.

What would Colonel Scott and Kris think of him now? They wouldn't be proud, he was sure.

Carter retrieved a small blue jewelry case from the bottom of the lockbox. The case clicked when the lid fully opened, revealing a medal. A ribbon—red, white, and blue vertical stripes—attached to the top of a golden-hued five-pointed star. Embedded at the center of that star was the silver star that gave the honor its name. Carter didn't remember the ceremony where he received the medal or the last names of the soldiers he dragged to safety while under fire; however, he vividly recalled the little boy's broken body at the bomb site in Fallujah.

He closed the jewelry case and slipped it into the pocket of his hoodie.

The last item Carter examined was another photo. This one, unframed and older, was tattered around the edges. Linda, his mom, sat on a sofa, flanked by Becca and him. His sister and mother resembled a painting he'd seen once portraying a peasant woman and her child. Beautiful in the way all good things are beautiful.

Then he remembered. Mr. Andy had snapped the picture.

Carter studied his house. Somehow, he had never felt at home here, anyway. Without looking back, he exited through the backdoor and cut across several yards to bypass Swan Avenue and his neighbors. He concealed his face with the hoodie and turned down the street toward the only safe place he had left.

***

"What the hell, man?" Chester said, touching Carter's shoulder and pulling him close. "They after you like you're a mouse in a cathouse."

"A cathouse?" Carter grinned as he examined Chester's appearance. His friend had peeled off the winter coat and seemed better than before, more vibrant and less unstable.

Chester grinned, shook his head, and said," You're all over the television news, buddy."

"I didn't kill anyone, Chester."

"That's obvious, my man. Anyone who knows you will vouch for that," he said. "The problem is, it don't matter how innocent you are when you're a convenient answer to the police's problem."

Chester guided Carter through the shelter doors and across the dining area toward the kitchen. On the way, Carter heard the television in the recreation room.

"...Sykes is a person of interest in the case. He is the principal at West Louisville Elementary School. The Louisville Police Department refused to comment on whether Sykes is a suspect in other murders and abductions plaguing Louisville and Southern Indiana. The school district declined to comment other than to say Mr. Sykes wasn't present for the last day of school yesterday."

Carter scratched his nose to conceal his face and walked with his back bowed to hide his usual gait. "Not present," he said. "It figures."

David's door was open. The social worker sat behind a desk, his left elbow ground into the desktop and his cheek resting on his palm. It propped up his heavy head, which Carter thought was filled with worry.

When Chester and Carter entered, it took a moment before David glanced at them and recognized his friend beneath the hoodie.

"Carter," David said, rising as if ejected from a cockpit. "Get in here." David hurried around the desk and glanced up and down the small hallway before shutting the office door.

Carter stood still as if awaiting the social worker's judgment.

"You're in a mess, Carter," David said. "If you did this, get out of here and turn yourself..."

"If he did this?" Chester said, his voice curt. "This man wouldn't hurt a biscuit with a butter knife, David."

"That's not how the world works, Chester," David said.

"He's right, Chester," Carter said, staring out the window near David's desk. He allowed the words to settle like the dust floating in the blades of sunlight. Carter shifted his gaze to David. The corkboard hanging on the wall blurred in the background. Carter recognized the framed photograph on the corner of David's desk. David held his beautiful dark-haired wife in his arms as the Manila city lights sparkled behind them. He towered over her, their broad smiles telling a story of happiness.

"What do you mean?" Chester said. "Did you have something to do with that dead girl?"

"Not directly," Carter said, his voice low. He pictured Kelsey the night at the Dirty Mint—her smile and the soft slope of her back. "Someone murdered her and planted her in my trunk to frame me as the Good Girl Killer."

David dropped back into his chair.

Carter spoke without emotion. "The first time I saw the Good Girl Killer, he wore a work shirt—the cartoon character near his pocket resembled a gray-haired Mario from the video game, but he carried a wrench. Nally's Auto Repair, I think. His girlfriend is Stephanie, a stripper at Banger's Club."

David's nose wrinkled. "I know he didn't introduce himself as a serial killer. How do you know it's him, Carter?"

"And how'd you meet her?" Chester added.

Questions. Perhaps the only things Carter dodged as much as touches were questions. Personal questions accelerated his heart. His mind shifted into high gear, swerving around the truth like a racecar on a crowded track. However, he had told the truth only ninety minutes earlier, which postponed his inevitable arrest.

The whole truth and nothing but the truth? The entire truth can be a vicious angel with razor-blade wings.

"I met her when I went to the strip club," he said. "I ended up seeing her with Honeyboy, I mean Kevin, the killer, and I met their friend, Kelsey." Carter swallowed hard. "I've visited the strip club many times, and I've even been to the sex club in the basement."

"Sex club?" David's brow wrinkled. "I've heard about the Dirty Mint. It's a sad place for sad people, I figure. You're risking so much going to such a place, Carter."

Carter didn't speak, but David read his body language.

"I've always sensed you had problems, my friend," David said. He ran his fingers through his wiry brown hair. "Plenty of times I wanted to talk to you, but you're so private, it's tough to have that conversation. I wish I had realized you were in so much pain that you'd take such risks."

"I know about the sex club, but..." Chester said. He wiped his face with his long, dark fingers. "Let's say I didn't expect that one. Not sure who you are, buddy."

Carter reached out and touched Chester's shoulder. The man's shirt felt soft and clean, although it hung from his lanky frame.

"You know me, Chester," Carter said. "Enough to tell me Chester's not your name but not enough to reveal the real one, right?"

"Where the heck have I been all this time," David said, staring at Chester. Shaking his head, he leaned back in his office chair. "I'm not a religious man, but these might be the end times my mom keeps warning me about."

"I could've left town, David," Carter said. "Ask yourself why I'm here instead."

David tapped the desk's brown surface. His gray eyes studied Carter.

Chester dragged a metal folding chair to the desk. His joints creaked, followed by a deep exhale as he sat down and stared at the two men.

"At the club, I overheard Kevin and Stephanie talking about a teenage girl he's holding at their apartment." It's odd when you hide your addiction for so long. Lies become more natural than the truth.

"Did you try..." David said.

"I tried the police," Carter said. "They didn't believe me and somehow concluded I might be their prime suspect."

"That doesn't explain the dead gal in your trunk, Carter," Chester said.

"When Kevin and Stephanie abducted me, Kelsey slipped in and cut me loose," Carter said. Shame and guilt turned his face crimson. "Kevin must have abducted her, murdered her, and planted her body in my car. Then he called the police." Carter paused, considering his following words. *Do I tell them Kevin isn't aware I know he's the Good Girl Killer? Do I even try to explain it?*

David brought his fingertips together like a chess master contemplating his next move. "So, this guy knows you've figured out he's the killer, so he's trying to pin the crime on you."

Chester nodded his head as though the story made perfect sense.

Carter peered at his worn running shoes and remained quiet. The convoluted tale sounded impossible even to him, and he had lived it. Chester wanted to believe, so he did. *We always find what we want to see in people.*

After the silence, David placed his palms on the desk and spread his fingers. His lips formed a thin line across his brown face. "Instead of fleeing, you came here, Carter. You're trying to set this right in some awkward way, but I sense you're leaving out important details. I hope it's for a good reason."

"Help me free the abducted girl," Carter said. "I need you both to believe me. We can save her."

Chester scooted the folding chair closer to the desk. "I'm in," he said without hesitation.

David stared at Carter. His gaze reminded Carter of the first time he met Colonel Scott. The Colonel's stare had penetrated his skin as if searching for value or a spark of hope. Somehow, the moral, hard-nosed Colonel found something valuable in him. Carter, especially during moments like this, often pondered what it was. Now, he needed David to see that same goodness.

Chester and David were most apt to believe him of all the people Carter knew. Perhaps he should have told them about Traps as he had Mona. But then they'd need proof. He'd venture into the hollowed-out place people with trauma create to house their pain—not to help, but to suffer with them—and then use the experience for his gain, just as he did with Mona. Chester's Trap was leaving his daughter behind in Oakland. David, often skeptical, would debunk any revelation Carter offered as evidence.

David blinked and exhaled as if resigned to what he had to do. Carter watched his friend's face soften as he interlocked his fingers and dropped his elbows onto the desk. "What is it you need from us, Carter?"

"First, I need to borrow your phone," Carter said. "Then, I'll share a plan."

CHAPTER 36

"Evil," Kevin said. "Pure evil, that's what he is."

Stephanie sat beside him on the gray sofa, her body leaning forward. Her hands covered her entire face except for her right eye, peeking between her fingers. Her shoulders rose and fell as if she was trying to fly without wings.

Kevin had just arrived home after being out all night. He smelled like sweat and cigarettes, but he'd cleaned his hands. Stephanie had made it home from the club at 3:30 a.m., so she'd slept until the afternoon. He'd woken her in a panic and brought her into the living room. He pointed the remote at the television and increased the volume.

The 11:30 a.m. news anchor spoke into the screen. "Ms. Wayfair, born in Elizabethtown, Kentucky, worked at Banger's Gentleman Club in Louisville as a hostess and a dancer. Witnesses at the club reported seeing Sykes, the principal of West Louisville Elementary School, and the victim arguing the day before police discovered her body in his car on Swan Avenue near downtown Louisville. Wayfair was twenty-seven years old."

Stephanie moaned.

Kevin clicked the remote, and the screen turned black. "Kelsey was such a fine person," he said. "I wish you'd have let me kill that dude when we had the chance."

Stephanie moaned again, prompting Kevin to embrace her. He pulled her face to his neck and shoulder. "Shush," he said, patting her back like a baby's. "You didn't know any better, Steph. I mean, you don't know killers like Sykes."

Her body trembled, and a guttural sob rose from her thin throat. Her legs bounced as if she might levitate as she spoke, but Kevin anchored her to his side. "Kelsey was my best friend, Kevin."

Kevin's tone changed as if her words pained him. "I'm your best friend, Stephanie. That's why you should listen whenever I tell you something. If you had..." He left the accusation hanging there like the clearest pane of glass. Her body became rigid, and she leaned deeper into his arms and chest. Kevin smiled as he patted her back.

"I'm gonna miss her so much," Steph said. She sniffed and fought to gain control. Her body shuddered.

"I'll miss her, too, Babygirl," he said. He mimicked her sniffling and crying, but his smile hung over her shoulder like some perverse photo of a grinning guard at a concentration camp. "I'm sure you feel terrible. I try to protect you from such feelings, but when you don't listen, then, well, we lose our friend. Maybe I should've forced you to listen. Then, I could have saved her."

An even louder moan than before escaped her lips.

"You've got me to set things right. I'll make Sykes pay like all those privileged bitches, so our Kelsey gets her payback."

"I don't know," she said. "You still got the black girl, don't you?" She tried to raise to speak more, but Kevin smashed her face against him. She tried to talk, but her muffled words became sobs again.

"I know you don't know, my love," he said, so close to her ear that his damp, darting tongue caressed her lobe. "If so, our special friend wouldn't be dead, would she?"

"You've released the girl?"

"Don't worry about her, Steph," he said, loosening his grip. "I'm not through with her yet. I'll get Sykes, too. The idiots around here can't beat me."

She pulled away, creating a chasm between them. Sensing it, Kevin wiped away the smile and donned the disguise Stephanie always failed to recognize as a costume. He retrieved a small plastic bag from his shirt pocket, waving it to show Stephanie. She grasped the transparent baggie, but Kevin didn't initially release it. He held it like a dog treat for several heartbeats, then relented.

Stephanie poured three white pills into her palm before tossing them into her mouth. He rubbed her back and neck with his oil-stained hand, drawing soft circles across her skin. Within minutes, Stephanie's body became putty. He lowered her onto her back, her head resting against a red sofa pillow.

"Sleep, Babydoll," he said, his voice filled with heartless, artificial compassion. He stood and glanced out the apartment window. Cars sped up and down Preston Street. May was ready to give June its glory. He had much to do before sunrise. Spring and summer always provided a rich hunting ground.

Kevin shuffled to the apartment door, retrieving the Lincoln keys from a small table.

"Don't leave again," Stephanie said, her voice thick like discarded motor oil.

"I've got to run by the shop to make a delivery," he said. "Rest, Baby."

He exited. When he arrived at his car, he knocked on the trunk lid three times and smiled when a tiny, muffled voice responded.

***

"Rest, Baby," Kevin said, "you've proven yourself special. I'm holding on to you longer than my other girlfriends, and I have a present for you."

Zara didn't react. She hadn't spoken to him since he drugged her and moved her to this new, smaller room where pungent gas fumes and the sweet, fruity smell of antifreeze sickened her. She stared ahead, her gaze fixed on a torn segment of beige and blue wallpaper across the room. The torn segment resembled South Carolina, which brought memories of playing on the beach at Hilton Head with her older sister, Amira.

Despite their essential jobs and hectic schedules, their parents never missed an opportunity to take them on vacations. They'd traveled to California, the Carolinas, Canada, Cozumel, and plenty of other places—family-only. She hated the end of the week because it meant the vacation would be over soon, and her dad and mom would return to their long work hours.

She'd also been with the pony-tailed man for a week or more. Although these days had not been a vacation, she dreaded the end. Despite his promises to release her, Zara knew he planned to kill her.

"Please, let me go," she had pleaded. "I won't tell anyone. I'll say I ran off with my boyfriend. Just don't hurt me anymore."

But Kevin—yes, he had told her his name, yet another sign she would never see her folks again—soaked up her tears like a sponge, puffing up more with each pathetic plea.

Now, Kevin caressed her face with the back of his fingers. She had become accustomed to how his hands smelled—motor oil and cigarettes, so she no longer responded to his touch.

The cheap mattress resumed its shape when he stood and exited the room.

Zara yanked the brown, plastic-coated extension cords tethering her to the headboard. It had become her habit to test the bonds each time he departed, as though that millisecond of hope nourished her spirit. However, it only reminded her how raw and scabbed her wrists had become. The bleeding ring of sores resembled the tattoos encircling Amira's wrists.

Kevin returned a few minutes later. He opened the door and said, "Are you ready for your surprise?"

Zara feared any surprise or present he might have for her. The light from the open door divided the small room. She searched the corners to find clues about where he held her but only saw a rusted vending machine filled with candy and chips and an ancient signed poster nailed to the wallpaper. It read, "Dr. Dunkenstein, Darrell Griffith." The picture showed a UofL basketball star on the 1980 Championship squad, Griffith, soaring over a helpless player. Griffith's crotch rose above the rival's head as he dunked the ball.

"Zara," he said. "I asked if you're ready." His voice blended a sing-song cadence and an explicit threat.

Zara grunted and nodded at the same time.

"Ta daaaaah," he said as he opened the door. He dragged, then pushed a young woman into the room as if she were a reluctant volunteer at a magic show. She wore a red blindfold, and her hands were zip-tied behind her back. Her blonde hair had escaped the barrettes, holding it tight against her scalp. The strands flopped onto her pale face like broken springs. The first four buttons of her white

Oxford shirt were missing, exposing the white bra underneath. Zara saw the bruises and red patches around her thin neck and cheeks. The woman's dark pants and black shoes were too large for her tiny body, and an untucked section of her blouse formed a triangle on her hip.

"This is new for me, Zara," Kevin said. "I usually...uh... release one girlfriend before I take another one. That's why you're special."

The blonde woman cried as he forced her toward the bed. Her blindfold slipped, enabling Zara to make eye contact with her. Both young women shouted against their gags, attempting to communicate with the other. The noises reminded Zara when her family visited the San Diego Zoo. One bear roared, and the other followed with growls and bellows as if they wanted to communicate but couldn't form words. Back and forth, Zara and the new girl cried out to each other with guttural sounds.

"Whoa, little ladies," Kevin said. "You'll have time to gossip about me when I leave. This place is my man cave. I'll let you get to know each other 'cause nobody can hear you down here in the Pit."

He laughed as he muscled the woman onto the bed. Part of Zara wanted to burrow into the mattress and cover her face so she couldn't see; however, another part urged her to shield the woman from harm. She had always been the compliant one. Amira rebelled and risked everything, while Zara tried to be helpful and made their parents laugh. That attitude didn't always work well. That's why she had responded when Kevin approached her outside Macy's department store. He asked her advice about the outfits he'd purchased for his disabled wife. His pathetic smile had triggered her compassion and drew her close. Locked inside the trunk of his humongous car, Zara vowed she'd never help anyone again.

But being tied like an animal can lead to self-reflection, she guessed. Was she ever really kind if a person could take it away? *What pain and indignity can he dish out that he hasn't already served?*

Zara growled, then threw her dark leg over the woman's body to protect her from Kevin.

Kevin gripped Zara's left thigh just above the knee. His dirty fingers sank into her flesh, pressing the muscle against the bone. Intense pain spiraled up her thigh like a staircase crumbling from the bottom to the top. Nonetheless, she bit down on the gag and refused to move.

The blonde woman trembled when Kevin touched her face, his hand drifting to her gagged mouth. He yanked the gag below the woman's chin, allowing it to become a cloth necklace, before adjusting the blindfold until it was tight around her eyes. The woman coughed several times and cried, "Why are you doing this?"

Zara growled when she heard the woman's voice.

"See," Kevin said, his tone as phony as his compassionate face, "y'all act like I'm hurting you when I'm just letting the new girl ask questions about the fine accommodations here in the Pit. Oh well."

"Don't hurt us," the blonde woman said. "I'll do whatever you want."

Kevin cackled. "Really? You're going to do me a favor?" He hovered above her, grabbed an errant strand of hair, and hoisted her head from the pillow. He grabbed her throat with his other hand, then lowered his head until their noses touched. "I tell you what," he said, his tongue slipping out to graze her lips.

Zara sucked air through her nose. Tears obscured her vision as if she watched Kevin through a prism.

Kevin said, "I have some business to attend, so I'll let you girls get cozy. You're like a couple of monkeys—one can see evil, and the other can say evil." He smirked as he pushed the woman's head onto the dirty pillow.

Zara remained gagged but saw the new girl's blindfold. She watched as Kevin exited the room but held her breath until she heard the door lock turn. She attempted to ask the girl's name, but only garbled grunts emerged.

Yet, somehow, the woman understood her.

"My name's Lenora," she said.

CHAPTER 37

"West Louisville Elementary." Vickie's voice sounded tired.

"It's me, Vickie," Carter said. "I had to ditch my cell. If someone's close, call me Mr. David."

"Hello, Mr. David," she said. "Thank you for returning my call."

"You'd be a knockout voice actor," Carter said. "Maybe a new character on the Simpsons."

"We're all worried, too, Mr. David," she said, her tone telling him to cut the jokes. Yes, I called to report a parent who needs assistance. She phoned several times but only left her first name and phone number."

"Are the police in the building?"

"Not here. But we're lucky to have Dr. Wallace from the Superintendent's office helping to finish our end-of-the-year procedures."

"I bet she's elated."

"The caller said she needed to contact you and maybe get a social services visit," Vickie said. "It sounded urgent. She said you would know her situation, so I didn't ask her much."

"Okay," Carter said. "I didn't do anything they're saying, Vick."

"I'm praying for our principal and hoping the police can uncover the truth. I'm telling everyone he wouldn't do something so evil. At least in my opinion."

Carter smiled.

"Hope," she said. "The woman's name is Hope. She said you had her number, but here it is." She read the phone number to Carter.

"Thank you, Vickie." His voice became a whisper. "I'm going to ask you to do something, but you're the only person I can trust to follow my instructions."

"I will do whatever God allows—you know I will."

"You'll receive a package at home soon. It will have some essential documents and explicit instructions that'll seem odd. Please do this for me when you can. You may need to use the signature stamp and have things notarized."

"David, you know our bookkeeper, Nan, don't you? She'll help, I'm sure."

"Yes," Carter replied, "I would never ask you to do anything illegal."

"I've always respected and trusted Mr. Sykes," she said. "I'm praying this works out the way it should."

Carter wanted to explain, but Dr. Wallace's voice interrupted from the background.

"Who's that, Vickie?" Wallace said.

Vickie's voice didn't change, but he sensed she wished to say more. "That's very kind, David. I'll let Dr. Wallace know."

Carter disconnected the call. He stared at David's phone and wondered if he'd ever speak to Vickie again.

CHAPTER 38

"Don't kill her," Hope said the moment he identified himself. "It's my fault. She didn't want to do it."

"What're you talking about?" Carter said.

"I'll do whatever you say, just don't..." Her voice became a tearful blubbering, and her breath came in rapid gulps.

Carter listened and processed her words. When she paused to breathe, he responded.

"Has something happened to Lenora?"

"Don't play with me, Carter," she said. Her anguish bled into outrage. "You're killing women, and my Lenora is gone. It doesn't take Einstein to put it together, especially since she told me you came by the house mad as hell."

"I haven't killed anybody, Hope," Carter said. "Stop for a minute. Where's Lenora?"

"I'm not stupid, Carter," she said. "You took her from the Denny's parking lot sometime yesterday. Just tell me if you've already murdered her. I have to know." She sobbed even louder than before, causing Carter to pull David's cell phone from his ear. As he waited for her to gain composure, he saw Chester and David inside the office. Chester gestured like a tomahawk chop as if attempting to persuade the sour-faced David the Earth was flat.

When Hope paused again in an attempt to compose herself, Carter spoke again. "I didn't do anything to Lenora. Tell me what you know so I can try to help her."

"She's gone," Hope said. Carter expected spit to drench him through the phone. "You're the only person with a reason to take her. She didn't come home from work this morning."

Carter's brain spun like a mower blade. *The bastard. Kevin's plan didn't stop with planting Kelsey in Carter's trunk. He must have followed me and saw my argument with Lenora at the duplex.*

"She's a good person, Carter," Hope said. "She doesn't deserve to die like the other girl. How could you kill Lenora, Carter? All because we asked for money? I'm just trying to stay in school and get on with my life." Her indignant tone suggested she was a victim of his greed and lust.

Carter didn't bother to refute her contention. Instead, he called himself a fool for misjudging Honeyboy as that little kid rocking back and forth in unison with his dead father's swinging feet, singing that silly children's song. Carter ran his hand through his hair and clenched his fist before striking himself in the chest.

"Do you think you can dislodge the guilt and shame from your heart, Big Brother," Kitchen Becca said as she grasped his arm to prevent another strike. Burgundy stains covered her yellow dress, and she stood so close to him in the shelter hallway that Carter smelled her blood's sweet, metallic odor. "Only one thing will remedy the hurt, I guess, Cartie. Save someone like you should have saved me. That's how your little boy brain thinks, right? You can't just walk away because of what happened to me. Pathetic."

Carter's body shook. His neck muscles tightened like overwrought cables on an Ohio River barge. He struck his chest again. Becca's words wound the overburdened cables into knots.

"If Lenora's still alive," he said, "I know who has her. I'll find her."

Hope remained silent for several beats before taking a deep and heavy breath and weeping again. Carter pictured Hope in the nightshirt at the duplex the night they were together and recalled Lenora's awkward behavior. Her handshake and silence weren't about him—Lenora regretted what she and Hope had planned.

"I know you've already killed her," Hope said as if her words were the gavel strike ending the trial. "They better give you the death penalty when they catch you, man. I'll reserve a front-row seat to watch them strap you to the gurney."

CHAPTER 39

Their legs resembled a Yin-Yang symbol. Kevin had rolled Zara and Lenora over onto their sides, back-to-back, and, with some force, he'd bent their knees so their bare feet touched, sole-to-sole. Once they were immobile, he'd given both an injection. The same sharp needle jabbed into their butt cheeks.

Lenora still wore the blindfold but didn't have a gag; Zara, the cloth stuffed deep into her mouth, remained able to see. Brown extension cords bound their wrists and ankles and secured them to the bed's headboard and footboard, making it impossible for either to change positions.

The drug faded some, leaving Lenora's mouth dry and raw. She managed a few words. "Where are we?"

Zara, who was less affected by the drug, heard her but could only grunt a response. The gag tasted like a wet sock against her tongue.

Lenora rolled her head toward Zara but not far enough to see her. Frustration and fear caused her to drop her head back onto the mattress. "It's okay."

She felt Zara wiggling beside her and heard the girl's indistinguishable sounds.

Lenora said, "I can smell burnt oil and gasoline. It's sickening. Do you think we're in a shed or a gas station?"

Zara produced garbled words again as though wishing to answer Lenora's question. The first word sounded like "yes," although Lenora could not be sure. After a pause, Zara made two noises while shaking her head back and forth against the mattress. The words sounded like "no-no."

"Okay," Lenora said. "I get it. One sound is yes, and two sounds mean no." She waited for a response, and Zara did not disappoint her.

The younger woman grunted a single time.

"Did he hurt you?"

Zara grunted once.

"I'm sorry," Lenora said. She held back tears as she curled her toes and rocked her back against Zara's. She hoped to pass support and sympathy to her but only tightened the cords on her ankles. "Do you believe he'll kill us?"

Grunt. It was Zara's turn to provide comfort. Lenora trembled before Zara's left butt cheek flexed against Lenora's backside.

Lenora responded by leaning her back toward Zara. They remained silent for a minute.

"Is anyone with him?" Lenora whispered. "A man with black hair. Older?"

Grunt-grunt.

Lenora wondered if Carter had paid this man to kidnap her so Hope would drop the scam. However, this girl's presence made it unlikely. When threatened, people often do desperate things. *Even those you like or love*, she thought. But that didn't explain the young woman tethered to the bed beside her.

Then fear surged through her as if she had fallen through the ice on a frozen lake. *What do they call the guy?* "The Good Girl Killer," she whispered.

Grunt.

CHAPTER 40

C hester and David stared as though Carter had asked them to skin him alive.

"That's your plan?" David said, his eyes so vast Carter feared they might shoot from his face like rockets. "Chester goes to the Post Office, and I pick you up after you rescue the girl from the killer's place? What comes after? Do you really think the serial killer will just let you do this?"

Carter displayed his pale palms. "What other options do I have?" he said. "Kevin has played me like a yo-yo. He killed Kelsey and is holding the other girls, waiting to set me..."

"Hang on," David said. "What do you mean, girls?" His back stiffened. When he stretched forward, his office chair squeaked against the silence.

Carter shook his head. He hadn't mentioned Lenora on the outside chance Hope was wrong, although that wasn't a bet he'd take. He'd outlined his plan and David and Chester's roles, but, in his haste, he'd failed to share the blackmail scheme and his confrontation with Lenora.

"I'm not hiding anything," Carter said. "However, it's possible the Good Girl Killer has taken another woman—one I know—to implicate me."

"Why not tell the police and let them handle this, Carter?" David stood from his desk chair and paced the office, taking four steps forward and back like a pendulum.

June offered sun and a warm breeze. Many shelter families with children had gone to the Central Park playground. Only several older men remained at the facility, lounging in the Rec room watching Pawn Stars or playing chess or Rook.

Carter and Chester sat in the metal folding chairs before David's desk. Chester's lanky frame angled toward Carter.

"I can't, David," Carter said. "I tried, but even the officer I trust most didn't believe me. She thought I might be the killer. Besides, time is running out. I've wasted too much time trying to pass the buck. If this guy kills again, it's my fault. I have to make up for...I just have to save them, even if it's the last thing I ever do." Carter pictured Mona when she released him. A civil war between her loyalties and instinct erupted. Carter wasn't sure if she would arrest him or shoot him; however, when she removed the cuffs, hope washed over him. Saving Lenora and Zara Turner became his responsibility and pathway toward redemption, no matter the cost.

Chester leaned forward in his chair. "The police won't understand, David. They'll drag him in, and when he helps them find the girls, they'll use it as evidence that he's the one who took them, especially if they're already dead. You remember that Jewel guy in Atlanta? They thought he was the bomber at the Olympics because he offered information."

David ran his long fingers through his dark hair, resting his hand on his head.

Carter prepared to agree with Chester but refrained when David spoke.

"I have to say this, Carter," David said as he gestured toward Chester. "I get Chester's point. I want to believe you like he does, but it's hard when you're holding back. It's tough when you're seeking some mysterious redemption. I've always known you were tight, but it still angers me that you've had this problem since last Thursday and didn't ask me for help."

Carter nodded when David paused to collect his thoughts. Carter fought the urge to apologize. Of course, his friend was correct. Living every moment feeding an addiction and wallowing in regret had sealed him tighter than the Berger family when they shipped him back to Foster Care.

David continued, "You don't have to be invincible, Carter. People know you're not Iron Man anyway. You only have to be..." David searched for the right word.

"Vulnerable," Carter said. Becca swirled inside his head like a therapist made of vapor.

"Vulnerable," she said.

"Brother," Chester said, shaking his head to disagree. You don't need to show weakness." He removed something from his deep pocket. You gotta show this."

Chester placed a 9 mm handgun on the desk.

CHAPTER 41

Hope had checked the door and window locks four times. She'd scoured the duplex for anything resembling a weapon before settling on a meat cleaver from a kitchen drawer. Now, she paced the floor, the dull kitchen tool in one hand and a cigarette in the other. The smoke followed behind her like the exhaust from a jet plane.

The empty duplex scared Hope. Without Lenora, the rooms were darker and colder, the fading sunlight piercing the windows like needles and thread. She marched into the kitchen and doused the cigarette in the sink. When she tossed the butt into the white trash can, she wondered if Carter Sykes had treated Lenora with similar disregard.

What have I done? She had considered Sykes an easy mark—she recognized sex addicts—but out of all the customers entering the coffee shop, he was the last she expected to be a serial killer. In truth, she had doubts even now.

Hope rolled her shoulders. "He killed Lenora, I'm sure of it," she said, watching thick water drops fall from the faucet and splash against the metal basin.

***

Mona's desk phone buzzed. The sound startled her. Her nerves rattled like a marble in a soda can. She feared her interaction with Carter might come to light, which, in effect, would end her career. Besides, her day had started long before sunrise, and she'd worked nonstop since Anderson called her. After releasing Carter, she'd roamed downtown to mitigate the damage done by looters posing as protestors. She hoped to complete her reports and get home.

"Officer Ridge," she said into the receiver.

"Mona, this is Grant at the front desk. You've got a walk-in."

"Unless he's carrying a flower bouquet or an Impellizzeri's pizza, I'm not interested."

"She says she needs to talk to you. Claims you know her."

Mona inhaled and paused before asking, "What's her name?"

"She won't tell me but says you have a mutual friend."

"Hell," Mona said, "send her to the west hallway by the vending machine. I'll go now."

When Mona turned the corner, she recognized Hope Leto. The woman wasn't wearing her barista apron or the sexy night shirt she wore when greeting Carter at the duplex door, but she was easy to identify. Her impossible black hair, cropped short, drooped onto her scalp like a field of dead weeds after a wind storm. She wore a classic black Radiohead tee shirt—circles and lines creating a bear with large triangular teeth.

Perhaps five years younger than Mona, Hope's rough night was evident on her face—the puffy eyes, as many lines as the logo on her shirt, and a caffeine-induced, wide-eyed urgency.

"Hello, Hope." Mona extended her hand. When Hope reciprocated, her hand was weak and clammy. "What can I do for you?"

"You can kill Carter Sykes," Hope said.

"I'm sorry, Hope," Mona said. "You'll have to get in line."

"What?" Hope said. Then, a slight smile crossed her lips. "Oh, I see."

"Yes," Mona continued. We're searching for him right now, but I'm sure you've seen it on the news."

Someone entered the hallway near the vending machine. Mona nodded at the officer and motioned for Hope to follow her into an empty waiting area.

When they were seated, the officer continued. "You know our friend isn't guilty of anything until he's convicted, right?"

Hope trembled. "He killed my..." She stopped. Then, she collected herself. "He killed my friend."

"Kelsey Wayfair?"

"No, it's my friend, Lenora Pace," Hope replied. Her voice faltered like a broken piano's note, off-key and shrill.

Mona slid a small notebook from her belt and a pen from her uniform pocket. "What leads you to believe this happened?" she asked, lifting the pen as if to take Hope's statement.

Hope's eyes stared down at Mona's hand. The officer saw her reluctance and the nervous twitch of her lip.

Mona waited, poised to write. Hope, unable to decide, continued to gaze down at the pen and paper.

Mona said, "I can't help Lenora if you hold back."

Hope lifted her gaze but didn't speak.

"How about this?" Mona said. "Let's talk off the record if you're afraid of Mr. Sykes. I want to know, more than anyone, whether he is the Good Girl Killer. Why would he choose your friend, Lenora, considering you had a relationship with him?"

Hope's face became a tumultuous sky filled with storm clouds. Tears flooded her cheeks, and her hands trembled. "I made a terrible mistake," she said. "It's my fault."

"Tell me what happened," Mona coaxed, her voice soft yet direct. "How do you know she's dead? Why would Carter kill her?"

"Lenora works at Denny's down by UofL," Hope said, trying to control the storm. "It's open twenty-four hours, and it was her turn to work the third shift on Thursday. The manager told me Lenora clocked out at 4:15 in the morning. Lenora always comes straight home, so she's home by 4:30, but she..." Hope's voice trailed off again.

Mona placed her hand on Hope's arm. "It's okay. Take a breath," she said. "So, she's only been missing for twelve hours. What makes you think..."

"Carter had that dead girl in his car, and Lenora told me he'd come by our house angry at us."

"Why would he be angry at you?"

Hope shut down again, unwilling to speak.

"Earlier, you said it was all your fault," Mona said. "I know he dropped by to see you on Saturday—and it didn't look like anger brought him to your door. It was more like pleasure."

The Hope's eyes grew wide, and she shuddered. The barista lifted her hands to her temple as if considering what to do.

"Hope, you must tell me everything. Lenora may be alive. Time matters."

Hope sniffled and glared at the floor as if contemplating a fork in the road.

"Lenora didn't want to go through with it after she met Carter," Hope said, her path chosen. "He'd been so sweet and kind, especially to Lenora. It was as if he wanted to protect her even though it was a wild night."

"I get it," Mona said. "He had a relationship with both of you. Wow."

Hope sniffled again. "Don't judge us. Lenora and I have been together for two years. We're secure enough to bring in a third person if they are sexy and funny."

"No judgment here," Mona said. *Carter Sykes. Sexy? Funny?* "So, what went wrong?"

"Carter gave me the idea. He said he'd give up anything, except coffee, to get that video off of YouTube, Instagram, and X. You know, the one where he pushes that protestor."

Mona nodded. She suspected the story's ending.

"I needed money for school and rent."

"You blackmailed him?"

"Lenora's only eighteen years old," Hope said. "I set up my phone to record the two of them going at it, and then all three of us."

Mona cleared her throat. She pictured Carter's uneasy posture at Hope's front door, his shoulders low and his back bowed as if trying to hide his presence from the world.

"Despite Lenora begging me, I printed a picture and sent him a letter demanding money, or we'd send the video to the news stations and the school district."

"I might kill you myself," Mona said. She patted Hope's leg again.

"I thought he'd pay, and that'd be it," she said. "Stupid, I know, but I didn't expect him to kill Lenora. I still can't picture Carter Sykes as a serial killer." Hope's lower lip protruded, and the tears commenced again.

"Carter Sykes is a conundrum, a player, a liar, and a fool," Mona said. "But I assure you of one thing: Carter isn't. That's Lenora's killer."

Hope's crying became a whimper. "How can you be so sure?"

"I had my eyes on him from 4:20 a.m. and remained well after Lenora would have arrived home. He couldn't have abducted her then."

"God!" Hope said.

Mona touched her arm. "Aren't you glad you didn't spread that video across the internet?"

Hope covered her face and mumbled into her palms.

Mona closed her eyes and lifted her fingers from Hope's arm. She'd translated the mumbles. Hope had said, "I've already posted it everywhere."

CHAPTER 42

When his pixilated rear-end flashed across the Louisville Tribune's website, and the WDRB-TV six o'clock lead story was "breaking news" about a controversial video involving the prime suspect in a Louisville murder, Carter held his breath. His secret life just took a Lewis and Clark-sized hike out of town. His picture, the video, and even interviews with people popped up like weeds poking through the West End sidewalks around his school.

David stood beside him in the Shelter's Recreation Room, eyeing his cell phone and the television.

The NewLou Observer, an independent paper, claimed anyone who attacked peaceful protesters like "Psycho Sykes" pretty much confessed to being a white supremacist and a murderer, so discovering he is also a pervert wasn't a surprise. Only one television station broke the news that the "minor" in the video had been missing since last seen leaving her job as a waitress at 4:30 a.m. Another station interviewed a parent from West Louisville Elementary who claimed she'd never felt comfortable around Mr. Sykes because he gave off "bad vibes." She pushed back her bleached blonde hair as she said it, revealing a crude tattoo of a cannabis plant on her pale white neck.

Next, the reporter introduced Vickie Burns, the Executive Assistant who worked with Principal Sykes before his suspension. Carter watched Vickie as she responded to the reporter's question.

"Mr. Sykes did great work at West Louisville Elementary," she said. Not a single strand of hair was out of place, and her soft voice added clarity and power to her words. "The teachers, staff, and especially the students respect him."

However, when the camera framed the young reporter again, she spoke with the gleeful tone of a movie star parading along a red carpet. "The Louisville Police Department has increased its efforts to find Mr. Sykes in connection to Kelsey Wayfair's murder. They ask anyone with information regarding Sykes to call the Crimestoppers hotline."

David stared at Carter. "My friend," he said, "this is escalating. I'm worried you'll get hurt if you don't turn yourself in."

"I'm more concerned what will happen if I do, David," Carter said. "This is a setup. If they catch me and Kevin stops killing, we can forget about justice for his victims. Besides, the Turner girl and Lenora may still be alive."

"Carter, please tell me the girl isn't a minor."

Carter saw the angst in his friend's face. It'd be difficult for him if he were in David's shoes. Hope didn't act like Lenora was under eighteen, that was for sure, nor did Lenora reveal her age. They had been a couple for a while. Still, he kicked himself for not assessing when Lenora's trauma occurred. The slight possibility that Lenora was underage made his brain ache.

"I pray she isn't, David," he said. "She seemed to be in her twenties to me, but I don't know for sure. It's another ton of embarrassment heaped onto the massive pile I've been shoveling."

"We'll need a shovel, all right." Chester's voice penetrated the Rec Room as he entered through the doorway. "The cops are buzzing around like hornets out there. We'll need a tunnel to get you out of here, buddy."

CHAPTER 43

David sat in his office chair, his elbows against the desktop and his hands folded as if praying. He didn't pray, but he did need guidance.

Carter and Chester monitored the police presence in the shelter attic. The continuing protests, riots, and the search for Carter left Louisville teetering on the edge.

David had marched with the protesters right after the shooting. However, his massive caseload and the Shelter responsibilities outweighed his time for social causes. Besides, urban crime, poverty, and competing identities led him to focus on what he could control, not the ideological feuds gripping Derby City.

At this moment, a different feud raged inside him. He had known Carter Sykes for years and considered him one of his best friends despite Carter's aversion to socializing.

He'd marveled at the man's uncanny ability to read people's pain. Over the years, they'd become quite a team, helping families like Ms. Gibson and Shandi survive on the city's fringes. He'd witnessed Carter's kindness but bumped against the man's quirky walls and fences. Carter always held back. In all their collaborations, David sensed his friend knew more than he would say, refusing to reveal trivial things, like how he knew what the family needed even when the evidence was unclear.

But this?

David's loyalties were at war.

David unclasped his hands, wiped his face, and picked up a yellow pencil. He leaned back and twirled it like a miniature baton. He dropped it and ran his fingers through his coarse, copper-colored hair.

Carter's explanations of the dead body, a serial killer setting him up, and another missing girl he'd argued with before she disappeared had all the makings of a Hitchcock movie—too coincidental to be accurate and too well-told to be impossible.

David knew Carter grew up in foster homes and had served in the military, and he'd gone to UofL to be a teacher and a principal. David's training in counseling helped him recognize his friend's mental health issues, perhaps even addiction. He wasn't surprised that Carter volunteered at the Shelter. Some people turned to crime due to complex experiences. Others become hypervigilant advocates who expect more from themselves rather than less. Both responses pose challenges.

David grew up in the West End and knew how his tumultuous background had shaped his own life, so he understood how Carter's foster home experiences and whatever caused him to be a ward of the state might affect him. David had at least grown up with a mom and dad at home, even though they were poor.

"However," David said as he stared at the pencil, "Carter's not a serial killer, is he?" Should he follow Carter's plan to rescue the girls and capture Kevin? David inhaled, his chest inflating. Then, he released the trapped air in measured bursts.

David rested the pencil on his middle fingers and gripped it with his pinky and index digits. As he pressed, the pencil curved. When it neared the breaking point—cracks forming on the yellow paint—David stopped.

His fingers dialed three numbers on his office phone.

After a moment, he said, "Yes, I have information about that school principal, Carter Sykes."

"Yes, I'm at the Jefferson Shelter, but he's not here. However, Mr. Sykes will be at Preston Highway Apartments in about a half hour, as I understand it."

He listened, then replied. "Because he told me, that's how I know."

The small voice emanated from the phone. David listened.

"I don't know what he'll do when he arrives."

He listened.

"The apartment number? I don't know," David said. He glanced at a piece of paper Carter had provided. "I know he's searching for tenants named Kevin and Stephanie."

David listened, then paused. "No, I don't know their last names, but I do know Mr. Sykes believes the guy is the Good Girl Killer."

He listened.

"Yes," he said, "Mr. Sykes is armed."

CHAPTER 44

Mona's mobile phone vibrated in the holder attached to the dashboard. "Captain Anderson" scrolled across the screen. She clicked the button on the steering wheel near her thumb.

"Yes, sir," she said.

Anderson dispensed with any niceties. "He's been spotted, Ridge. Dispatch received a call saying Sykes was en route to Preston Highway Apartments near Indian Trail and Outer Loop. We're calling an all-units alert to that location very soon."

The captain's rapid breathing and whispers made him sound like an obscene phone caller.

When she didn't respond, he continued. "I'm giving you a head start. You can arrive first and take him down. Say we arrived before the all-call because we started tracking him well before the informant phoned the station."

Mona ignored Anderson and plugged Preston Highway Apartments into her GPS.

"I'm on the way, Captain," she said, her voice monotone. Mona couldn't fathom how this turned out well for her. *If he reveals how I*

released him from custody, my career will crash and burn. She attempted a deep, cleansing breath, but her worried brain wouldn't permit it.
Instead, worry clawed inside her thoughts like a cat against a closed
door.

Should I kill Carter? Am I everything I hate?

She stretched her neck right and left. Survival was important, but
these thoughts weren't hers—they came from an unfamiliar darkness
that resided in her but was not her.

Besides, she knew Carter didn't abduct Lenora Pace because that's
when she held him in custody. Still, one word from Carter's defense
attorney and her career was over. Everything she worked to achieve
would be gone.

"You with me, Officer?" Captain Anderson said.

"Yes."

"Then move, Ridge. Stop acting like your head's so far up your butt
you can't..."

"What apartment, Captain?"

He paused before answering. "B106. Stephanie Freel is the renter.
The other name wasn't on the lease."

"Was that name Kevin?" she said.

"Yes," he said. "How did you..."

Mona ended the call and raced toward Preston Highway.

CHAPTER 45

Looking through two dusty oval windows, Carter and Chester watched the police cars creep along the streets. The Shelter attic smelled like yellowing newspapers and yellow-stained sheets. The sun resembled an orange balanced on the horizon's blade, sinking slowly.

"Carter," Chester said as his nose touched the glass. "What're you after here?"

"We're waiting for the cars to leave so we can finish this, Chester. You know that."

"That's not what I mean."

Carter gazed at Chester's bony cheeks and sunken eyes. Granted, he appeared healthier and more alive now than last Sunday, but he still carried the weariness like a second skin.

Chester said, "If we succeed and clear your name, which is a long shot, what's your mission objective?"

Carter shifted and glared through the dirty window pane again, smiling at Chester's military jargon. He answered the question as though a commanding officer had asked it. "Save the girls, sir."

"Is that right?" Chester said in a tone that erased Carter's smile. "If this goes all Charlie Foxtrot and the cops catch us before we get those kids out, you're screwed, and me with you—and I'm not talkin' about the kind of screwin' you do in that sex club."

Carter's skin prickled.

"I let someone down. I don't think I can survive if I do it again."

"What?" Chester said. His dark brow wrinkled. "You're crazier than I am."

Carter swiveled to the right to stare at his friend again.

"You see, Carter, I know more than you think. For instance, I met a guy named Gomez who served with you in the Gulf. He passed through Louisville, and I tried to help him at the Shelter. He saw you in the dining room, and I thought he'd jump up and salute. Gomez said you dragged four soldiers out of harm's way when an IED blew up, even though you'd taken shrapnel, then killed three Iraqi guards. He claimed you got a Silver Star."

"Do you believe everything you hear, Chester?"

"I've learned the deeper the secret's hidden, the truer it is when somebody uncovers it. I'm afraid you don't care about yourself anymore. That makes you a dangerous soldier to have on a mission."

Carter smiled. "Chester, what is it you want? You're right here with me, risking exposure and worse. Haven't you been hiding, too?"

Chester chuckled but didn't respond. "I'll never leave anyone else behind."

Carter didn't need to ask what Chester meant. Long ago, he'd lived Chester's trauma alongside him in a Trap. It didn't happen in the Middle East. Instead, it transpired at a Greyhound bus station in Oakland, California, where a little girl wriggled to escape her mother's arms to reach Chester. The woman held her back as a younger Chester boarded a near-empty bus. He fell into the back seat and cried as the little girl and her mama shrank as the bus rolled away.

"Talk about hiding things—you've not even told me your real name," Carter said.

"Cops are leaving like a donut shop caught fire." Chester nodded toward the window.

Carter saw two police cars burn rubber, their sirens whining and lights flashing as they sped toward the interstate.

Chester and Carter scanned the streets below.

"Looks like your plan's working," Chester said. "They're scooting out of here."

Chester started toward the attic hatch, but Carter grasped his sleeve, holding him in the sun's rays. "Tell me why *you're* risking so much to help me."

The man's dark eyes softened, and his voice sounded bittersweet. "You don't treat me like I'm invisible," he said. "Maybe if I help you do something good with whatever time's left, you'll make sure my little girl sees me, too."

CHAPTER 46

"Kevin sent me," the man said. The Banger's DJ was so loud Stephanie leaned toward the black man. She wasn't sure, but he resembled a homeless man she'd seen near the interstate ramp. It surprised her that Allan's bouncers let him in the place.

She examined the man's face and his ancient thrift store clothes. "Why didn't he come himself?"

The man shrugged. "Kevin said to tell you it's about the girl. Zara or Tara, I think. He said you'd understand. He gave me twenty bucks to bring you home because he needs you. Something's got him all worried."

That's why the boys let this guy in—an emergency. Stephanie's heart rate spiked. She pictured the girl breaking free and summoning the cops. It'd be over for Kevin and maybe even her.

"Is he at the apartment?" She wanted her voice to sound calm, but panic swelled inside her throat.

"He said he'd be back by the time you got home," the man said. "I'm tellin' you, Lady, he didn't seem too good when I left him. He told me to hurry and said he didn't have time to call you 'cause he had to look around outside the apartments."

"Let me tell the manager and get my stuff," Stephanie said. As she hurried toward the Banger's dressing room, she thought, *Kevin is my life*.

***

Stephanie had worn her stiletto shoes to the club that night. Nonetheless, she managed to stride step for step with the messenger as they exited Banger's and bolted toward the parking lot.

"I parked near the alley," he said, pointing toward a Toyota Prius at the end of the lot.

"The Prius?"

"It's my friend's car," he said. "He lets me borrow it to earn money."

When they arrived at the vehicle, the man opened the door and motioned for her to sit in the front passenger seat.

"Let's hurry if this damn thing can," Stephanie said as she wiggled into the seat. She watched the man rush around the green hood. The sun had set, replaced by darkness and the pinholes of light adorning the night sky.

When the man slid into the driver's side, Stephanie started to speak, but rustling in the back seat startled her. As she attempted to turn, a strong arm encircled her throat. The touch, hot against her skin, caused her to ground her stiletto into the floor mat and buck her hips into the air. Her knee struck the dashboard and glovebox, and her hands flew to her neck. She dug her acrylic nails into the attacker's flesh.

The man rose from the back seat to adjust his right arm around her throat. He tightened his grip and held her in place.

The driver watched as the man slipped forward to increase his leverage.

Stephanie thought the black man seemed as surprised as she was. She tried to scream, but it was no use. Idaho realized she'd never see Kevin again.

She pictured Kelsey dying alone. Now, it was her turn.

As darkness narrowed her vision, she rolled her head just enough to see Carter Syke's face before the world disappeared.

CHAPTER 47

Since Carter described the car accident with Papaw, Mona's brain recycled memories she seldom summoned. That moment, playing like a safe driving video for traffic school, made her queasy and off-balanced. The drunk driver's blood-smeared face and dead eyes, the pain exploding throughout her body, and her grandfather's slumping shoulders left her heart an insect splashed on her cruiser's windshield.

Yet, here she was, staring through the glass at the apartment complex. Several three-story buildings bordered the unlined parking lot—the white brick facades marked by tar bleeding from the tan roof. Mona pictured mascara running down a woman's cheeks. At the front entrance labeled Building B, a blue double door at the top of five concrete steps displayed large golden handles with the word "Pull" etched above them. Hedges lined the perimeter along the ground—the unkempt edges sprouted green fingers, but mostly, the anemic bushes clung to life.

The street lights flickered above the complex as if teetering between dusk and night. In June, the evening didn't start its shift until around nine o'clock, so Mona remained hidden behind a clump of Bradford Pear trees. She didn't anticipate doing anything until the other units reached the scene, but she was ready if a crazed suspect shoved a bound and gagged girl through the doorway.

On the way, she had wrestled with the question, what if Carter proved to be the Good Girl Killer all along? What if he appeared in that doorway pushing the abducted kid down the front steps, her fingers bleeding and her eyes covered? Then, she had to shoot him, right?

"Real classy, Mona," she chastised herself for such corrupt thinking. Of course, she'd decided she wouldn't kill him to conceal her professional ignorance, even if the opportunity arose unless the shot saved the girl's life or her own.

"Only shoot to preserve life." She recited it from her days at the Police Academy at Eastern KY University. She concluded no job is worth a person's dignity and integrity. Instead, she'd work as a private investigator or dog groomer rather than live with a contaminated and compromised soul.

Despite the captain's advance notice, she'd wait for other officers. What did Anderson expect her to do—rush in and take down a serial killer alone, like Denzel Washington or John Wick?

She massaged her temples.

Besides, Carter was the same guy she'd had in custody and released into the wild. If that came to light, she couldn't explain it without trading her badge and gun for a cot in a jail or a mental health facility.

Nothing made sense anymore. Carter's eerie trespass into her memories, the irrefutable evidence that he hadn't abducted Lenora Pace or the legitimate shock and sadness he had exhibited when they discovered Kelsey's tortured body in his trunk. Even the girl's severed fingertips, part of the Good Girl Killer's signature, surprised Carter in a way too complicated to fake. Besides, the anonymous tip was too on the nose to be authentic. Kevin and Stephanie living here together? Was Sykes being set up as he claimed?

Sirens blared in the distance, and the sky grew darker.

Mona stared into the windshield again, seeing the encroaching night and the cold, dead eyes from long ago.

CHAPTER 48

"You know what to do," Carter said.

Chester didn't stir or even respond. He stared back as though he didn't recognize Carter.

Carter realized his friend had been surprised by what he did to Stephanie, but the situation and the stakes demanded it. One call to Kevin or a nosy neighbor seeing her in the car might spoil the entire plan and endanger everyone. Carter couldn't allow that, no matter what steps he had to take to prevent it.

"Are you alright, Buddy?" Carter said after opening the passenger-side door, "Tell me if..."

"Get the girls, Carter," Chester said, nodding. "I got you. It just surprised me to see you so violent." He rolled forward a foot or two in David's Prius. Carter nodded and closed the door.

***

Carter faced the building's north side. He jogged toward several blue industrial-sized trash cans beneath a window. The sunset illuminated the Bradford Pear trees and the parking lot, but the shadows provided enough to obscure Carter's actions.

He repositioned two trash cans and climbed onto the lids. They wobbled, but he caught his balance by grasping the window ledge and pushing his face against the glass. After steadying himself by widening his stance, Carter tried to raise the blackened window. It didn't budge. Breaking the glass wouldn't provide easy access, so he reached into his hoodie pocket and retrieved the kitchen knife Kelsey had used to free him at the Dirty Mint.

Kelsey's disfigured body—her fingertips missing and her head battered and swollen—crossed his mind. He shut his eyes to erase the image. When he opened them again, his reflection stared back from the glass.

The knife blade slid between the old window frame and the seal. Carter dragged it back and forth, loosening the dried paint. He dug the knife into the decaying wood until his hands fit between the frame and the sill. Carter squatted and pushed upward. The wooden fragments scraped his knuckles, but he continued to drive with his legs and arms until the window squealed and raised. He paused and glanced around, hoping the noise hadn't drawn attention. Carter's final shove pried the latch from its perch, opening the window enough for him to shimmy through.

Before entering, he checked the surroundings. Only the Ehrler's Ice Cream shop across the street had customers—most were protestors. Several masked young men and women formed a circle and appeared too busy to notice him, and since protesters had been breaking windows all week, his actions weren't out of place. El Acapulco Mexican

Restaurant and the Dollar Tree store on the corners were open, but their parking lots were vacant.

Carter dragged himself through the open window, face first, like a guilty lizard scurrying into a crevice.

CHAPTER 49

The young man licked the Rocky Road cone as if he were still ten years old instead of twenty-three. The taste brought memories of when his father took him and his sister for ice cream. His dad's scarce attention excited them so much that they acted giddy. However, when the photographer from his father's newspaper arrived at the ice cream shop and directed the family into so-called impromptu moments, Kyle and his older sister realized they were props to persuade the minions that the wealthy media mogul, Mr. Watterson, was just a regular dude who gave his kids treats all the time.

Sure, Dad's newspapers, websites, and television stations adopted a social justice stance, but Kyle knew what dear old Dad said at the dinner table. Fight The Man? His dad was The Man.

Besides, Kyle wasn't a fool. He recognized how his father hated him. Hatred and disappointment pretty much defined their relationship. No matter how long either lived, the son would never meet the Old Man's standards.

By the time he was a junior at Trinity Catholic High, Kyle had figured he'd do his part to destroy the establishment—after all, it was everything his father represented. Once society decomposed, the new world would grow back, with people like his dad and stepmom no longer the kings and queens.

When he saw Sykes at the school, the principal reminded him of his father—the shirt and tie, the authoritarian supremacy, and the Hitleresque pose—and he had to react. The fence and the man both needed to be toppled. Kyle ended up embarrassed but not defeated. He would get another crack at Sykes or someone like him—he knew it.

His body tingled with urgency and opportunity as he watched the man wobble like a tightrope walker on the trash cans and break open the window across the street.

A gift, that's what it was—another crack at Sykes.

A young woman, also dressed in black, talked to another protestor. Kyle grasped her elbow mid-conversation and yanked her to his side. "Check this out, Queenie," he said, pointing at the man across the street.

"So?" Queenie said, her voice tinged with irritation. "Dude's gettin' his. We've been doing that for a week."

"He's not with us, Q," he said. "You don't recognize him?"

"Let's eat our ice cream, and then we can get back to it," she said. "Everybody's tired." She returned to her friend and continued their conversation.

Kyle Watterson tossed the remainder of his cone in the trash can near the Erhler's entrance and lifted his red neon mask. Then, after the principal slithered through the open window, he yelled to his crew.

"Circle up, comrades," he said. The laughter and talk petered out as they gathered around him. "You see that place over there? The owner is one of the biggest white supremacists in Louisville. What you say we light him up?"

CHAPTER 50

"You were here first, Ridge," Detective Vincent said. "You get the honors."

Mona nodded at the tall detective and stepped between two uniformed officers. She directed her colleagues to the sides and did another visual confirmation of the apartment number.

Rust-colored numbers read B106, so she tapped her knuckles against the door.

"Ms. Freel," she said. "We're with the Louisville Metro Police Department. We have a warrant for the arrest of Carter Sykes. Please open immediately."

She listened and stared at the peephole. She holstered her firearm so anyone inside, especially Carter, would see she offered no threat—at least not yet.

No response. Mona glanced at the detective and spoke again. "Mr. Sykes, if you're inside, please come out so we can talk. Stephanie, are you okay? What about you, Kevin?"

Mona rapped her knuckles against the door again, with greater force.

No response.

She announced, "Please stand clear of the door. Pursuant to the warrants, we are entering the premises."

She stepped to the side.

The shorter and stockier officer behind her lifted a solid pipe-shaped object from the floor and shuffled forward. He swung the ram by the handles and struck the door near the knob. The wood and metal cracked and bent. The second blow splintered the wood and separated the door from the lock and frame.

The taller officer, gun in hand, lifted his foot and kicked open the door, revealing the darkness.

CHAPTER 51

Carter hunkered down in the darkness. A weak glow seeped beneath a doorway in the distance; however, shadows shielded the rest of the room. His drop from the window to the floor had jarred him and ignited pain in his knee. Bent over, he rubbed the side of his leg before stretching his toe into the blackness like a blind man's cane, tapping his foot to ensure solid ground awaited.

The door's dim light became his focal point and target. He smelled a thick, acrid odor that reminded him of rotten eggs mixed with pine tree car fragrance. The smell caused Carter to cover his nose with the crook of his elbow.

He hoped it wasn't death and Pine Sol.

***

Officer Ridge and Detective Vincent followed the two officers into the apartment, their guns drawn.

Vincent's voice boomed, "Show yourself, hands up." He surveyed the living room to the right, then pivoted toward the small kitchen to the left.

Mona trailed the two officers into the short hallway. The stocky one knocked and opened the first door on the left, and the other officer did the same to the right. Mona continued down the hall toward the third door facing her at the end of the puke-colored carpet. She approached it and tapped the brown plywood entrance. Her hand rested on her gun.

No response. Mona turned the knob and waited.

***

Carter's walk around the dark room's perimeter felt endless. Each step posed a potential danger. For all Carter knew, the Good Girl Killer waited a few steps away, prepared to add him to his list of victims. He'd then claim Carter murdered the captured girls, and then...

That's a slippery slope, Sykes.

Carter edged into the darkness.

***

Mona pushed the door with her foot. The rusted hinges and the friction against the carpet sounded like a timid mouse and a slithering snake. She held the gun at eye level and walked her fingers along the wall to her right to find a light switch. The officer's footsteps patted the hallway carpet behind her as she flipped the switch with her index finger.

***

Carter sidestepped, focused on the illuminated line under the floor. Outside, loud noises sounded closer to the building, but he refused to hurry. Each advance in the darkness led him closer to the door. Perhaps the light emanated from a closet. He shivered, and his heart skipped a beat.

What will I do if Kevin is inside that room?

He slipped his hand into his pocket.

***

Officer Ridge bent her knees, moved forward, and kept her finger on the trigger. She swiveled right and left, scanning each corner for a potential threat. She kneeled to peek under the bed, her shoulder rattling the night table—the small lamp rocked like a bowling pin that refused to fall.

She stood and surveyed her surroundings again.

When she confirmed the empty room, she said, "Clear."

***

Carter paused when the cars and trucks roared down Market Street. David had come through for him, diverting the police to Preston Highway and Kevin's apartment. David's recorded voice would serve as evidence that they'd sent the police. The worst-case scenario was that they'd discovered nothing connected to the girls. However, if they captured Kevin with the girls or with proof he was the abductor, it would be a real win for him and Mona.

Carter expected the door to be locked, but it released with the weight of his hand. When he opened the door, he didn't find the light source he anticipated—at least not one bright enough to have guided him to the Nally's Auto Repair office.

A coffee maker on a table produced a faint glow above the carafe to show the organized sugar packets and cheap Walmart powdered creamer containers. Beside the table stood a pair of twenty-five-cent bubble gum machines. The small globes were faded reds, blues, purples, and green. Also, a clock on the wall cast just enough light to establish 9:20 p.m.

He found the light switch near the counter and flipped the tiny lever. Posters of Continental Tires and Magnaflow Exhaust Systems adorned the wall. The smell of new rubber, stale smoke, and motor oil led Carter to hold his breath. The cash register sat where most auto shops had a monitor and keyboard, beside an old 1980s hand-processing credit card imprinter that belonged in an antique store rather than on an auto repair shop counter in 2023.

Who has time to run a business and pay taxes when there are so many girls to murder?

Carter opened the bathroom door near the front desk. Empty. He walked behind the counter to check for anything that might help him locate Zara and Lenora. He'd believed the girls would be here instead of at the apartment. Sure, Kevin might take them to his home first, but this site seemed the most logical place to hide them and torture them. The garage had plenty of space, and the hours posted online said repair service was "by appointment only." Kevin had parked a few expensive foreign cars behind the shop—Porsches, BMWs, and Aston Martins. Kevin had a van or a truck, or at least a car with a giant trunk, to transport his prey here when he needed to move them. And to haul their bodies after he killed them.

Carter shuddered before walking to the front door leading to the parking lot. The June night spread across the city; vehicles zipped by, and protesters wandered outside like zombies. He turned the latch until it clicked, unlocking the front entrance as he'd planned. Then, he returned to the light switch and flipped it down before stepping back through the door he used to enter, closing it behind him.

Carter found the light source. The light didn't shine beneath the door but rose from under the office as if hell existed, and the last Nally's Auto Repair sat above it.

CHAPTER 52

"Yeah, but we got a tip that Sykes would be here," Detective Vincent said. "I had to turn away some units because it was overkill. I've posted two unmarked cars in the parking lot and three units several blocks out. You sure your cruiser won't scare him away?"

"May I speak frankly, sir?" Mona said. Vincent was a veteran—well over twenty years on the force—but Mona sensed something different about him. He wasn't much taller than her, and the gray streaks at his temples stood out against his thinning brown hair and browner skin. Unlike Captain Anderson, Detective Vincent appeared more concerned about saving lives than finagling promotions and publicity.

"Of course, Officer Ridge," he said. "But make it quick in case Sykes shows. We should surprise him instead of the opposite."

She nodded. The officers and two detectives searched for evidence around the three-bedroom apartment. The lifted sofa cushions glanced beneath tables and chairs and peered behind the large television near the front wall.

"Something's off about the call and this apartment," Mona said. "This isn't Sykes' place—and the best I can tell—I don't see anything you'd expect in a school principal's home. I know the guy, and this isn't him."

"No one said this was his place, Ridge," Vincent said. "The caller said he's coming here."

"But what if someone sent us here not to catch Sykes but to find something that connects the tenants to the killings?"

"Like what?" The Detective gestured toward the kitchen and the hallway. "So far, we've found zero evidence of anything illegal except the wicked weed smell in the carpet. If I worked for Louisville schools, I'd take up pot myself. Besides, who'd make such a call? Wait, do you think Sykes called the station? Why?"

"Maybe to distract us? Or to have us find something here? I don't know."

Mona gazed at the kitchen and then the hallway carpet. She recalled Carter's words about seeing the girl tied up in the background. To be exact, he'd said, "tied up in the back bedroom."

"Let's recheck the bedroom," she said. Before Vincent replied, Mona rushed from the living room into the hallway. She heard the Detective exhale as he followed her to the back bedroom.

At least he didn't ask if I was menstruating and storm out the door.

The blue and white blanket covering the bed matched the curtains and the wallpaper. However, something seemed out of place. Although someone had made the bed with great effort and care, the three pillows leaned against the headboard at odd angles. Two pillows crossed each other on the right side while the other stood upright against the left bedpost.

Mona lifted the two pillows on the right. The post rose toward the ceiling, peaking several feet above the mattress in a pineapple shape. The smooth brown wood had been dusted and polished.

Mona glanced at Vincent, his arms crossed as he stood at the foot of the bed. Without speaking, she hustled past him to the left side of the headboard. She batted the pillow, rolling it to the side.

"Damn," Vincent said as he walked toward Mona.

The bedpost displayed deep grooves and wear in the wood. More cuts and faded wood encircled the post at different levels—clear evidence that someone used ropes or cords to restrain someone—and the victim (*victims?*) fought to break free.

"Wiseman, get in here," Vincent said. A moment later, another plain-clothed detective entered the room and faced his older partner. "Forget what I said about hurrying. Let's go over this place inch by inch. Get the lab here for prints."

"I've got an idea where to start," Mona said as she kneeled beside the headboard and examined the floor. "Look at how the carpet's worn away as though someone dragged the bed back and forth many times." She leaned against the wall, attempting to peer behind the headboard.

Vincent and Wiseman approached her. Mona produced a flashlight and handed it to Wiseman. "Stand on the bed and shine this down," she said. When he stared at her without moving, she added, "Please."

Vincent said, "Don't stand like you're constipated, Ray. Do it." Wiseman crawled to the middle blanket and shined the light behind the headboard.

"There's a vent on the floor," Mona said. "I never forget what they taught us at the Academy—had we checked Ignatow's vents, we would've found swift justice for Brenda Sue Schaffer."

Detective Vincent nodded. He turned to the younger Wisemen and said, "Ignatow killed his ex-girlfriend, but the jury found him innocent due to the lack of evidence. Years later, after Ignatow had sold his house, a carpet installer discovered film canisters in a vent. The pictures showed Ignatow to be the monster law enforcement thought he was. He even owned up to killing that beautiful woman, but he couldn't be tried again for the same crime."

"Double jeopardy," Wisemen said, nodding his head.

The two detectives lifted the bed frame and slid it away from the wall. Mona retrieved a small screwdriver from her belt and crawled toward the vent. Without delay, she removed the shiny new screws securing the vent cover. She tossed the cover aside and reached inside.

"Be careful, officer," Vincent said as he watched over her shoulder. "It could be rigged."

"I don't think so," Mona replied. "It appears to be a fake vent." She slipped her latex-gloved hands into the hole and lifted a rectangular floor section.

"Is that a toolbox?" Vincent said.

"It is," Mona said.

CHAPTER 53

The sliver of light beneath the office door wasn't enough to illuminate the garage, so Carter searched for another button. He rubbed his palm on the dark wall until he bumped against a row of light switches. He flipped them all. Within seconds, the ceiling lights buzzed and brightened the garage.

Even though he'd read that this shop was the largest in the Kentuckiana region, the room stretched farther back than anticipated, and the ceiling rose high above the lights attached to the rafters. The buzzing fixtures lighted the garage but cast dark shadows in the corners.

Orange oil drums covered the other side of the garage. Gas cans, boxes of spark plugs, oil filters, and different car parts lined the metal shelves nearby in precise order.

Carter scanned the workbenches around the work area. The garage resembled a museum exhibit. Someone had arranged the rills, oil cans, and cleaning rags as if creating a display rather than a work site. Above each bench, wrenches, rachets and sockets, tire gauges, and other tools created a symmetrical arrangement more organized than any auto parts store he'd seen. The work surfaces were cleaner than Carter's kitchen counters and pantry. Beneath the benches, several air compressors, two steel car jacks, and two metal carts touched the wall.

The three retractable doors facing the building's front had sections that folded on the tracks whenever activated. They mirrored the doors at the back of the garage, where cars exited after Kevin finished the repairs. Two trenches were visible between each set of doors. These pits gave mechanics access to the underside of vehicles. For Carter, it provided access to the basement beneath the garage floor.

The bright basement lights made it easy to see the metal scaffolding in the pits and the concrete underground floor. Although an easier route existed, Carter lowered himself into the pit using the metal steps and scaffolding. He bent his knees because he expected very little headroom in the concrete tomb, but that wasn't the case. The basement had eight-foot ceilings.

I've never seen a garage this huge. It's more like a military airplane hanger with large repair pits for accessing vehicles' undercarriages.

Carter eased himself off the scaffolding onto the basement floor. "Catacombs," he said. The basement stored even more barrels and gas cans; however, used containers littered the basement corners, and he stuck to the floor as if walking on fly paper.

He surveyed the basement to get his bearings. Judging by the location of the upstairs office and the light that guided him across the garage, Carter expected to find a door to a room in the corner of the basement.

That wasn't the case. Instead, another workbench, secured to the drywall by wooden braces, jutted from the wall where Carter estimated the door should be. Other workbenches were attached to the bare drywall at different points. Kevin, or someone, had wedged a mammoth-sized Coke machine between two benches near the other end of the basement. The light falling through the pits illuminated the space—the surfaces held chemicals, gas cans, gloves, and a few tools, except for the bench near the Coke machine. An open red toolbox sat on the bench by the lighted soda machine. The tools—large wrenches, bolt cutters, a cordless drill, and a handsaw—jutted from the box like kindling on a campfire.

CHAPTER 54

Mona and Detective Vincent stared at the toolbox extracted from the floor vent.

"Do we open it, sir?" Still on her knees, she stared up at the detective. She realized his dilemma. If the warrant didn't cover the toolbox, it might prove problematic if they found something illegal yet unrelated to the case. However, it could also connect Sykes, Idaho, and Kevin and provide information needed to rescue the abducted girls.

Almost as soon as the thought took hold in Mona's mind, Detective Vincent made the call. "Crack it open," he said. "We need to find those kids."

Wiseman stepped forward, carrying a crowbar and a hammer. Mona leaned back as he slid the bar into the latch and swung the hammer. After three blows and three clangs that caused Mona to blink each time, the bolts holding the lock in place fell to the carpet.

Wiseman stepped away.

Vincent nodded. "Let's see what they're hiding, Officer Ridge."

Mona released the broken latch. She cautiously lifted the toolbox lid and pushed aside a thick icepack, like those found in high-end coolers.

Mona winced as though the hammer had struck again. Wiseman leaned away while Vincent moved closer and put his foot against the box to turn it. Before Mona could catch it, the toolbox tipped over. Plastic zip-lock bags spilled from the box onto the floor—each tightly sealed bag contained colorful and manicured fingertips crusted with dried blood.

CHAPTER 55

"In the belly of the beast," Carter said.

He stared at the drywall and the workbench as if the door he had expected to see would materialize from the plaster. Leaning against the protruding surface, he tapped the wall and listened. It sounded hollow, but no one knocked back.

Carter rubbed his chin and walked parallel to the workbench, examining every foot of the wall above the sections. He recalled the old haunted house movies he watched with Becca on their tiny television—her precious jumps followed by laughter so loud he warned she'd wake up their mom. On TV, the characters always discovered secret doorways in haunted houses by shifting a statue on the mantel or by removing an ominous book from a shelf. Often, the entire bookshelf swiveled, revealing the villain's lair or a mysterious passageway.

The soda machine wedged between the final two workbenches glowed and hummed. *Did I turn it on when I hit the switches upstairs, or does Kevin always keep it powered?*

Carter crawled under the benches beside the soda machine, searching for the power cord, but didn't find one. The machine was flush against the drywall, the cord disappearing behind it. Carter lowered his shoulder and tried to push the machine forward, but the heavy machine refused to budge as though embedded in the plaster and concrete.

Carter stood again, tapped his index finger against the metal, and walked to the machine's front. He approached the toolbox on the workbench and selected a long, flat-edge screwdriver and a hammer. When he returned to the soda machine door, he wiggled the tool into the gap between the rubber seal and hammered the tool's handle. The screwdriver sunk into the gap, and, with little effort, Carter pried the machine open.

Gutless. The soda machine contained no soft drinks, no inner mechanism to deliver cans or bottles, and no back. Instead, the machine was an outer husk with electricity lighting the buttons and a Coke symbol on the door. But it did have a purpose. The machine served as a doorway through the wall into a hidden hallway—its darkness, tempered by soft light, stared into Carter like a Trap turned inside out.

CHAPTER 56

Carter followed a black power cord through the humming machine and the rectangular hole. He turned to his right and saw the door he'd expected. As before, the pale light escaped around the door frame, illuminating the six-foot wide, twenty-foot-long concrete hallway.

As he edged toward the entrance, Carter listened for voices and scanned the walls. Extension cords, strips of black cloth, and duct tape rolls hung from hooks to his right. Below the hooks, a metal cart rested against the wall. He saw gauze, bandages, bottles of alcohol, and syringes scattered on the rolling cart's surface.

A wooden workbench, smaller than the ones upstairs and in the adjoining basement, butted against the left wall. Carter paused to examine the iron vise attached to the surface. Its metal crank and heavy jaws appeared coated in rust and dark honey.

As Carter moved past, he realized it wasn't sweet honey or rust. Carter remembered Mansfield, Ohio, and the coppery odor rising above his sister's tiny body.

He'd spent too much time searching for this door, so he decided to forego the knock. Instead, Carter raised his foot to kick beside the silver knob with his right leg, then remembered the lingering ache in his knee. He switched to his left leg and front-kicked the same spot.

The jolt cracked the wood near the doorknob. Muffled moans and garbled words followed at once. Carter kicked again, with more force than before. The cheap door separated from the latches and swung open like a gate in a hurricane. The equal and opposite force pushed Carter backward. Without hesitation, he planted his foot and burst through the entrance.

***

The shackled young women resembled conjoined twins attached at the butt. They wiggled and pushed against each other as if the movement might set them free. The tall Black girl—Zara Turner—wailed through the gag, her panic tinged with defiance. Lenora's shriek was pure surprise. She faced away from the shattered door so she didn't see the trespasser.

Carter hurried toward them—pungent sweat, blood, and urine odors filled Carter's lungs.

"Don't worry," he said. "It's not Kevin. I'm Carter Sykes."

Lenora's surprise morphed into terror—her cry sharper than broken glass.

"Lenora," Carter said. "I'm not here to hurt you. I've never planned to hurt you."

He glanced around the room. Five feet away, a microwave rested on a wobbly metal table, and a Darrell Griffith poster adorned the wall above it. Extension cords hung on nails like wreaths across the room, and a black metal chair leaned against the sparse wallpaper covering a section of the plaster.

When he refocused on the women, Carter ached. The bedsheets were blood-soaked. Zara's tee shirt hiked above her belly button, was ragged and dark red, like a burgundy canvas. Lenora faced the other wall, but the long blonde hair he remembered from the night at the duplex pressed against the blood-stained pillow. Her bound, bloody hands, forced into prayer, rose toward the metal bars of the headboard.

Zara was closest, so he kneeled beside her first. He touched her trembling shoulder and retrieved Kelsey's kitchen knife from his hoodie pocket. She resumed her frantic gyrations when she saw the blade.

"Don't worry, Zara," Carter said, showing her the knife. "Watch." Slowly, he sawed at the cords restraining Zara. The girl's onyx eyes, encircled by red, resembled burning coals.

When he severed the cord, Carter ripped the remains from her body and cut the gag. As he did so, Zara cried and covered her face.

"I'll get you out of here," he said as he glanced at Lenora wiggling beside Zara on the bed. Her guttural moans stabbed his heart.

Carter rose and turned toward the foot of the bed. Zara's left hand shot forward before he took a first step, landing on his wrist. Carter heard her hoarse voice say, "Don't leave." He had no choice but to stay, and he never did when he fell into a Trap.

***

She expects to die but hopes she won't. As she watches the door, Carter feels the uncommon merger of fear, hope, and resolve. Lenora sinks into the mattress, motionless beside her, and the decrepit table with the microwave is in a different place now. The Dr. Dunkenstein poster hangs on the wall. It's last night.

Zara sees the doorknob as it turns, so Carter shares her dread. She bites her lip and causes herself pain before Kevin inflicts his. When Honeyboy Kevin struts into the room, he stops and smiles. "You're waiting patiently, my good girl."

Zara stares at him with the dispassionate gaze Parisians offer American tourists.

He stares at Lenora but speaks to Zara. "Don't you worry about your bed-mate. She'll be visiting dreamland for a while."

Zara rocks back and forth. She wants to see Lenora but can't. Zara prays that Lenora is alive, but his cruelty taints the truth whenever Kevin speaks. She fears Dreamland might mean death. Or worse.

"That gives us time," Kevin says. "You know I'll release your fine self soon, so I want to make memories we can cherish forever." His face, a distorted mask of lies, causes Carter to push against the Trap's walls. He tries to form a fist with Zara's soft hands but fails.

Bile rises in Zara's throat; however, she refuses to satisfy her abductor. She hurls hate with her stare but regulates her face so he sees nothing, not even the hellfire crackling inside her. Carter hadn't experienced such control and resolve in any Trap he remembered. She denies Kevin the ecstasy of dominance he craves. Amazing.

Kevin's smile evaporates. As Dr. Wallace would say, noncompliance has consequences.

He stomps toward Zara and untangles the knots holding her to the bedpost. When he grabs her hair, pain permeates her scalp. But she doesn't cry out—no ecstasy for you, Honeyboy.

Kevin drags her to her feet and pushes her toward the door and into the hallway.

Carter predicts the destination—the vise—sticky with honey and rust.

"I agree with you, rich girl," Kevin says into her ear, his fist still tangled in her thick hair. "I can tell you're too good for people like me. But it's not always been that way. My family used to travel in the same circles as yours. My daddy built himself an empire, and my mama's people had fat stacks in the bank, just like yours."

Zara shivers. A photo splashes across her mind. Her dad, mom, sister, and Zara are at a fancy hotel. Their smiles speak of happiness and love. Carter realizes Zara's sister is the protest leader behind his school. Damn. The image pushes her to the edge of tears, but she knocks over the frame and regains control.

Without warning, Kevin tightens his hold. Carter feels the explosion on Zara's scalp as he yanks her messy hair and stares into her stoic face. He tilts her head back. Carter sees Kevin's sharp teeth, smokey blue eyes, and the hallway ceiling. He feels the tears rolling from Zara's eyes onto her temples.

When Kevin pushes her to the steel vise bolted to the table, Zara's head lurches forward as if riding a rollercoaster. He grabs her wrist and shoves her face so that her nose grazes the vice's ridged metal jaws. Carter hears her heart beating like a rainstorm on a car's roof—his heart matching hers beat for beat. A gasp escapes her lips. Her terror shows itself now. Carter experiences it as she does.

"No!" she cries when Kevin grabs her wrist, pulls her head back again, and jams her thin, black wrist between the vice's parallel jaws. Carter wills her to pull away, but Kevin's too strong. The killer releases her hair and grips the metal crank. He rotates the crank three times, capturing Zara's arm and hand. Carter figures he had measured her wrist in preparation for this moment. She attempts to escape, but the tool's teeth and jaws bite into her skin. She yelps like a fox in a bear trap.

Carter knows some traps you can't escape.

Kevin slows his pace now that Zara can't move. He adjusts his pony-tail and pops his knuckles, then hums the children's song again—the same tune he sang while his dead father's lifeless body hung above him in the bedroom. Carter strains to remember the lyrics, but his mind swats it away like a swarm of hornets.

Kevin's hand disappears beneath the bench but reappears with a wooden box. After he removes a high-grade cordless jigsaw, he slides the box beneath Zara's helpless hand.

Zara doesn't understand, but Carter does.

However, when Kevin powers on the cordless, handheld saw, Zara not only understands but screams in terror before slumping toward the bench. The wailing resonates in Carter's ears until Zara's shock and pain overcome her consciousness, freeing Carter from the Trap.

***

Carter reached across Zara's body and gently lifted her other hand. He held his breath, struggling to control his emotions as Zara had when confronted with evil. Her hand was cold, and the tips of her pinky and ring finger were gone—bloody gauze melded to the remaining knuckles like paper mâché. He rested the mangled hand on her bare stomach and caressed her cheek.

"It'll end today, Zara," Carter said.

Carter circled the bed to Lenora's side. Despite the cloth blindfold, her pale skin revealed her distress. As he uncovered her eyes, he examined Lenora's fingers. Kevin had wrapped her left hand in gauze, too. The crusting bloodstains told him Lenora had lost the same fingers as Zara.

Carter sliced the cord and shook Lenora's shoulder. She moaned, but whatever drugs Kevin had injected were stubborn. Despite her earlier flailing, she wasn't fully conscious—her lids fluttered, and drool stretched from her lips to her chin. He clasped her shoulder and rocked her back and forth.

Carter rechecked his watch, then glanced at Zara. "Can you walk?" he said.

Zara nodded and dropped her bare feet onto the concrete floor. The bloody, white shirt reached her knees like a dress when she stood. She shuddered and shifted her stance as if boarding a canoe for the first time. Dark red and white patches alternated on the shirt's front, and sweat painted the underarms yellow. Her muscular legs trembled but then accepted the weight.

Carter slid his right arm behind Lenora's neck and slid his left beneath her legs at the knees. He lifted her from the filthy mattress, holding her in his arms.

"Lenora," Carter said, "we're leaving this basement. Do you understand?"

Lenora shook her head, and her eyes opened like window blinds. "Help her," she said, turning toward Zara.

"He is helping us," Zara said. Despite her wounds, she smiled at Lenora and touched her knee.

Carter glanced at his watch. "It's time. Let's go now. Follow me, Zara." He hurried out the broken door, still carrying Lenora. The light illuminated the hallway, enabling Carter to see even more of the Good Girl Killer's tools lining the path. As he rushed toward the makeshift hole to enter the other part of the basement, he glanced over his shoulder.

Zara lingered behind. She stared at the vise where Kevin had hurt her and Lenora. Even from fifteen feet away, Carter saw her body trembling, and her breathing quickened her chest's rise and fall.

"Lenora," he said, using a sharp tone to stir her. "Can you walk?"

Lenora gazed at Zara. "I will," she said.

Carter leaned Lenora against the drywall. She squatted several inches and lifted her shoulders so her back and head touched the wall. After a few seconds, she straightened and nodded to him.

He dashed to Zara's side, placing his hand on her shoulder. Her skin was cool yet slick with sweat.

"Zara, we have to go," he said.

She said, "This is where..." Her words sounded dry and gritty, like a desert floor. She paused and swallowed.

"He's evil, Zara. Pure, unadulterated evil. He'll pay, don't you worry. But right now, we're taking you and Lenora to safety."

Zara turned. "Have you ever hurt so much that you feel like pain's replaced who you are—your soul, I mean?"

Carter remembered Becca's empty shell lying at his feet in the Castle. He often wondered if her soul had risen like vapor and if, as it ascended, it drew out all the goodness and happiness inside him, leaving behind only his pain and addiction. It was his turn to shudder.

"Happiness waits for you, Zara," Carter said, squeezing her shoulder. "Your mom, dad, and sister will remind you who and what you are. Go to them."

"You've talked to my family?" Her eyes were hopeful.

Carter constructed the lie in his mind—how he met her family and Lenora's girlfriend, and they asked him to find their girls and bring them home—but he caught himself. He'd lied for too long to others and himself.

"No," he said. "But I know they love you and are proud of you. I would be if you were my family."

She sniffed and touched his sleeve.

"Come on."

"You are a frigging conundrum, Sykes." The voice bounced against the concrete floor and unfinished plaster.

In one fluid movement, Carter's hand flashed to his belt. He stepped between Zara and the speaker, squared his shoulders, and aimed Chester's .38 Special.

Carter targeted Kevin Nally's smirking face.

***

Kevin's grin sickened Carter nearly as much as the bloodstains spotting Lenora's unbuttoned Denny's shirt. He used both hands to steady his aim—pointed at Kevin's right eye five paces away.

"I mean, I don't get you," Kevin said. "Always stumbling into my business." Kevin adjusted his hold on Lenora so she shielded even more of his muscular frame. He bent down and planted his nose in her messy blonde hair until only a portion of his face remained visible.

"You wanted Stephanie so much I figured if I played my cards right, you'd be a solid scapegoat for my hobbies," Kevin said. He hugged Lenora's chest and shoulders with one arm as he wedged a cordless drill under her jaw. The bit tilted toward her brain—his finger trigger-ready.

"I guess that wasn't the case at all. I've been catching these little divas for a long time, and nobody's suspected me. I've been too smart. Now you show up at my little funhouse like you've been chasing me all along. Not even Steph knows about this room. Hell, you've put me in a bind. I couldn't even get my gun because the cops were all over my house like roaches. I'm betting you sent them."

Carter clenched his teeth. In the Marines, he had qualified as a Marksman with a pistol and rifle, but that was long ago. He hadn't fired a gun since then. Besides, it was too risky with the drill so close. What if he missed and killed Lenora? He'd never forgive himself.

"It's really like we've been partners, Sykes," Kevin said. "You set 'em up, and I knock 'em down."

"No, we're not partners," Carter said, moving the gun barrel a half inch. "You won't hurt these girls again."

Kevin laughed, although he dipped his face even farther behind Lenora. "How'd you figure out what the police can't? I expected you to be in jail by now—everybody calling you the Good Girl Killer—but look at you."

The Traps had told Carter all he'd needed to track Honeyboy. Stephanie's reaction and the organized apartment told him Kevin didn't hold the victims there long. When Carter saw the emblem on Kevin's shirt at Banger's, it required one Google search to find the last standing Nally's Auto Repair. But he didn't need to explain any of that to Kevin. Carter snarled and stepped closer to the target.

Kevin pulled Lenora with him as he backpedaled toward the door leading through the Coke machine.

"I saw your porno with this little one right here," he said, shaking Lenora with his thick arm. The drill bit indented her jawline. "Dude, you ended your career on the spot. See, you're not that different from me. Both of us like to take chances."

Kevin backpedaled toward the exit without warning, dragging Lenora by her heels. When she cried out, he tightened his hold and lifted her feet off the floor. Fear twisted her face, and blood dripped from her hand onto her bare leg and the concrete.

Carter advanced, step for step—his finger on the trigger. He figured Kevin wanted to get through the hole and the soda machine and close the door before Carter could intervene. He couldn't allow it.

Kevin disappeared into the drywall, yanking Lenora into the machine's empty frame.

Carter sprinted toward the opening, his gun leading the way. He pounced as Kevin dragged Lenora into the basement and attempted to shut the door. Carter caught the metal frame inches before it closed with his free hand. He didn't pause. Instead, he crouched lower like a running back breaking into the endzone.

Carter's shoulder and head struck the door, driving it into Kevin's body. The metallic thump rattled the machine and forced Kevin to stumble backward.

Kevin hissed as he struggled to regain his breath. The drill flew from his hand and spun under a workbench.

Lenora staggered, fell to her knees, and crawled beneath a different bench near the door.

As Carter emerged from the machine, Kevin stomped toward him. On the way, he retrieved a heavy wrench from his back pocket. He lunged at Carter, swinging the silver wrench toward Carter's arm. Carter dodged it, but the tool collided with his revolver. The loud metal-on-metal collision catapulted the weapon from Carter's hands onto the concrete under Bay 4.

Instead of scrambling for the gun, Carter set his sights on Kevin. The two men were equal in stature, although Kevin was younger. Strands of Kevin's hair escaped his ponytail and rose like a cobra when he bounced. Carter focused on his Nally's center torso to see the wrench and the killer's other hand.

Kevin danced, raised the wrench chest-high, and pointed the heavy end at Carter. The bold move revived his breath and his smirk at the

same time. "You're too old for this, Sykes. Why didn't you stay at the
Dirty Mint instead of running like a coward? I could've already ended
your pain, and who knows, I might have left Kelsey and Lenora alone."

"I'm not some little girl you've drugged, Momma's Boy." Carter
touched his brow and examined the blood on his fingers. He'd cut
himself on the soda machine door. He wiped his hand across the
hoodie and shifted his weight onto his back leg while raising his
clenched fists.

Kevin smiled. "Momma's Boy?" he said. "She'd be so proud of me."

"I bet she's a lot like the girls you kill, right?" Carter said. He slid a
little closer. "I bet she still uses those long fingers and manicured nails
to tuck her little boy in at night."

Kevin's smirking lip glitched, and his shoulders rose.

"Oh, I've touched a nerve," Carter said. "You still got those scars
she dug on your back and arms?"

Kevin attacked. He charged toward Carter, landing a punch to
Carter's head rather than swinging the wrench. The punch connected
with Carter's cheek and knocked him off balance. When Kevin raised
the wrench and brought it down like a hammer, Carter deflected it
with his forearm. Pain reverberated from his elbow to his wrist.

Hidden beneath the workbench, Lenora screamed like she'd been
struck instead of Carter.

Carter attempted to stumble away, but Kevin continued his assault.
He shifted toward Carter and snapped a kick to his left thigh. The
thud sounded like a baseball bat against a sandbag. The hurt was bone
deep.

Carter imagined a purple footprint on his leg.

Kevin raised the wrench and strode toward Carter again. However,
he stopped when breaking glass, a flash of bright light, and indecipherable voices echoed from the garage upstairs. A single column of

smoke rolled like dirty fog above the open bays overhead. Both men used the distraction to recoup.

Lenora scuttled further under the workbench by the soda machine. Her whimpers refocused Carter on Honeyboy.

Kevin searched the floor for Carter's gun. Carter seized the moment, driving his left fist into Kevin's jaw and following with a right uppercut to the killer's chin. The blow knocked Kevin onto his heels. He stumbled but didn't fall.

When Kevin shuffled toward him again, swinging the wrench, Carter slipped away from the blow to his left, but Kevin had anticipated his move. With a boxer's speed and footwork, the younger man shifted his feet and grazed Carter's left shoulder with the wrench's head. Pain burrowed into his muscle and bones, and he sucked air through his teeth as he bound away.

Kevin tossed the tool in the air like a juggler, watching it spin two times before he snatched the handle and lunged at Carter again. He swung the wrench with his right hand. Instead of a downward arc as before, he targeted Carter's head with a sidearm swing. Carter leaned away from the strike. The open-ended adjustable wrench, nearly two feet long and solid, passed an inch from his nose, so close the breeze touched his skin.

Carter swayed but regained his balance at once. He grabbed Kevin's hand and used it as a lever to twist the killer's wrist and arm. Kevin yelped in pain. The sound reminded Carter of a hyena's cry. The wrench dropped to the concrete floor, its metallic clang echoing around the basement.

Kevin yanked his hand away and backpedaled to create distance between them.

"This is fun," Kevin said with a laugh as he shook his injured arm. The mechanic repositioned his feet and rolled his shoulders before reaching into his side pocket and producing a box cutter. His smirk returned, and he flicked his thumb against the cutter without looking. A two-inch blade, razor-sharp, emerged from the handle and glinted in the basement lights.

This sucker has training in boxing and maybe martial arts. Carter's shoulder and arm ached, and his bruised leg tightened. He glanced at Lenora under the workbench and imagined Zara cowering in the hidden hallway. He rotated his shoulder and stretched his knee as he stared at Kevin. *I don't have much left in the tank.*

A tiny, familiar voice in his head said, "Kick his ass, Cartie."

"Something's not quite right about you, Sykes," Kevin said. He slapped the boxcutter against his left palm. "I just can't put my finger on it."

"Says the man who saws off the fingertips of girls who've done nothing to him." Carter glanced upward through the closest bay as he spoke. What he saw told him it was time to end this.

"It's about time those girls pay—and their parents, too," Kevin said. "They've had it easy and…"

"What about Kelsey? Is that why you killed her?" Carter said.

Kevin laughed, throwing his head back. "She betrayed me by cutting you loose. That's what got her killed," he said. "I had my plan—setting you up to play the sad loser and going somewhere else to start over. She jeopardized my future. But that was only some of it. Kelsey was too hard to resist."

"And Stephanie? Are you taking her for your new start?"

He laughed again. "Steph's been my Plan B since I realized I could pin all this on your stupid ass. You see, Idaho will be your last victim, Mr. Good Girl Killer."

"You'll pay."

"Really?" Kevin said. "You think the handful of girls the police know about are the only ones I've played with? I'm the victim here, Sykes. My dad built this palace. When I took over, I realized he was a great man, but people treated..."

It was Carter's turn to smile. He cleared his throat and sang, "This old man, he played one; he played knick-knack on my thumb; with a knick-knack paddy whack, give the dog a bone; this old man came rolling home." Carter stopped. "Is that the old man you're talking about?"

Kevin's smirk disappeared. Shock replaced it; his so-called sympathetic eyes and smart mouth opened as wide as his father's had years ago. Kevin's chest heaved like a caged animal might burst from inside.

Carter poured more salt. "Was it when Little Kevin watched his daddy hanging that you decided to kill your mother, Momma's Boy? But boys don't kill their mommies, do they, Kevin? Even if she locked them in a room with their old man's corpse swinging overhead. Oh, you've cut off her sharp fingertips and murdered her plenty of times, but..."

The beast was uncaged. Kevin's body shook with anger and confusion. He charged at Carter, his eyes bulging and his teeth bared.

Carter was alert yet patient. Sergeant Doogan had taught him combat in basic training and beyond. He always said, "It's easier to redirect a tank than stop it, so Carter held his ground and waited for the younger, quicker man to charge toward him without any control.Ke vin jabbed the blade at Carter's stomach with rage-stoked strength but little precision. Carter blocked the thrust with his arm, but as Kevin pulled the boxcutter back, the silver blade slashed through Carter's hoodie sleeve, opening a shallow gash on his forearm.

Carter ignored the wound and followed the cutter's path into Kevin's space. He stopped and grasped Kevin's elbow, catching the man's arm before he could stab again. Kevin, still enraged, raised his knee, but Carter sidestepped far enough that Kevin struck Carter's hip rather than his gut.

Just as they had taught him in the Marines, Carter clung to Kevin's arm and maneuvered his leg behind the man's knees. Kevin fought to keep his balance, giving Carter enough leverage to strip the boxcutter from his hand, sending it clattering onto the gray floor.

Kevin stumbled backward, a groan escaping his lips. Carter closed the gap between them again and punched with his right hand. However, his fist passed Kevin's face. Instead, Carter pounded him above the eye with a solid elbow strike. It rocked Kevin, causing his knees to buckle. As Kevin bent over to catch himself, Carter grasped the ponytail close to the man's scalp and dragged Kevin's head downward while smashing his knee into the killer's face. The snapping and flattening cartilage indicated the blow broke Kevin's nose. Blood spurted from his face like a soda fountain. Carter followed with a front kick to the mechanic's chest. He heard Kevin's panicky gasp as the breath abandoned his body.

Kevin dropped to the concrete floor, moaning. However, he rolled to his left and grasped the boxcutter off the floor.

Carter's legs wobbled, and his entire body strained, but he remained standing, his hands clenched into fists, glaring down at the blubbering man.

CHAPTER 57

Find the gun. Find the gun. Carter's mind repeated the mantra. *Do it before he regains his will to fight.* He averted his eyes from Kevin and turned to retrieve the gun.

"You looking for this?"

Carter spun toward the voice near the scaffolding at Bay 4. The rumbling and the dark rolling smoke on the floor above resembled a storm-filled sky.

Stephanie emerged from the darkness. She aimed the gun in Carter's direction. Black mascara ran down her face, creating lines from her inflamed eyes through the thick makeup on her cheeks to her faded red lipstick and narrow chin. Carter's sleeper hold and the nap in the back of David's Prius had matted her hair and wrinkled what little clothes she wore. Somewhere along the way, she'd kicked off her heels.

Carter raised his hands to surrender and stared at the gun barrel and the girl he first knew as Idaho.

However, when Chester stepped from the same darkness behind her, Carter shifted his gaze. An inexplicable tingle rippled across Carter's skin, and a deep breath involuntarily expanded his chest.

Throughout his life, he'd expected little from others, even those he considered his family. The repeated disappointment and loss made expectations too risky. But he trusted Chester. Now, Carter was like the climber from Tennessee the Colonel had described—clinging to the mountain, unsure what to do. Chester stared at Carter as Stephanie pointed the pistol toward his stomach. Carter ignored the gun and fixed his vision on his friend's eyes, probing and questioning.

His friend held eye contact, and his expression changed from sullen to frustrated. The change startled Carter. Chester subtly motioned with his hands as if sweeping Carter away, silently mouthed, "Get out of the way."

Carter lowered his hands and stepped to the left, leaving a clear line of sight between Stephanie and Kevin. She didn't adjust her aim. Now, the barrel targeted Kevin rather than Carter.

Chester, his eyebrow raised, offered a confused nod and shrugged his shoulders as if to say, "Why're you looking at me?"

Carter's lip trembled, and he suppressed the sob rising from his throat as gratitude filled his heart. He'd feared Chester might let him down, but he had not.

When Carter looked back at her, Stephanie spoke. "You guys brought me to this basement to hear this?"

Carter and Chester remained silent.

\"I'm so glad to see you, my love," Kevin said, sitting on the floor behind Carter.

Stephanie glared at him and kept the gun aimed at his chest.

"Shoot him, Baby," Kevin said, motioning toward Carter. However, Carter read her expression. Broken. Hopeless. Betrayed.

"Why'd you kill Kelsey?" Stephanie said. Her voice quivered like an unsteady branch in a windstorm. "She was my only friend."

"I didn't kill her. It was..."

"Enough, Kevin," she said as she slid her bare feet across the rough basement floor. "I heard you."

"I'm your only friend, Stephanie," Kevin said. His head tilted, and he slipped on the mask of kindness and sympathy. "I saved you from the streets. I've planned a good life for us in..."

"Your plan?" she said. "Chester made sure I heard that, too. You're going to kill me like you did Kelsey and all the other girls. I've loved you since we met. I convinced myself I didn't know what you did with the girls so I could turn away. But Kelsey? Me?"

Kevin shed his disguise, replacing it with his true nature. Cold eyes, snarling lips, and smug superiority. "If I'm in jail, you'll be a street whore in no time, I-da-ho. That's why I gave you the name." How he pronounced each syllable reminded Carter of Mona at the coffee shop, her fingers creating air quotes. "You better keep me out of prison, or you'll be dead long before I leave Death Row. Besides, who else is going to love you? It sure ain't Sykes."

"You're right," Stephanie said as she turned to Carter. "I can't let you go to prison." Chester crept closer behind her, preparing to take the gun, but she swiveled enough to freeze him in place.

Carter braced for whatever might happen next. In that moment, peace embraced him. He'd lost everything he cared about. The sex video Hope had released ensured his job was gone, taking away his purpose, and Mona's pals might still lock him up, taking his freedom. Nonetheless, Carter wanted to live. He raised his hand to stop her.

"Damn you, Sykes," Stephanie said. "I wish I'd never danced for you."

Stephanie pivoted back to Kevin. His eyes grew large as his hand flew upward like it had wings. His lips parted as if ready to speak.

Her first shot struck his thumb before continuing into his shoulder just above his father's cartoon image on his work shirt. His shoulder retracted, and he folded onto the concrete, propped on his elbow. The second shot entered his stomach and disappeared into his wriggling body. He tried to breathe, but he only gasped and then gurgled, blood and bile streaming from his mouth. Stephanie's final bullet penetrated his throat, passed through his head, and skipped across the concrete like a stone on a pond. It left a trail of blood and gray matter that resembled an open hand with five fingers cradling Honeyboy's head.

CHAPTER 58

Lenora cried as Carter's shadow covered her. "Are you with me?" he said. She nodded yes, so he touched her elbow and helped her to her feet. The drugs were wearing off; however, Carter could tell her hand reclaimed its pain.

Nonetheless, Lenora hurried to the Coke machine and yanked the door open.

"Zara, please come out," Lenora said.

Within a moment, Zara stepped through the opening. She embraced Lenora and gazed at Carter.

"Is he dead?"

"Yes," Carter said, stepping aside so she could see Kevin's dead body.

Chester stood beside Stephanie, his hand on her shoulder. She held the gun at her side, the cloud of gunpowder dissipating, but its rotten smell lingered in the air.

Carter smiled when Chester gently pried the revolver from her hand. But it dimmed when Stephanie trudged to Kevin's lifeless, bloody form. She planted her bare knees on the concrete and lifted his shoulders, propping up his bloody head.

***

Chaos is like a balloon, Carter thought. *It can only inflate so far until it explodes.* The shouting on the top floor suggested this balloon neared its limit. The smoke thickened, and more people ran between the bays, destroying the garage. Police sirens wailed, and their oscillating, high-pitched yelps urged Carter to action.

Lenora and Zara leaned on each other—not from weakness, but due to shared strength. They'd forever share a bond forged by unimaginable experiences. Their injured hands would not be the only damage lingering with them for a long time.

Carter pulled them close and said, "It's time to get out of here."

Carter motioned for Chester and met him halfway.

They stood face to face beneath Bay 4. "The rioters are crawling all over this place," Chester said, his voice amplified. "They've broken the windows and doors. We didn't need the front door unlocked—they'd already busted through. It's not bad yet, but barrels, tires, and gas cans are everywhere, and several kids brought homemade bombs to the party."

"That's why you'd better take the girls, Chester."

Carter read the confusion on his friend's face.

"You mean *we'd* better get them out of this mess?" Chester said.

"No. It has to be you who saves Zara and Lenora. I'll try to get Stephanie." Carter glanced at the women again. "The cops are on the way, and the media are close behind. I'll follow my plan. Soon, I'll be missing in action."

Chester shook his head. "Doesn't make sense, Sykes. You're not MIA. You just saved two girls. When they hear the real story, Louisville will vote you in as mayor."

"I've got nothing here anymore, buddy. Besides, no one's interested in truth anymore," Carter said. "I drew Lenora into this; she almost died. Kelsey did die. My mistakes haunt me enough already."

"But you..."

"I committed a moral crime, Chester. I had sex with Hope even though I saw the scars on her wrist," Carter said. "Life damaged her, but I ignored it to avoid my pain."

"You didn't make those things happen, Carter."

"Just like you didn't kill that store clerk."

Chester remained silent.

"Walk Lenora and Zara out of this hellhole. It will help your daughter understand that her dad is a hero. Leave here with your head high. Tell them who you are."

Chester's gaze lowered. "What about you?"

Carter laughed. "I'm not brave or dumb enough to challenge the cops, and I sure don't plan to do myself in, Chester. I've learned that living isn't looking back and trying to make amends for what you can't control." He leaned toward his friend. "David's waiting for me at the Prius where you parked it."

Chester coughed. The smoke increased in the garage. "Let me give you something then," Chester said. He retrieved a faded, legal-sized yellow envelope. It reminded Carter of the blackmail note he'd received from Hope.

"What's this?" Carter said.

"It's a fresh start—all you need to become Chester Price. A birth certificate, some old bills, a social security card, a government identification, a credit card I use once a month to keep it active, and a military identification card a buddy of mine in the service made."

"You still need this."

"Nope, I'm Mitchell Moore, from Oakland, California."

Mr. Moore and Mr. Sykes hugged each other.

"Nice to meet you, my old friend," Carter said.

Mitchell Moore smiled and helped Zara and Lenora ascend the steps and scaffolding to the garage above.

CHAPTER 59

"Hey, Sykes." The yell echoed from the bay into the pit. "Remember me, asshole?"

Carter recognized the masks, black clothing, and even blacker boots from the protest behind his school, but he recalled the speaker's red neon face-covering best. All seven stared through the Bay into the pit. Most appeared to be male, but at least two were women. With their dark attire and heads tilted downward, the gang resembled a plague of grackles sitting on a tree branch.

"Never seen you before," Carter said. "Are you a new boy band?"

Neon Red removed his mask, both dramatic and annoyed.

Kyle Watterson, fortunate son. "Sorry," Carter said. "Don't know you."

Watterson's anger raised his voice several octaves. "I know you," he said. His foot stomped the floor, and spittle shot from his mouth onto the scaffolding and ladder. "Fire," he said to one of the other birds on the branch. The male held a jar with a cloth hanging from the cap.

The young man didn't move, the Molotov cocktail still in his hand.

Watterson stomped again, pushed two birdies aside, and marched toward him. "Fire and toss, Nolan."

Nolan said, "I'm not killing anybody." He shoved the Molotov cocktail into Kyle's chest and held it there.

Watterson trembled with rage. He yanked the jar from his friend, produced a lighter, ignited the damp cloth, and held it as the flame grew. He smiled at Carter and tossed the burning jar into the pit.

The jar smashed against the concrete. The alcohol vapors ignited, creating a fireball that shot above Carter's head. The remaining alcohol splashed onto the floor toward Stephanie, where she held Kevin's bloody body.

Carter stumbled away from the heat. A wall of fire and smoke separated him from Stephanie. "Run, Stephanie," he yelled, but she didn't move. He saw her through the flames, rocking Kevin's limp body on her lap as if she never intended to leave.

"Stephanie," Carter said, his voice straining against the commotion upstairs and the fire's roar.

She raised her chin and gazed at him. Her eyes, as dead as Kelsey's had been inside his trunk, confirmed her intentions.

Carter covered his nose with his hoodie sleeve. The smoke followed his needed route—climbing to the garage floor and escaping into the night. However, as he watched the smoke waft upward, he saw Kyle and his gang. They were rolling two barrels toward the bay. Both rusty containers appeared heavy, with burning cloths hanging from the barrel's pour spouts.

Giant Molotov cocktails.

Carter's heart pounded. The basement would be an inferno in a few moments. He saw the steps to Bay 2 on the other side of the room. To exit, he'd have to climb the scaffolding and the stairs and take the Emergency Exit to the lot where David waited.

He glanced at Stephanie a final time. She waved as the flames and thick smoke moved closer to her Honeyboy.

Carter shook his head and glanced up at Neon Red's crew. One girl stood toe-to-toe with Kyle, her finger stabbing at his nose. He swiped her hand away, stepped toward one of the barrels, and pushed it with his black boot. It rolled into Bay 4. The rusty metal first struck the scaffolding and then tumbled into the pit. The landing sounded like a plane crash, although the barrel didn't explode. Instead, the lid and flaming wick broke free and clattered against the concrete. The fifty-five-gallon drum emptied two things onto the basement floor.

First, a yellow and brown liquid flowed from the spout, rolling across the burning cloth. An acidic odor filled the air before the liquid ignited. Carter realized it wasn't gasoline at all but acid. Bones, including a human skull, rode the wave of acid into the growing flames.

Carter ignored the body parts and the flames and focused on the scaffolding beneath Bay 2. He mapped a route through the fire to the Bay.

When he stepped in that direction, he heard Watterson's boot against metal again—the falling barrel eclipsing the light.

***

Carter dove to his left and tumbled as the second barrel smashed into the floor. Again, the acid inside flowed across the floor, trailed by flames and the skeletal remains of Kevin's victims.

Not even the adrenaline rushing through Carter reduced the pain exploding in his body. His knee bore the worst of it, twisting as he rolled away from the acid and the growing flames.

Carter feared he might crack open like the barrel, sending his bones scuttling across the basement like dice on a casino table.

A femur and hip, along with the upper portion of a skull, spilled from the yellow and green soup escaping the drum. Carter pictured all the barrels stacked upstairs and in the basement, wondering if Kevin had filled each with a victim.

The approaching sirens and the likelihood of fatalities sent Neon Red and the other grackles into the wind.

Carter stood. However, he managed only two limps before the excruciating pain in his knee dragged him to the floor again. At once, he attempted to rise and walk to the scaffolding beneath Bay 2 but only managed to lean against a support column.

Come on; don't fail me. Carter massaged his knee. He could no longer see Stephanie or the workbenches behind him. The fire and smoke grew thicker. He tore his sleeve where Kevin had sliced him with the boxcutter and wrapped the fabric around his nose and mouth to filter the air. Carter willed himself to stand on his left leg while protecting his right knee; he limped for three steps and fell against another of the basement's load-bearing columns. The bay was twenty feet away but might have been as far as Mansfield, Ohio. He clung to the column like his sister attached herself to the base whenever they played tag in the yard.

"You're it, Carter." The voice, tiny yet strong, came from the opening overhead. Kindergarten Becca stood at the Bay's ledge as if painted onto the rising smoke. Her dress was vibrant, the sunflowers alive. She twirled around, her arms raised like a ballerina's. In one hand, she held the rag doll he had promised to repair so long ago. However, it was new when she pulled the toy to her chest. Becca's wounds weren't visible either, only her vivid dress, long, silky raven hair, and gentle grace.

"Come on up," she said.

"I can't make it," Carter said. He leaned his back against the pillar.

"It's time, Carter," she said, her hands on her hips. "You're ready to let go now."

"I'll fall if I let go," he said.

"I'm not talking about that, Carter," she said. Her voice sounded like gray-haired Becca, but in form, she was still the little girl in the closet. "It's time to let go of me."

Carter shook his head as if rearranging his thoughts. *Am I Frozen to the Face?* Colonel Scott's voice rang in his mind: "You have to let go. It's scary but necessary if you want to advance."

"You saved those girls," she said, her voice tender. "You've never been responsible for what happened to us but carried it anyway. You don't need to carry me anymore."

"I can't," Carter said. Tears. Pain. Hurt. Heat.

"I'm in the castle, Carter—the one we dreamed about. I'm the princess. Please find your castle, Carter, even if you have to crawl from this hole and build it yourself."

Her figure dimmed, and the smoke covered her until the sunflowers disappeared.

"Don't, Becca. Please don't..."

"My Cartie, you know it's time," she said. "You know."

Her thin arm rose, and her fingers extended toward him as if she wanted to touch him like always, but the smoke lifted her farther and farther away.

Carter Sykes dropped to his knees like he had done that day in the castle when the Traps first touched his life.

Chapter 60

Behind the Asian woman holding the microphone, Nally's Auto Repair lay in ruins in the early morning darkness. Thick smoke seeped from the collapsed girders, blackened barrels, and roof shingles. Debris had fallen into the four rectangular holes on the floor and now rose from the basement like broken bones, finally revealed.

"Thank you, Candace.

"As you can see, a fire demolished the last Nally's Auto Repair shop in Kentuckiana. The station, located at Slevin and Market, was the flagship of Nally's that dominated the local market during the 1980s and 90s.

First responders describe the scene inside as gruesome and horrid. One source claims the firefighters discovered barrels containing human remains. Another described incinerated bodies located in the basement. The fire department captain refused to comment on the casualties inside and the cause of the fires.

The police credit Mr. Mitchell Moore's heroic actions with rescuing two women who had been reported missing during the last two weeks. Moore, a resident at the Jefferson Homeless Shelter and a war veteran, entered the structure and led two unnamed injured abductees to safety.

In a startling turn, witnesses, including Mr. Moore, claim Carter Sykes, the local school principal police consider a "person of interest" in the murder of Kelsey Wayfair, was present and may have perished in the fire.

The police spokesperson refused to comment on Mr. Sykes's role in the abduction and the fire. However, the unnamed women and Mr. Moore assert Mr. Sykes helped the abducted girls escape.

We will provide more details as they become available. Back to you, Candace."

***

Vickie Burns rested her head on Denzel's shoulder as he clicked the remote, and the image on the screen disappeared.

"Vick," Denzel said, "it's best to rip off the band-aid. Open it now." He reached across Vickie, lifted the sealed package, and placed it on her lap.

EPILOGUE

D etective Mona Ridge was on a stakeout. She watched the entrance to the Restore Furniture and Thrift Shop from her Ford Explorer. The store had been easy to find after she passed the "Welcome to Quicksand" sign. However, finding the West Virginia town had been a challenge. She'd crossed the West Virginia border and traveled those famous country roads John Denver sang about to Greenbrier. From there, she navigated the twists and turns into the beautiful Appalachian Mountains. When her GPS lost its mind, she stopped and asked for directions three times.

Nonetheless, Mona arrived in Quicksand with time to spare, beginning the stakeout at 3:17 p.m., well before her 5:00 p.m. deadline.

Transparent raindrops tapped her windshield, although the warm February day teased the upcoming spring. A coal truck's horn blasted in the distance, and houses on both sides of the street gave way to an Ace Hardware, a Vape shop, a Dairy Queen, and the thrift store. A diner called Augie's and a brick church stood on the other side of the narrow street. Quicksand Christian Church had a majestic bell tower that appeared out of place for such a rural town.

The bell tolled at 5:00 p.m. Mona sat taller in her seat and gazed at the store's glass entrance. Less than a minute later, the doors parted, and a man emerged.

His dark hair escaped his Marshall University baseball cap and raked against his ears and collar. His beard, flecked by gray patches and sawdust, suggested he was a mountain man or a biker. He stopped, stared at the spitting sky, and removed the varnish-stained work apron shielding his slim body. He wore unnaturally blue work pants and sandy-beach-colored boots. Steel-toed, Mona figured. The man folded the apron over his arm, and, she was sure, he smiled.

The man's stride had a purpose. He glanced right and left before jogging across the road toward the diner, as he did daily. He ascended the steps onto Augie's porch two at a time before entering the wooden door.

Mona glanced at her holster and the gun it cradled, contemplating how to handle this situation.

***

A bell jingled when Mona opened the door. The diner reminded her of a coffee shop in downtown Paintsville—booths and tables, nooks and crannies, empty and quiet. Of course, the man selected the padded booth near the back, close to a ceiling-high window. The silver-haired waitress, an orange apron hugging her thick body, stood a little too close to the man as she smiled and filled two coffee mugs. Ghosts shimmered above the cups.

Mona sighed and walked toward the man's booth.

When she arrived, he didn't glance at her. Instead, he studied the menu.

She searched her mind for something clever to say, like, "Don't you have the entire menu memorized by now?"

However, before she delivered the quip, he spoke. "I took the liberty of getting you a coffee, officer. Please sit down."

Mona removed her blazer and slipped into the seat facing him. "Quicksand?"

"I might ask you the same thing, officer." His face expressed playful joy and suspicion when he finally stopped perusing the age-old pictures of meatloaf, pork chops, and grilled cheese.

"When did you know I was here, Carter?"

He lifted the apron beside him and pointed to the name badge attached to the chest. "I'm Chester Price, remember?"

Mona smiled. "So you are. But that doesn't answer my question."

"Jeff, the furniture restoration manager, told me a woman had called asking about veterans doing furniture repair. That caught my interest. Also, if anyone tracked me down, it'd be you. I figured a smart person could connect "Chester"—he formed rabbit ears as he enunciated each syllable—"and me with the credit card. I reminded myself that the only person that smart is Officer Ridge."

"I'm Detective Ridge, remember?" She pointed toward her badge.

His grin widened, but the suspicion remained. Mona realized she should've left the gun and badge in the vehicle.

"I always believed in your skills, Mona. Besides, you found me in Quicksand, didn't you?"

Mona laughed. "It wasn't easy. It took forever to persuade Vickie Burns I had no nefarious intent. Finally, she showed me the packages you sent. Pretty generous, renting your home to Ms. Gibson and Shandi for a dollar a month and creating a fund to pay the property taxes. Then, donating to the Jefferson Shelter where Mitchell Moore, alias Chester Price, lived. Very kind."

Carter lowered his gaze.

Mona said, "I finally convinced Vickie and Mrs. Gibson to grant me access to your house on Swan Avenue. She insisted we visit together and prohibited me from opening drawers or cabinets. She even threatened to claim I forced her to let me search without a warrant. The house had changed owners, so old warrants didn't apply. I told her she'd make a great defense attorney."

Carter glanced across the table and smiled as if proud of Vickie.

"But she did make one slip up," Mona said. "She said you always felt you had to fix things. I know she meant people, but I recognized the same thing about your house."

"I wasn't very good at repairing people, especially myself."

"Vickie showed me your Silver Star, Carter. It always made her cry for some reason. She couldn't explain it."

"See, I even cursed her, didn't I? Is that why you found me, Mona—to protect and serve others who might get caught in my web of deceit?"

"Carter, you silly man. This meeting is a social call. You're safe with me." Mona nodded and grinned to put him at ease. "I know you're seeing a counselor at the Comprehensive Care Center. I can imagine why with the suffering you've seen—your own and the trauma of total strangers. I also know about Rebecca and your mother. You've sacrificed enough for all of us."

Carter's face turned red. His furrowed brow, steady gaze, and the wrinkles around his eyes resembled a cherished photo of her grandfather.

Mona placed her palms down on the table.

Carter leaned closer to her, his fingers beside his coffee cup. "You risked so much for me and even trusted me, Mona. I've thought of you every day since..."

"Louisville is a long distance from these mountains. The past is even further," she said.

Mona stared at his fingers and carefully glided her hand across the tabletop.

Carter Sykes didn't pull away.

ACKNOWLEDGMENTS

M y wife, Kathy, and son, Daxon, have encouraged and been patient with me during the process. Kathy's input and a keen eye for details helped tremendously. Besides, she is the best reader I know.

This book would not have been possible without my brother James's gifted brain. His support and advice lit the path along the entire endeavor. He's the natural storyteller of the Hensley-Mollett clan. Also, my brother Jerry amazes me with what he can do—he and Janet raised Tara, Jaret, and Amy to be good, intelligent, and strong. They make me proud.

My lifelong friend David (aka Big Dave) has always been someone I idolized and loved as a brother. He has spent his life helping broken men and women like those found inside these unworthy pages.

My new friend, Judy P., provided great editing, "feed-forward," and encouragement.

Finally, we don't build public schools with bricks and mortar. The building blocks are the teachers, administrators, and staff inside them—the ones compassionate enough to be tough and tough enough to be compassionate. They demand kids demonstrate the better angels of their nature but recognize when the child's success means allowance and empathy. They focus on student achievement rather than their own convenience. The best teachers refuse to believe poverty, trauma, and dysfunction are insurmountable. Teachers, administrators, coaches, bus drivers, cafeteria workers, secretaries, and volunteers were the ones who expected my best but didn't give up when they witnessed my worst. You made all the difference at every level. Thank you, Neil, Lee, Roger, Alice, Don, Steve, Randy, Virgil, Dr. Gesner, Dr. Fong, Dr. John Fischetti, Jeann, Marjorie, Dr. Gage, Dr. Shaunessy, Jerry Hay—there are so many more I will need to write a dozen books to thank you all. If any educator, including bus drivers and lunchroom staff, ever wonders if they made a difference, let me dispel your doubts. You do, and you did

About the Author

Dewey Hensley is an educator, writer, and speaker. He lives in La Grange, Kentucky, with his wife, Kathy, son Daxon, cat Hobbes, and dogs Cricket and Birdie. You can reach him by email at deweyhensleywrites@gmail.com.

Made in the USA
Middletown, DE
10 September 2024

60671704R00159